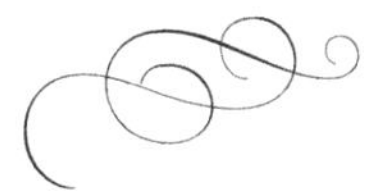
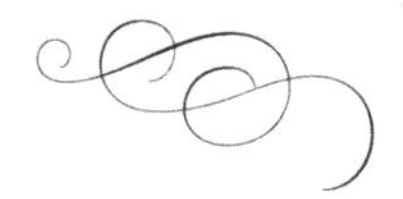

Murder at Arleigh

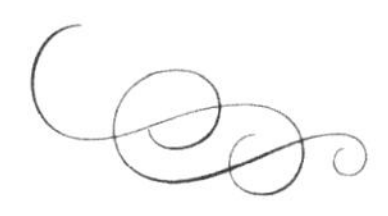
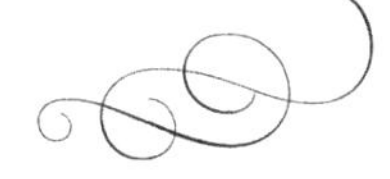

Books by Alyssa Maxwell

Gilded Newport Mysteries
MURDER AT THE BREAKERS
MURDER AT MARBLE HOUSE
MURDER AT BEECHWOOD
MURDER AT ROUGH POINT
MURDER AT CHATEAU SUR MER
MURDER AT OCHRE COURT
MURDER AT CROSSWAYS
MURDER AT KINGSCOTE
MURDER AT WAKEHURST
MURDER AT BEACON ROCK
MURDER AT THE ELMS
MURDER AT VINLAND
MURDER ARLEIGH

Lady and Lady's Maid Mysteries
MURDER MOST MALICIOUS
A PINCH OF POISON
A DEVIOUS DEATH
A MURDEROUS MARRIAGE
A SILENT STABBING
A SINISTER SERVICE
A DEADLY ENDOWMENT
A FASHIONABLE FATALITY
TWO WEDDINGS AND A MURDER

Published by Kensington Publishing Corp.

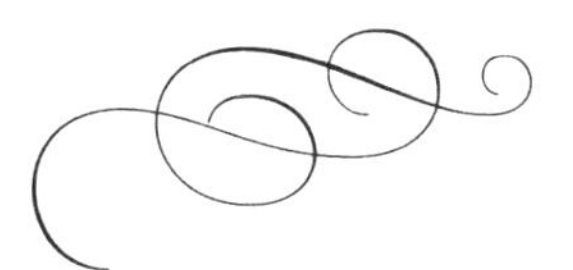
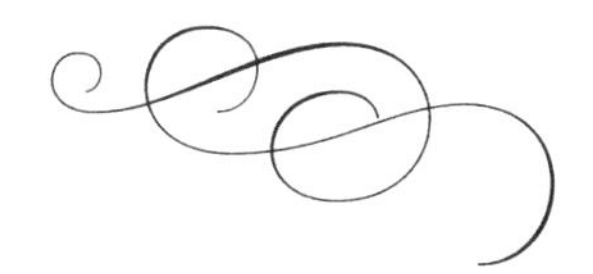

MURDER AT ARLEIGH

ALYSSA MAXWELL

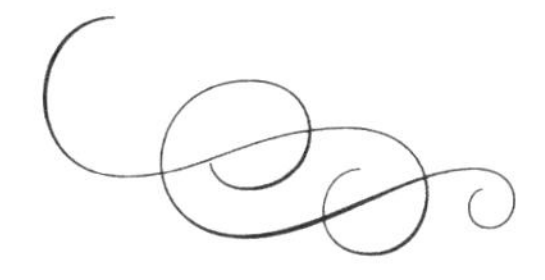
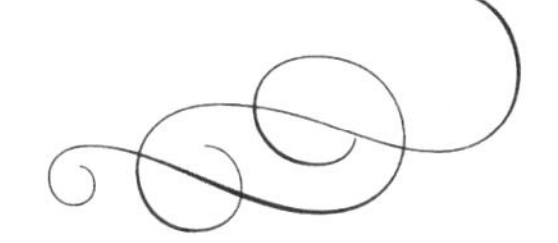

KENSINGTON PUBLISHING CORP.
kensingtonbooks.com

KENSINGTON BOOKS are published by

Kensington Publishing Corp.
900 Third Avenue
New York, NY 10022

All Kensington titles, imprints, and distributed lines are available at special quantity discounts for bulk purchases for sales promotion, premiums, fund-raising, educational, or institutional use. Special book excerpts or customized printings can also be created to fit specific needs. For details, write or phone the office of the Kensington Special Sales Manager: Attn. Special Sales Department, Kensington Publishing Corp., 900 Third Avenue, New York, NY 10022. Phone: 1-800-221-2647.

Library of Congress Card Catalogue Number: 2025935024

KENSINGTON and the K with book logo Reg. US Pat. & TM Off.

ISBN: 978-1-4967-5325-0
First Kensington Hardcover Edition: September 2025

ISBN: 978-1-4967-5327-4 (ebook)

10 9 8 7 6 5 4 3 2 1

Printed in the United States of America

The authorized representative in the EU for product safety and compliance
is eucomply OU, Parnu mnt 139b-14, Apt 123
Tallinn, Berlin 11317, hello@eucompliancepartner.com

In memory of Victoria Thompson, a brilliant author whose work paved the way for so many historical mystery authors, and a beloved member of Sleuths in Time. Her talents were surpassed only by her generous spirit and eagerness to help her fellow authors succeed.

Acknowledgments

With Arleigh being one of Newport's "Lost Cottages," and one that hasn't been widely written about, I was left to piece together its history through a number of sources, including countless archived newspaper articles from the period. What those sources revealed to me was that, despite the wealth of information available about Newport during the Gilded Age, many of its secrets have either been lost to time or have become hidden behind the more obvious glamour of what has survived. For readers who would like to know a bit more about Arleigh and the Lehrs, as well as other lost cottages and families, I recommend:

Lost Newport by Paul F. Miller
The Barons of Newport by Terrence Gavan
Wicked Newport by Larry Stanford

And, most important to me of all, *King Lehr* by Elizabeth Drexel Lehr, whose own words shed insight into what it was like to be married to the man called America's's Court Jester.

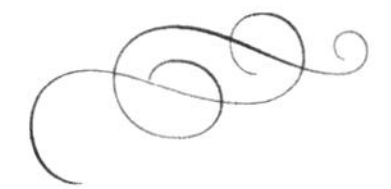
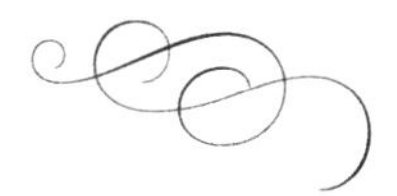

Murder at Arleigh

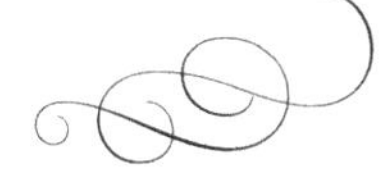

Chapter 1

April 1903, Newport, Rhode Island

A peevish burst of wind and rain pursued me beneath the porte cochere and through the front door of Arleigh, the midcentury Queen Anne–style manse about to play host to my cousin Reginald Vanderbilt's wedding. Even with its double-gabled, asymmetrical design, punctuated by an impressive turret, as if to put an exclamation point on an astonishing fact, Arleigh couldn't hope to emulate the grandeur of Reggie's parents' cottage, The Breakers. Surely, I couldn't be alone in wondering why Reggie and his bride, Cathleen, had decided to hold their nuptials here.

Inside, however, I discovered that Cathleen's mother, Isabelle Neilson, had spared no expense to create a fantasy tableau fit for a princess. Multitudes of fragrant and exotic spring blossoms, mostly white, festooned nearly every surface in stark but pleasing contrast to the entry hall's dark wood paneling. Urns of flowers, interspersed with gleaming satin bunting, adorned the grand staircase and the railings of the overlooking gallery. A pure white carpet runner lined the steps like a fresh blanket of snow.

With the chill clinging to me, I felt loath to hand over to the waiting footman the silk and velvet pelisse I'd tossed over my gown upon leaving home. But then my husband, Derrick, stepped into the foyer behind me, slid the garment from my shoulders, and replaced its warmth with the touch of his hand at the small of my back. The footman took my wrap, along with Derrick's top hat and gloves, and we moved farther into the entrance hall to make room for others streaming in behind us.

The hall itself might have been considered a salon, being spacious and square, with a built-in, cushioned seat beneath a vivid stained-glass window—or what would have been vivid if not for the dreary weather—as well as other seating along the perimeter walls. However, from what I could see, a parlor lay through a doorway to my left. To the right, ceiling-high pocket doors had been slid wide, leading into the wide expanse of a drawing room, from where one might drift through another such opening into a music room. A dining room lay directly ahead and appeared cavernous. I surmised each room led into the next and back into the hall, creating a continuous flow that allowed guests to move about freely. Footmen circulated, offering small delicacies and coupes of champagne punch.

The hearths were ablaze, and that, along with some 150 guests—small by society's standards—heated the house adequately enough. As I'd expected, more than a few expressions mirrored my puzzlement over the day's event. Smiles appeared barely pasted on, about to slip at any moment; brows gathered above sideways glances. I tried to ignore the cynics and instead studied the profusion of floral garlands that climbed the walls, encircled the sconces, edged the gilded tables, and draped the doorways.

Yet, Derrick's whisper in my ear gave voice to the very doubts I myself could not banish. "So, why do you suppose we're here and not in New York? What's he gotten himself into now?"

"Shh!" But he was right. That we were here, a relatively small gathering in the leased home of Harry and Elizabeth Lehr, and not at St. Patrick's Cathedral in the heart of Manhattan, could not be a simple case of the bride being Catholic and the groom Episcopalian. Yes, mixed marriages could be complicated, but not irresolvable, especially considering the Vanderbilt millions. And while Newport did play host to the cream of society all summer long, this was *April*, and the only fashionable place for a society wedding at this time of year was, inarguably, New York City.

So, why *were* we here?

"Mr. and Mrs. Andrews, welcome to Arleigh. I trust you are both well?" Elizabeth Drexel Lehr, a tall, slender woman, with rich, nearly raven-black curls and aristocratic features, which were sometimes beautiful and sometimes bordered on haughty, extended her long-fingered hand to me. Her husband stood beside her, a hand at her bent elbow, while he stretched out his other to Derrick.

"Lehr, old man." Derrick gave his hand a hearty shake. "Awfully good of you to lend Reg and his girl the use of your house."

"Well, it's not really ours, is it?" Harry Lehr gave a cavalier shrug. He was clean-shaven, his light brown hair parted in the middle and slicked back. Though trim of figure, his features held a softness, a certain slackness in the jowls. It suggested corpulence later in life. "It's only leased," he told us, referring to the house, "and it seems the pair were in something of a bind, don't you know. Needed a convenient place to get hitched, and Mrs. Lehr and I said, 'Heck, why not?' Isn't that so, m'love?" he added with a fond look at his wife.

"Indeed, though *Mr.* Lehr should receive all the credit, as it was his idea." She linked her arm through her husband's, and he gave her hand a pat, as if to secure it within the protective crook of his elbow. Society spoke of the Lehrs as a perfect love match, their affection for each other evident wherever they went. At a previous meeting, I had thought I'd detected a hint of discord between them, but perhaps I'd been wrong. Then again, what married couple didn't disagree, at least once in a while?

"That was *very* kind of you," I said with emphasis, and it was true. The Lehrs had been inconvenienced all week, having to vacate their own home—leased or not—while the wedding preparations commenced. While I debated whether or not to inquire *why* Reggie and Cathleen were in want of a place to *get hitched,* Mrs. Lehr unwittingly supplied an explanation.

"They never actually mentioned why they wished to wed in Newport," she said with a delicate, well-bred laugh, "but only that it was important to them that they do so. I thought it wonderfully sentimental. I can only surmise that both harbor only the fondest memories of their summers here."

"That must be it," I agreed; although as soon as they walked away, Derrick and I traded looks that declared us both firm nonbelievers in *that* theory. I slipped my arm through his. "Let's go say hello to Aunt Alice and the others."

We wound our way to the front of the crush in the drawing room. Here, a string ensemble grouped off to one side played only loud enough to provide a gentle cadence above the hum of voices. An elaborate arch of white flowers framed a mullioned window overlooking the sodden side garden, faced by a few rows of chairs for the immediate family. Everywhere else—the remainder of the drawing room, the music room, and the entrance hall—offered standing room only.

Aunt Alice, flanked on either side by her sister-in-law Florence Twombly and my cousin Gertrude, stood in the aisle between the rows. Alice's son Alfred, his wife, Ellen, and Gertrude's husband, Harry Whitney, hovered close by. Gertrude's beaded and flounced Worth gown successfully camouflaged her pregnancy, her third. After a girl and a boy, she and Harry were hoping for another daughter.

Missing, of course, were Alice's eldest son, Neily, and his wife, Grace, for the family schism caused by their marriage had yet to heal, if it ever would. Also missing was Alva Belmont, formerly Vanderbilt, ostracized forever since her divorce from Uncle William eight years ago. I spied Uncle William, however, across the room, as well as his two sons: Willie, all grown up and married himself, and Harold, not yet twenty. Their sister, my dear cousin Consuelo, had been unable to make the trip from faraway England, where she presided over Blenheim Palace as the Duchess of Marlborough.

But as for Aunt Alice—I approached her with slight trepidation. Did she know or suspect anything amiss about today's proceedings? Did she, too, find it strange to be here in Newport?

She wore her typical half mourning, though enlivened today by a glossy silken sheen and vibrant shades of violet trim. But it was her smile, filled with the self-satisfied pride of an indulgent mother, that assured me that if Reggie had found himself in some kind of trouble again, she knew nothing about it.

I breathed a sigh of relief, for her sake.

"Emmaline, Derrick, how good of you to come." She opened her arms to us, embracing each of us in turn. Though my branch of the Vanderbilt family was far less illustrious than those who still bore that name, they had always been kind to me, included me in their summer activities, and filled in as needed, once my parents had departed our shores to live as expatriates among Paris's artist community.

"Isn't it wonderful to see Reggie taking on a man's responsibilities with such a lovely young wife?" she simpered, then called out to Alfred, her second eldest son, who had replaced Neily as head of the family upon the death of their father. "You simply must find a place for Reggie now at the New York Central."

"Of course, Mama. Just as soon as he's back from his honeymoon." Alfred caught my eye an instant after those words left his lips and hoisted an eyebrow. We both knew Reggie had no interest in working for the New York Central Railroad. Or anywhere, for that matter.

Derrick and Harry Whitney exchanged greetings, and once he and I had drifted away to mingle with other guests, he murmured, "Did you know he was arrested yesterday?"

"Who? Reggie?" I shook my head in dismay. "What was it this time? No, let me guess. Since we're in Newport, it must have had something to do with that new Winton-Tourer of his."

"Right you are, my dear. Caught racing it down East Main Road—with someone else in the car with him."

"So reckless and thoughtless." Though acquiring both touring and sporty automobiles had taken society by storm, I had yet to become enamored of them. Oh, I certainly enjoyed the exhilaration of a brisk ride through the open countryside on the mainland, where there seemed to be ample space for them. I knew that, for the most part and in the right hands, they were a relatively safe, if somewhat undependable, mode of transportation. But here, they seemed out of place, a noisy, smelly encroachment on the peace and quiet of our island.

Derrick had nonetheless joined the ranks of the motorcar owners the year before, purchasing a little Peugeot phaeton in shiny maroon with brass trim. We'd had to enlarge our barn to accommodate the vehicle, which kept our two carriage horses company. I hadn't minded, but I had made it abundantly clear that while I might ride in it occasionally, I far preferred our reliable horse and buggy—and I utterly refused to allow our baby daughter to be a passenger.

Before I could ask who had been with Reggie during this race, Derrick leaned in and lowered his voice. "It was one of the bridesmaids, Miss May."

I stifled a gasp and spoke lower still. "Mable? Was Cathleen also there?"

Derrick shook his head. "Not that time, although there was an incident of racing last week and Cathleen was with him then."

"He's going to kill someone, one of these days. Who was he racing against??"

"One of his groomsmen. Ely Forrester." Derrick pointed to a young man standing in a group of equally youthful men, all of whom looked as though they wished to be elsewhere. I knew of the Forrester family, but they were not summer Newporters, so I was not acquainted with Ely. Taking his measure, I judged him to be in his early twenties. He was of slight build, with sloping shoulders and a slouchy posture that diminished his stature even more. He appeared oblivious to those around him as he fidgeted with his tie and cuffs and tugged at his morning coat.

"Well," I said with a sigh, "at least Reggie and Cathleen are leaving immediately on their honeymoon. That should keep him out of trouble for at least as long as the voyage."

Derrick snorted. "Trust me, there's a host of trouble a man can get up to on a cruise."

"Speaking from experience, are you?"

He was saved from having to reply when the orchestra went suddenly silent, and then struck up a few warning notes. This caused a subdued commotion as the guests took up their desired positions to witness the nuptials. The opening notes of the Lohengrin March effectively stifled any remaining conversation. Reggie, accompanied by Alfred and his groomsmen, including Mr. Forrester, stepped up to the floral arch, under which now stood a priest I recognized, Father Meenan, of St. Mary's Catholic Church. Along the gallery on the upper floor, the first of the bridesmaids appeared, dressed all in white with a darling picture hat perched just so over the upsweep of her hair. Behind her came the next three. Following was the maid of honor, my youngest cousin, Gladys, looking as flushed and ebullient as a bride herself.

The music surged, and Cathleen descended the staircase—floated really—on the arm of her uncle, her father having passed away several years earlier.

"How lovely she is," I whispered to Derrick. In white silk chiffon, she was an ethereal confection, crowned by diamonds and orange blossoms and a veil of antique lace. With each downward step, her wide, tiered sleeves fluttered like the wings of a tiny bird. Another thought struck me, one I didn't voice. How very young she looked. Young, eager, and so unaware of anything beyond the glory of her wedding day. But at eighteen, how could she envision anything but a perfect life with her new husband?

I stole a glance back at Reggie. In his tapering black morning coat and white silk cravat, he looked handsome, self-possessed, and aristocratic. Also, *sober.* Was he? I prayed so.

When it was done, I felt as though the entire assemblage let go a subtle sigh of relief. It had been a short but lovely ceremony, a nuptial mass having been dispensed with in deference to the mix of faiths present. We toasted the bride and groom, and the wedding breakfast was served. The guests found seats where they could, either at the dining room table, or on chairs and sofas that miraculously appeared from where they had been previously pushed against the walls.

While Mrs. Neilson presided over the festivities, the Lehrs also acted as hosts, making the rounds of each room to ensure the guests had all they needed—or wanted. Harry Lehr was quick to send footmen repeatedly down to the wine cellar, which they had stocked for the Season. With a glance at Reggie, I wished he wouldn't. A telltale redness tipped my cousin's nose and his heavy-lidded gaze melted hazily over his surroundings. And as his eyes lost their focus, his voice gained an edge, his laughter bellowing through the house and prompting Cathleen to watch her new husband with a bewildered expression. Alfred and Gertrude glowered at their brother, while many of the guests sniggered into their hands or rolled their eyes, being all too familiar with Reggie's antics. Only Aunt Alice seemed not to notice, continuing to beam with pride at her favorite child.

While the rain continued lashing the windows, spirits inside remained high. Derrick and I wandered for a time in separate directions, each of us catching up with acquaintances. I had just left young Flora Twombly's side when I noticed Mr. and Mrs. Lehr tucked into an alcove at the rear corner of the entry hall, partially hidden by a sweep of velvet drapery. By this time, most of the company had squeezed themselves into the drawing and music rooms, leaving the hall virtually empty. Except for the Lehrs.

Though his back was to me, I could see that Harry Lehr held a hand quite near his wife's face and gesticulated forcefully, enough to make her startle and pull back. She didn't cower long, however, but replied with a glowering look and words whispered too low for me to make out, but which shot like arrows from her tight lips. I eased back into the drawing room doorway, yet didn't—couldn't—look away.

Was this the couple everyone termed a love match? Oh, we all had our moments, even Derrick and I, but never with such open animosity.

Mr. Lehr suddenly pivoted away from his wife, leaving her blinking as if he'd flashed a bright light in her eyes. As he strode in my direction I turned and attempted to blend into the nearest group. But the moment he entered the room, his scowls melted away; smiles and laughter replaced his bad humor. He moved past without noticing me, speaking with guests as he went and playing the proper host. I gazed across the hall to find Mrs. Lehr standing where he'd left her, still blinking. Were those tears? There was no mistaking the vulnerability that, for an instant, stripped away her cultivated, dignified veneer to reveal . . . something that, from my vantage point, bordered on heartache. Devastation. Then she, too, pivoted and vanished beyond the drapery, into, I presumed, a hallway.

I found myself unable to turn away from the empty space where she had been. With a brief look around me, I located Derrick in the music room, deep in conversation with Aunt Alice and Alfred. My feet conveyed me across the hall.

I found Mrs. Lehr in the sort of short corridor I had surmised would lurk beyond the alcove. My knowledge of Newport's houses was such that I often could find my way around one I had never entered before. Mrs. Lehr stood in front of a gilt-framed wall mirror beside a closed door, her hands braced on the marble-topped console beneath it. The sounds of the wedding seemed far off here. The mirror reflected the watery gloom of the rain-streaked window opposite. It also reflected her troubled countenance. But she was not checking her hair or jewelry, but, rather, staring down at her hands. Her satin-gloved fingers trembled against the marble. I was about to call her name, but she straightened, opened the door beside her, and stepped inside.

Had she heard me and endeavored to escape my good intentions? When she didn't close the door behind her, I hesitated several long moments before taking the liberty of following her into what appeared to be another small parlor or perhaps a morning room.

"Mrs. Lehr, are you all right? You seem . . . indisposed. Is there anything I can do?"

When she didn't reply I became aware of other voices—two of them, both male—coming from behind yet another closed door on the back wall of the room we occupied. She turned to peer at me over her shoulder, her features strained and her face gone pale. Before I could ask what had so dismayed her, the swinging door burst open and a man came striding out of a pantry that apparently connected this room to the dining room and the kitchen.

I recognized Ely Forrester, Reggie's groomsman—the one who had been racing with him down East Main Road the previous day. He came to a halt, obviously startled by the sight of Mrs. Lehr and me. His nostrils flared, and his thick eyebrows gathered like thunderclouds before he resumed his brisk stride past us.

I looked beyond Mrs. Lehr to find Reggie hovering in the doorway, looking equally as startled as Mr. Forrester, but where Mr. Forrester had displayed anger, Reggie looked sheepish. His coat was unbuttoned, his tie askew.

"Ah . . . how much of that did you . . . uh . . . if you'll excuse me." Shoving his hands into his trouser pockets, he hunched his shoulders and walked determinedly from the room.

I moved to Mrs. Lehr's side. "What was that all about?"

She gave an infinitesimal shake of her head. "I've no idea. It doesn't matter. Men always have their secrets."

Her face had gone paler still, and a strange brightness lurked behind the moisture in her eyes. In an act of over-familiarity, for we were barely acquainted, I pressed a hand to her wrist. "Are you quite all right?"

"Yes, of course. I merely needed a quiet moment." She made a pitiful attempt to smile. "It's grown awfully hot and stuffy, and all those voices." She slid her hand out from under mine and touched her fingertips to the elaborate piles of raven-black curls that made up her coif. "Goodness, my head was beginning to ache. But I'm fine now."

"If you're certain . . ."

"I am. But it's awfully kind of you to inquire."

There was that word again—*awfully*. She'd used it twice. Was it a word that described the day for her? Her marriage? Her life?

No. I was getting carried away, seeing ill tidings where there had only been a tiring day, an exhausting week, and a married couple feeling the strain of opening their home to a host of outsiders.

"I can't help but wonder what my cousin and his friend were up to," I said, loath to leave her alone. "Was it me, or did they seem perturbed to find us here?"

"Probably discussing some business or other. You know men. They believe their concerns to be unfit for ladies' ears, not to mention doubting our ability to comprehend." She shrugged. "I should be getting back. Will you accompany me, Mrs. Andrews?"

On our way to rejoin the festivities, she asked me about Derrick's and my daughter. Born in February of the previous year, Annamarie was toddling about the house now and delighting herself and us with a few newly acquired words: Mama, Papa, Nana, and, perhaps most darling of all, Pat-pat, her interpretation of our dog Patch's name.

Once in the drawing room, Mrs. Lehr thanked me again for my kindness and signaled to someone across the room. "Excuse me, won't you?" she said, and started away, presumably to whomever it was she had waved to. But when I turned to see whom she approached, there was no one, and Mrs. Lehr had gone in the opposite direction.

I didn't speak to her again that day, or see her for weeks afterward, until quite unexpectedly she came to call one day at Gull Manor, our home on Ocean Avenue.

Since Annamarie's birth, I had begun working at home some days, and on others, splitting my time between home and the offices of the *Messenger,* the local newspaper Derrick and I owned and ran. Technically, Derrick owned it, having purchased it while it was little more than a floundering broadsheet a few years back. With his business acumen, my reporting skills—if I might be so bold to boast—and the expertise of our editor-in-chief, Stanley Sheppard, our subscriptions had flourished, as had our list of weekly advertisers. My working from home as often as I did might not have been ideal, and to be sure, my male counterparts at Newport's rival papers looked down their noses at me, but what were a few sneers when it meant being a mother—*truly* a mother—to our happy, bright, perfect girl?

One morning at the beginning of June, as more arrivals in town began breathing life into the summer Season, I took Annamarie out to our rear garden overlooking the Atlantic Ocean. I needn't worry about my darling girl running into the water. The edges of the property were bordered by boulders that required one to climb them before gaining access to the water. On her short, tottering legs, Annamarie would be hard-pressed to make that climb before I swooped in to scoop her up. And should I be tardy in reaching her, our dependable spaniel mix, Patch, would catch the hem of her dress in his teeth and refuse to let her move another inch forward.

That day, we sat on a blanket I had spread out on the grass. Patch had accompanied us outside, wandering off to explore, only to come trotting back every so often to check on his people. Since Annamarie's birth, he had taken on the role of protector, rarely far from her side and sleeping next to her crib at night.

We had brought along her rag doll, Mimi, along with her favorite stuffed pony, which she called Pommi, and a wooden choo choo train given to her by Aunt Alice. It even said NEW YORK CENTRAL RAILROAD in gold letters on its sides. But today Annamarie's interests wandered to the sunny yellow daffodils I had planted along the border fence of the kitchen garden. To my vexation, she pushed up onto her plump legs and toddled over to them. I had a sense of what would happen next.

As I watched each precarious yet nonetheless successful step, I pondered how much she had changed our lives. How she had worked her way into our hearts so effortlessly—that mere days after her birth we could barely remember life before her. Or how her slightest achievement—an attempt at a new word, her first steps, putting on her own hat—brought such joy as I had never imagined. It had been a difficult birth, but I regretted not an instant of it. She had changed the way I looked at everything, brought a new brightness to the world and new meaning to my own achievements, because I saw them now as gifts to her, a way to show her that her life might be whatever she wished it to be.

When she reached the flowers, at first she merely touched her fingertips to what must have appeared to her young eyes as flecks of gold swaying in the spring breeze. But then, to my dismay, her hands closed around the two nearest blossoms and she gave a great tug, followed by a burst of laughter.

I reached her just as her tiny fingers opened to release the shreds; they floated, spiraling, to the ground at her feet.

What fun, my inquisitive daughter must have thought. She laughed and tried it again. Patch caught wind of her delight and came loping over. The next batch of shredded petals landed on his nose and made him sneeze. None of my coaxing with Mimi or Pommi or the choo choo could divert her. I considered simply lifting her in my arms and marching her in another direction, but I realized they were only flowers, with not much longer to live, so why deprive her of the experience of sprinkling gold around her feet?

Thus, with my daughter squealing with delight and me sitting on the grass, sighing with resignation as my daffodil border shrank, Mrs. Lehr found me. She had apparently knocked at the front door, and Nanny, my housekeeper and so much more, had led her through the house to the kitchen door. What must Mrs. Lehr have thought? Why hadn't Nanny offered her a seat in the parlor and a cup of tea before coming to inform me that company had called? What kind of household ushered guests through the kitchen?

Our household, I'm afraid. We were frightfully informal here at Gull Manor, hopelessly lax when it came to propriety and protocol. Nanny—Mary O'Neal—had been with me since my earliest days, sometimes more of a mother than my own had been, and now the grandmother I still often needed in spite of my being a wife and a mother. Or perhaps because of that. Our maid-of-all-work, Katie Dillon, had come to us after being dismissed from The Breakers through no fault of her own. She had become indispensable to Nanny and to all of us, and seemed more a younger sister to me than a servant. Would the women of the Four Hundred find fault in my familiar ways with people who were, technically, in my employ? Indeed they would. Even Aunt Alice had found cause to be mortified, occasionally, by my lack of decorum.

So be it.

Gathering Annamarie in my arms, I stood as Mrs. Lehr

came down the two steps from the kitchen door, stopping to steady herself on her high-heeled boots when she reached the grass. I noticed she, too, held something in her arms: something furry and black that lifted its head to regard us, but made no move to free itself of its mistress's embrace.

"Goggie!" Annamarie also spotted the small dog Mrs. Lehr carried and waved a daffodil-filled fist. Holding her on my hip, I made my way over.

"Mrs. Lehr, I'm so sorry. Had I known you were coming . . ."

"Nonsense. I'm at fault for not sending ahead." Both she and the pooch in her arms regarded me with earnest gazes.

"Come, we'll go inside. Would you care for tea?"

In answer, she reached out to chuck Annamarie beneath her chubby chin. "Hello, you. You must be Annamarie. Let's do stay outside and play." She smiled into my daughter's bright green eyes. "When your housekeeper told me where you were, and with whom, I insisted on being led outside to you. I see you've a blanket. Shall we go and sit?"

Nanny hadn't been at fault, after all. Once we'd settled, Mrs. Lehr lifted the stuffed pony and pretend-galloped it onto Annamarie's lap, which sent my child into a fit of laughter. "Mah!" my bossy daughter cried out. Mrs. Lehr, understanding the utterance meant *more*, obliged. Then it was Patch's turn to inspect these new arrivals, which he did with a quivering nose and a wagging tail. Mrs. Lehr indulged him with a thorough petting. Patch showed mild curiosity toward Mrs. Lehr's dog, but not a great deal of interest. His lack of regard was returned in kind.

"And who is this darling one?" I offered my hand to the furry little beast on her lap, who sniffed first and then allowed me to pet it with just the sort of hauteur one expected of small dogs who served little purpose but to be pampered by their owners. It had the most extraordinary ears. When standing straight up at attention, they looked remarkably like a butterfly's wings, an illusion created by fringes of wispy hair some several inches long.

"This little fellow is Hippodale," she replied, holding him up for our inspection. "He's a papillon and quite the lapdog. Not the adventurous sort like yours." Her gaze followed Patch, who had decided to run off again in search of more interesting quarry.

Adjusting the ribbon of my hat beneath my chin, I asked, "What brings you to Gull Manor, Mrs. Lehr?"

She lowered her gaze and nodded as if in unspoken acknowledgment that we were not the sort of close acquaintances who visited each other regularly. In fact, we barely knew each other. With obvious reluctance, she raised her chin and met my eye. "Mrs. Andrews, I'm here because I need your help."

"My help?" I probably sounded surprised, but in truth, I wasn't. Not particularly. She was not the first woman in Newport to speak these words to me. I waited for her to elaborate.

She blew out a long breath, staring down at the toy pony and continuing to trot him up to Annamarie, raising him up to plant a kiss on my daughter's dimpled cheek, then pulling him away quickly before starting again. My child became entranced with the game, all her attention centering on the pony as she paid us grown-ups little mind.

"One hears things," Mrs. Lehr began. Despite the game she played with my daughter, her demeanor had changed entirely from when she had arrived, as if thick clouds had scurried across the sun. "That's how I know you might be able to help me."

Yes, I'd heard those words before, too. My reputation as someone with the tenacity to find the truth of a matter, no matter how deeply it lay, had become well known in Newport, especially among the women. I leaned a little closer to her and lowered my voice, not out of fear of being overheard, but to assure her she had the whole of my attention. "How might I help you, Mrs. Lehr?"

She compressed her lips and cast a frown at Annamarie.

"She can't understand you," I reminded her. "Now tell me, what is troubling you?"

"Mrs. Andrews, someone is trying to kill me."

A short, sharp breath scraped my throat. "Good heavens. Who?"

Her gaze seared into mine as her arms tightened around Hippodale. "My husband. Harry Lehr."

Chapter 2

For several moments, neither of us spoke. Even Annamarie, perhaps sensing something amiss, fell silent. One little fist edged toward her mouth, and I noticed a few petals stuck between her fingers. I stilled her hand before it reached her lips and studied the refined face before me. Mrs. Lehr's features showed no trace of humor or anything short of utter seriousness.

I slowly unhinged my mouth. "Surely, I heard you wrong."

"Oh no, Mrs. Andrews. You heard me quite correctly. My husband wants me dead. He's tried more than once."

Was this the great love match engineered by my aunt Alva and her fellow society matrons Tessie Oelrichs and Mamie Fish? Married two years ago, the Lehrs were still the toast of society, with all the makings of a fairy-tale couple. Or so people said.

I thought back to Reggie's wedding, when I had accidentally witnessed something I was quite sure Harry and Elizabeth Lehr did not wish to have witnessed.

"Mrs. Lehr, perhaps you should start at the beginning.

What makes you believe your husband would wish ill on you?" In my arms, Annamarie began to fuss, tugging at my sleeve and making whimpering noises. Ordinarily, I would have gotten up and walked her about the yard, distracting her from whatever displeased her. Or considering the time, I might have taken her upstairs for her morning nap. But I dared not move, not before Mrs. Lehr made sense of the shocking accusation she had made

Her fingers combed through Hippodale's silky fur. Her brows drew tight above her slender nose and her teeth nipped at a corner of her lip. "It . . . is difficult to speak of."

"I can't help you if you won't confide in me."

At that moment, the kitchen door opened and Nanny came down the steps. She carefully picked her way over to us. "Time for the princess's nap," she said, and reached down to take Annamarie from me. Annamarie, gripping Mimi by the foot, did indeed yawn and went without a fuss, for which I was grateful. Had Nanny been observing us out the window and noticed the change in our encounter? Had she sensed the abrupt turn of our mood? Dearest Nanny had always possessed a knack for knowing when I needed her.

Once she had disappeared back into the house with my daughter, I returned my attention to Mrs. Lehr. Again I waited silently for her to continue.

"He despises me."

Her vehemence sent such a start through me, I flinched. "Surely not."

"No, it's quite true, Mrs. Andrews. He has told me as much."

"In anger, perhaps, but an unschooled tongue isn't always to be believed."

"There was nothing unschooled about my husband's tongue when he told me I repulsed him. He wasn't angry in the least." She paused, stroking Hippodale's head with her fingertips. "In fact, he was quite nonchalant about it. It was our wedding night."

"Your . . ." I couldn't bring myself to confirm what she had just told me. "But everyone believes the two of you to be . . ."

"A love match. Yes. In public, Harry treats me with the utmost affection and respect. It's an act. Quite simply, he married me for my money and nothing else. Oh, many a couple marries for money, but they find a way to make it work. Harry and I don't work, Mrs. Andrews. Only on the surface, when people are watching. At home, we have no relationship at all, other than Harry hounding me for money."

"But . . ." I thought back to society column articles featuring Harry Lehr, some written by our own Ethan Merriman at the *Messenger.* He had always been described as perfectly attired, sporting all the latest in watches and hats and all the accoutrements of a wealthy man. He dined at New York's finest restaurants. "I don't understand. He's reported to have always been at the forefront of fashion. He frequented dining establishments like Delmonico's and Sherry's regularly. Surely, he has his own money."

She shook her head. "Those were luxuries Harry enjoyed for free. As a bachelor, and as the good friend of the likes of Lina Astor and your own aunt Alva Belmont, Harry was all the rage for a time. Proprietors considered it a privilege for him to be seen toting their wares and sitting at their tables. His popularity fueled their own popularity."

"Then what changed?"

"He's no longer a bachelor about town. Married men aren't nearly as interesting, are they? They're not as good for business." She gave a shrug. "So now he must pay for what he wants."

This explanation still left me thoroughly confused. "Why did he get married, then?"

She shrugged again, looked down at Hippodale, then out at the undulating ocean. Anywhere except me. "Societal pressures. Men of a certain age must marry, mustn't they? Or people will talk."

This left me as mystified as before, but I didn't press her for further explanations. I could see by her expression that doing so would have mortified her. Instead, appalled by the circumstances in which she had found herself, I said, "I'm so sorry."

"Yes, well. I believe he's finally gotten it in his head to do away with me altogether and attempt to take full control of my finances. For the most part, my father's and my first husband's wills disallow that while I'm alive. The terms of the trusts are quite specific. But when I'm gone, Harry might petition the courts for custody of my son and control of what will be Johnny's inheritance, once he's reached his majority. That is something I cannot let happen, Mrs. Andrews. I *will* not."

"You have a son . . ." I had heard she did, now that I thought about it. A shadow passed across her eyes, and I remembered something else I had heard: There had been a child, born to Bessie and her first husband, who had died in infancy. For the briefest moment, I shared in her grief. Only since becoming a mother, did I completely understand what utter devastation it would be to lose a child.

But what about this son, Johnny? Was he in danger, too? "How old is he? Is he here in Newport?"

"Johnny is eleven. And no, he's not here. He's with my mother when he's not at school. I won't let him anywhere near Harry if I can help it. He must remain free of his influence."

That, at least, filled me with relief. And then I remembered that Harry Lehr had spent time with Alva and her sons when they were younger. They had thought of him as their uncle, someone with whom they could rollick at places like Bailey's Beach, and simply be boys without the pressure of meeting their father's expectations. "Uncle Harry" had fulfilled a need in their childhood left vacant by their parents' divorce. Surely, if there had been any ill effects for Willie and Harold, Alva would have perceived it and put a stop to it.

Now, this woman's claims shattered every impression I'd ever formed of the man, known to be a jokester, but not a monster. "What has happened to make you believe Mr. Lehr wishes to harm you? Has he ever . . . struck you?"

"No, Harry strikes with words, at least up until now. But he doesn't seek to *harm* me, Mrs. Andrews. He wishes to *kill* me." For a moment, she let her attention lapse, and Hippodale clambered down from his perch and was attempting to chew on blades of grass. She lifted him back onto her lap and held him close. "At our home on Long Island, there is a balcony off my bedroom overlooking the gardens with views all the way to Long Island Sound. I often spend time out there, standing at the railing and enjoying the view. Before we left for Newport at the end of March, the railing inexplicably broke away and I almost went over. I might have broken my neck, had not my lady's maid and companion, Miss Thorton, been present to catch me and pull me away from the edge."

"A frightening experience, to be sure. But could the railing have been coming loose for some time, and on that particular day finally gave way?"

She shook her head. "I don't believe so. At any rate, that's not the only incident. Just after your cousin's wedding at Arleigh, I was coming down the staircase one morning, only to find the runner at the topmost step so loose it slid beneath my foot. Again I nearly tumbled down—quite a distance as you yourself saw—except that once again, Miss Thorton was with me and caught me before I fell." She paused, and just as I was about to ask if there had been anything else, she said, "And then there was the automobile accident."

"You mean when your man-of-all-work was killed?" I had heard about it, as had all of Newport. We had run an article and an obituary in the *Messenger.* The car's brakes had failed on Bath Road, a short distance down from Bellevue Avenue, and the poor man, Ellis Jackson, careened into a rock wall. "Wasn't that purely an accident?"

"It shouldn't have been Jackson in the car that day. I had plans to shop along Bellevue Avenue, and Miss Thorton always drives us in the car. But she noticed the motor behaving strangely, so I'd asked our man-of-all-work to take it to a garage in town to have it looked at. That's why Jackson was driving it. So you see, it should have been me careening into that rock wall."

"My goodness."

"You see my point."

Did I? These three occurrences were nothing out of the ordinary and could easily be explained as purely accidental. Coincidences, yes, especially happening in such rapid succession, and tragic, certainly, but not necessarily malign.

"Mrs. Lehr, if you suspect your husband in this manner, your best course is to go to the police."

"Good heavens, no!" Her little dog jumped at her sudden outburst. She soothed him and began more calmly, "Going to the police would cause a scandal, especially if I don't have enough evidence to make them believe me. They'll likely dismiss me as a hysterical female."

I sighed, unable to reassure her on that count. She wouldn't be the first woman the police failed to take seriously.

She watched me, searching my face, her own expression seeming to say, *You know I'm right.* Then she said, "I cannot have people saying I've become unhinged. Wouldn't

Harry love that? Then he could have me committed. No, Mrs. Andrews, for the sake of my son and my mother, I won't risk the family's reputation until I have proof of Harry's treachery. And that is why I need you." Securing Hippodale in the crook of her arm, she reached out the other hand to take mine. "Will you help me?"

I returned to Arleigh the very next morning. Mrs. Lehr met me at the door, whisked me inside, and hurried me to the morning room, the very same room where she and I had caught Reggie and Ely Forrester having their illicit conversation. While that episode of eavesdropping had been accidental, today's would not be. The morning room was fairly large, with a seating arrangement, as well as a small circular table with four chairs around it. Breakfast had been served, as evidenced by the savory aromas and the chafing dishes, as well as two platters on the marble-topped buffet on the wall opposite the windows. It was to one of those windows, deeply inset and hung with multiple layers of drapery, that she hurried me.

"You'll stand here."

"I'm to hide behind the curtains?" I began to reconsider the wisdom of the plan she and I had concocted the day before.

"How else are you to hear how he treats me?"

"What if your dog should come along? He'll be sure to catch me out."

"No worries there. I've arranged for Hippodale to have a bath this morning. One of our footmen has him—he's the only person able to handle Hippodale during his bath—and they'll be occupied for the next half hour at least."

"Yes, but hiding like a child . . ."

"Please, Mrs. Andrews. He'll be down any minute. I wouldn't ask this of you if I weren't afraid for my very life."

I nodded. She arranged the draperies just so around me, while I stood, feeling all of eight years old, pressed against the wall behind me. In fact, I could remember playing hide-and-seek with my half brother, Brady, and making use of the curtains in our parlor in just the same way. He had always found me. Would Harry Lehr?

As she had predicted, her husband soon entered the room. I heard his dragging footsteps, his irritable sighs, and his lack of response when his wife bid him good morning. A cover came off a chafing dish, then another. I could hear liquid, presumably coffee, being poured. Then the sound of a chair dragging against the carpet and the creak of Mr. Lehr settling into it.

"I hope you slept well?" Mrs. Lehr inquired cordially enough.

"Do you? I'm surprised you care," he quipped in return. A noisy slurp reached my ears, making me wrinkle my nose in distaste. "After the hash you made of our evening last night. Good God, woman, I don't know how I'll show my face among our friends and acquaintances for the remainder of the Season."

"Whatever are you talking about, Harry? We had a perfectly lovely time at Rosecliff last night."

"Did we? You, with your stupid questions and mundane conversation. It's a miracle you didn't put everyone to sleep."

"You're being unfairly critical and you know it."

"No, I'm not. And that dress you wore. Hideous. My grandmother wouldn't have worn such a monstrosity."

"Good heavens, Harry, can I do nothing right in your eyes?"

"You can advance me some money. I'm short this month."

"You're always short."

"A man has expenses. What do you expect me to live on?"

"Your allowance is more than adequate."

"For whom? A beggar? I should have known better than to marry a woman as miserly and dour as you. Why, you resent my ever having the slightest bit of amusement."

"Amusement—is that what you term it? Carousing, drinking, gambling? Buying trunks of clothing you don't need? Between your own expenses and what you spend on your so-called friends, you've already gone through more than my investments will bring this month. We cannot go on this way, Harry."

"You are quite right, my dear. I cannot go on being the most ill-used husband of the Four Hundred and continue to suffer in silence. If people only knew the truth. Well, perhaps I *should* tell them what a farce our marriage is. How my wife keeps me tethered on a short leash for no other reason than she enjoys watching me beg. Is that it, Bessie? Shall I tell all of society that? What *would* your mother think? That her daughter possessed no concept of wifely duties. Is this how she raised you, Bessie? Is it?"

"Enough!" Mrs. Lehr's weary sigh drifted to me through the layers of silk damask between us. "Please spare me any more of your haranguing. How much do you need?"

He named a sum that made me shudder. I expected Mrs. Lehr to protest vehemently, to simply refuse.

"Very well." She gave another sigh, this one wafting with defeat. "I'll write you a check. You can cash it in town."

"I'd prefer the cash now."

Something in her must have snapped, for she retorted with barely restrained fury. "I haven't got it on hand, Harry, so you'll simply have to make do."

I heard another drag of a chair followed by the swish of skirts along the carpet. Then rapid, clattering footsteps in the hallway. Within moments, they returned, first clacking, then thudding once she reached the carpet again.

"Here. Now leave me alone."

"Gladly, my dear. I've places to be this morning anyway." Heavier footsteps announced Harry Lehr's retreat.

I waited a long moment before shifting the curtains slightly and peeking out. Mrs. Lehr sat at the table, her chin in her hand. Her husband's breakfast lay abandoned across from her. I slipped into the seat beside hers.

"His demands for money never cease," she said after a moment. "My husband has an insatiable hunger for all of life's finer things, with no capacity for earning them. That is why he needed me. King Lehr, some call him." She chuckled grimly. "Have you ever heard that? King Lehr, with society as his domain and me as his pawn."

"I'm so sorry."

"It's humiliating, having someone witness his greed and his cruelty. But I needed you to hear it if you're to believe my husband is capable of murder."

To be fair, nothing I had overheard convinced me of that. That Harry Lehr was a cad and a wastrel had been made evident. That no woman deserved to be shackled to a man like him—of that, I had no doubt. But a murderer?

"Mrs. Lehr—"

"Please, it's Bessie. My family and friends all call me that. The one person I wish *wouldn't* call me Bessie is Harry. But you've seen too far into the reality of my life to remain on formal terms, don't you agree?"

"Bessie, then. What I do see quite clearly is that your marriage is making you exceedingly unhappy. Have you considered . . . perhaps . . . a divorce?" I held up a hand to forestall her objection. "Now, before you protest, divorce isn't quite the scandal it once was. My aunt Alva remedied that several years ago, didn't she? And to be frank, sometimes a bit of social stigma is worth it if one gains one's freedom and peace of mind in the process."

She shook her head with each word I spoke. "No, Emmaline, a divorce is quite impossible. Were it merely social stigma facing me, I wouldn't hesitate. But you see, I was raised a Catholic. And my mother is so devout that my being divorced would utterly break her heart. She would despair of my soul, of my ever achieving salvation. So you see, it's quite impossible—even if Harry is proven to be an attempted murderer."

"I . . . yes, I do see."

"Then you'll help me, Emmaline?"

I smiled sadly and nodded. "I prefer Emma, if you please."

"Emma, it is." She returned my smile, equally as sad as my own. "Now then, how shall you begin?"

"Which automobile repair garage do you use in town?"

"I don't know, actually. Harry always handled that sort of thing. When I asked Jackson to take the motorcar in, I assumed he knew where to go."

"All right, we need to find out which repair shop it is." I sat back and considered. "Does your husband keep an appointment diary?"

"Yes, in his office."

"That seems the best place to start."

Bessie came to her feet. "Follow me."

I hesitated. "What about your husband?"

"I'll check with Bagley, our butler, to make sure Harry's already gone out."

Once she had the butler's assurances, she led me back into the entrance hall and to the staircase. We made our way up, and at the top walked along the gallery to a small room tucked away near the end of the hallway, where another door led into what I assumed to be the service corridor.

"In here."

The door to Mr. Lehr's office stood open, quite as though he had nothing in the world to hide. The room, decorated in dark greens, beige, and rich wood tones, was little larger than a walk-in closet. The air smelled of cigar smoke, macassar oil, and leather books. His desk stood in front of the window, facing the door. I quickly walked around it and began sifting through the papers that littered its blotter.

"I . . ." Bessie clearly looked uncomfortable, her lips rolling between her teeth as she watched me. "Perhaps I'll wait downstairs."

I stopped rummaging and looked up at her. "I shouldn't be long. You don't expect him back anytime soon, do you?"

She frowned. "I don't believe so, but one never knows with Harry. I'll keep watch, and should he return, I'll give you a signal."

"Speak loudly," I suggested, "and I'll understand. That door at the end of the hallway—is it unlocked? And where does it lead?"

As I'd suspected, she confirmed that the door led into the upstairs service corridor. "And it's never locked during the day. What's more, there shouldn't be anyone in that area just now."

"Good. If I must make an escape, I'll go that way."

She left me alone in the empty stillness. No sounds came from the bedrooms. The beds must have been made and the linens collected while the Lehrs and I were in the morning room. That meant there would be no servants telling tales of an errant visitor found in Mr. Lehr's office.

After finding nothing of interest on the desktop, aside from several unpaid bills from merchants in town, a few threatening legal action unless paid in full immediately, I opened the drawer above the kneehole. I'd feared it might be locked, but it seemed Harry Lehr was nothing if not confident of his privacy. More fool he. Right inside, on top of yet another untidy pile of papers, I found the appointment diary I'd been searching for.

I sat down in the chair with the diary open on my lap. First I scanned the entries for the current week. Concluding that Harry Lehr enjoyed an extremely active social life, I worked my way backward, past the time of the accident that killed Ellis Jackson, peering at entries for luncheons, dinner parties, golf, sailing, sea bathing, etc. I assumed Bessie must accompany him to some of these activities to keep up the charade of a happy marriage, but the man hardly kept a spare hour in the day.

Suddenly there it was. My finger speared the entry: Ocean House Automobile Garage. It was five days before the accident. I knew the place; it was on Bellevue Avenue and East Bowery Street, quite close to Kingscote. Quite close to Arleigh, for that matter, merely a straight jaunt up Bellevue. Why would Jackson have passed the establishment and turned onto Bath Road? Had he decided to make another stop in town? Or had he simply been prolonging the experience of driving a motorcar?

Or had the car already been seen to? But if so, how could the braking mechanism have failed after the mechanic had performed the maintenance?

"Have we somewhere to be this evening, Harry?" came Bessie's voice from the entrance hall below. I couldn't make out his response, for he spoke more quietly than his wife. As we agreed, she had raised her voice loud enough for me to hear her.

I snapped the diary shut and slid it back into the drawer. My fingers rode roughshod over the papers on the desktop as I attempted to restore some semblance of Harry's organized mess. Was he on his way upstairs?

Suddenly my fingers went still. From the surrounding disarray, I'd unearthed a bill from the Ocean House Automobile Garage. The occasion I'd found in the appointment diary was listed, but below it were several more maintenance charges for his motorcar, as well as hers, all marked overdue, going back to two weeks before Reggie's wedding.

Bessie's raised voice once more reached my ears as she asked her husband another question. She was telling me I had better hurry. I hadn't a moment to spare as I darted from the room and to the service corridor door. Odd, but when my hand reached the knob to turn it, the door opened easily inward, as if it hadn't been clicked shut. Again I had no time to wonder about that, but slipped through, making sure to close the door softly behind me. The corridor appeared empty, but as I'd stepped across the threshold, I thought I heard a skittering noise ahead of me. Mice?

The corridor extended a few yards before turning. Behind me, I heard muffled footfalls I assumed were Harry's as he reached the landing. I hurried forward. There would be no reason for him to open the separating door, but I didn't wish to test that theory. At the corner, I made the turn—

And collided with a black-clad torso.

"Oh!"

"Ack!" A young man grasped my shoulders, then just as quickly released me and lurched backward a step. "Terribly s-sorry, m-miss!"

In an instant, I'd regained my bearings. I'd run into a footman and apparently startled him as much as he had startled me. He was young, probably no more than twenty, with dark hair that contrasted starkly with his pale, freckled skin and bright blue eyes.

"I'm sorry, I didn't think there would be any . . ." I stopped just short of admitting I hadn't thought anyone would be in that part of the house. Instead, I clasped my hands together at my waist and pulled myself up straighter. "That is, I seem to have taken a wrong turn."

"Then may I be of service, ma'am?" That he had amended *miss* to *ma'am* spoke to his keen observance in noticing the wedding ring I wore beneath my lace glove. He gestured toward the door through which I'd just fled. "If you'll follow me."

"I . . . uh . . ." I followed as he started walking, realizing I couldn't very well run in the other direction without him raising the alarm. I hoped against hope that Harry Lehr had gone to his bedroom instead of his office, or, if the latter, that he'd closed the door behind him. My heart climbed into my throat with each step we took, for what excuse could I give to the master of the house not only for having been in the servants' area, but being in the house at all? Not that I feared him. I most assuredly did not. But I feared the repercussions for Bessie, should she be caught out in a lie or, at least, an omission of the truth. What reason would she give for my being at Arleigh without having informed her husband of my presence? Would he spend the next hour or so haranguing her as he had done earlier?

We came into the main hallway, our footfalls muffled by the plush runner. I must have looked like a frightened rabbit, my eyes wide as they searched for a sign of Harry. A breath of relief poured out of me at the sight of his empty office. Every other door along the hallway was shut, and from somewhere I could hear water running.

At the top of the stairs, I turned to go down, but the young footman stopped me. "It's this way, ma'am." He pointed a few doors down.

"What is?"

"The . . . uh . . . powder room." A blush suffused his complexion, clashing with his freckles. "I assume that was where you were going, ma'am."

"Yes. Indeed. But I'm fine now. I'll just be going . . ." I placed my foot on the top step, but hesitated at the sight of a black shadow racing up toward me. It began to bark. Actually, to yap, but fiercely. The sound echoed off the stairwell walls and the coffered ceiling above me. Hippodale, a fluffy ball of shining coal-black fur, had apparently finished his bath. Suddenly a door along the hallway opened.

"Hippodale, here, boy!"

Gasping, I turned to regard the now-open door. Inside I spied the brocade draperies on a corner of a four-poster bed, but I saw no one. Harry, perhaps in a state of partial undress, must be standing behind the door, which stood open only a few inches. Another call came. "Hippodale, get in here, you foolish, ridiculous rascal!"

The dog darted past me and streamed through the narrow gap between the door and jamb. The door shut. Once again, relief emptied my lungs of air.

Chapter 3

Armed with the information I'd found in Harry Lehr's office, the next morning Derrick and I stopped at the Ocean House Automobile Garage, on Bellevue Avenue near Kingscote and Stone Villa. I knew Ella King could not be pleased to have this establishment encroaching on the pastoral setting of Kingscote, but much had changed in this part of town since the house had been built, with commercial interests having crept ever closer over time. I also wondered how James Gordon Bennett found the intrusion of oil, grease, and gasoline practically under his nose. Then again, being directly across the street from the Newport Casino, he must have grown used to the recent influx of automobiles, with their noxious fumes, juddering engines, and honking horns.

Harry hadn't been secretive about his appointments with the garage. This suggested he had nothing to hide, except for unpaid bills. But if I judged him by how he treated his wife, he was a man who felt entitled to the good things in life without having to work—or pay—for them.

"I understand there's a new proprietor since the last time I was here." Derrick guided the carriage into the dirt yard that fronted the building and maneuvered between the motorcars waiting for maintenance. A large bay door stood open to the morning air, and the scraping and clanking of tools could be heard from within. A small office occupied about a quarter of the brick building, while the repair shop comprised the greater share of the structure.

We clambered down and followed the sounds into the shop, where a sporty Pierce Motorette stood in the middle of the space lined by workbenches, shelving, and cupboards. The motorcar quite resembled our carriage, with tufted leather seats, a tilted footboard, and a collapsible canvas roof. All it lacked was the hitch for the horse.

Though the sound continued, I detected no one in the vicinity. Not until a male voice uttered something unrepeatable. A wrench hit the cement floor and spun out from beneath the vehicle. It was then I noticed the feet and legs lying on the floor, the torso hidden beneath the chassis.

I took a step closer to the automobile. "Hello?"

To my surprise, the individual slid quickly out from beneath the Motorette. Closer inspection confirmed that he was lying on a board that had been mounted on wheels.

"What a clever innovation," I mused.

"The underside of a motorcar has a lot more workings than a carriage," Derrick pointed out with a shrug.

The man who had rolled out nearly at our feet gazed up at us with a mixture of curiosity and annoyance. "Can I help you folks?"

"As a matter of fact," I began.

Derrick stuck out a hand. "Need help up?"

The man hesitated a moment before managing to scramble to his feet without assistance. Then he held up his hands, both smudged with black grime. "You'd be scrubbing all day if you were to clasp one of these. Now, what is it you need? Did you bring your motorcar in?"

"No, not exactly." I suddenly recognized the dusky-complexioned man standing before us. "Oliver? Oliver Prescott? I didn't know you'd returned to Newport. Gayla and your parents must be delighted."

"Why, is this Emma Cross? *Little* Emma Cross?" He began to extend his hand, but, remembering about the grease, pulled back again.

"Goodness, Oliver, how long has it been?"

"I've been gone nearly eight years now."

I suddenly remembered my manners. "Oliver Prescott, this is my husband, Derrick Andrews. Derrick, you've met his sister, Gayla Prescott, who works for the telephone exchange."

There occurred a scant moment when the two men looked each other over; Derrick with friendly anticipation, Oliver with a touch of wariness lurking within hooded eyes.

Derrick spoke the deciding words. "A pleasure to meet you, as it always is to meet any of my wife's longtime Newport friends. But . . ." He grinned. "Pardon me if I don't shake your hand—this time."

Oliver's circumspection melted into a grin of his own. I understood. The Prescott family boasted an African ancestor going back a few generations, a great-great-grandmother, and while they were a firmly established and respected Newport family, occasionally there were those who judged them solely on that history. "The pleasure is mine, Mr. Andrews."

"Derrick. Tell me, Oliver, is the shop yours now?"

"It is. Learned the trade and earned enough down in New York and Pennsylvania to come back here a businessman. Took the place over at the beginning of the month. Not the cleanest work, I'll admit, but plenty lucrative."

"How wonderful for you," I exclaimed. "But I can't imagine how I didn't know this. Gayla never said a word." Which I found exceedingly strange, given the operator's garrulous nature.

"Don't worry, she'll catch you up soon enough. It was a bit of a surprise when I showed up. Took the family off guard—happily. But something tells me you didn't come here merely to renew an old acquaintance."

"That's true, Oliver." I glanced around. "Are you alone here?"

He nodded. "At the moment. One assistant is delivering a car, and the other comes in later."

"Then I'd like to ask you a few questions, if I may. About a customer who came in a few weeks ago. I suppose you'd have just taken over."

"Let's go into the office." He led us outside and to the smaller section of the building. Inside were a desk and two chairs for visitors. From a shelf on the wall, he plucked a rag and wiped his hands. "This is where I do business with my customers. Now, who are you curious about, Emma? I won't ask why," he added with a wink. "Yeah, Gayla's kept me informed about goings-on here in Newport."

Which only confirmed my suspicions that this city's main daytime operator sometimes—and perhaps inadvertently—listened in on the telephone calls she connected.

"Do you know who Harry Lehr is?" I asked after Derrick and I took our seats. "He's—"

Oliver laughed. "Emma, there's nobody in this town who doesn't know who Harry Lehr is, and yeah, he came in not long after I got here. Brought in his wife's motor, a little Spaulding Runabout, two-seater, gasoline powered. Or was, I should say. Isn't that the vehicle his man-of-all-work was killed in?"

"It was," Derrick said. "Why did Mr. Lehr bring the Runabout in? Any particular complaint?"

"None that he mentioned to me." Oliver tented his fingers, tapping them together as he spoke. His expression once more showed annoyance, this time not directed at us. "Just wanted me to look it over for safety's sake, he said. Strange thing was, he hung around the entire time I was at it."

"What do you mean, 'hung around'?" I asked.

"Breathed down my neck is more accurate. Observed everything I did. Insisted I check over the engine, pistons, gasoline line, you name it. Said he merely wished to ensure his wife's safety."

I only just refrained from snorting. "And he watched you the whole time?"

"Yessiree."

"What about the brakes?" Derrick asked him. "Did you work on them?"

"I took a look, but I never touched them. Didn't see that I needed to."

Derrick nodded in acknowledgment. "Did the police question you about the vehicle after the accident?"

"Believe me, they did. But they had no reason to find fault with my work. I keep detailed accounts of all the repairs I do. And one of my two assistants was here that day. He agreed the Runabout left here in fine working condition."

"What about Mr. Lehr?" I asked next. "Did he try to blame you for the accident?"

"Most certainly. Claimed I'd overlooked some defect in the braking mechanism and that caused the accident. He's threatened to sue and demanded a full refund for the work."

"Does he owe this shop other money as well?" Although I couched this as a question, I very well knew the answer.

"For services going back a few months now, ever since the Lehrs came to town. The previous owner couldn't get it out of him and wished me luck." Oliver made a sound with his tongue and shook his head.

"The motorcar must have been examined after the accident," Derrick commented. "What conclusions were reached?"

Oliver shrugged. "I heard they brought it to the Engineering Works over on Thames."

"The Newport Engineering Works?" Derrick repeated. The company had long since been building and repairing marine and locomotive engines, and in recent years had added automobile maintenance to their services.

"That's right. My competition, or one of them."

"And does anyone know what they concluded about the brakes?" I asked.

He gave another shrug. "You'd have to go there and ask."

"Oliver, I have one more question." I leaned forward. "Did Ellis Jackson bring the Runabout in to have the brakes looked at the day he died?"

"No, I never saw him, and neither did either of my assistants. Why?"

"Because Mrs. Lehr sent him here to have the Runabout looked at after her lady's maid told her it was behaving strangely. I would assume he'd bring it here, being so close to the house. Yet he crashed on Bath Road."

"Now, that *is* strange." Oliver passed the back of his hand beneath his chin. "Could be the man didn't think there was anything wrong with the motorcar and wanted to test it before bringing it in. Forgive me for saying so, but most men don't believe ladies know one end of a motorcar from the other." He offered me a sheepish grin.

"That does make sense," I agreed, and had to admit he was right. Most men maintained that women had no business owning or driving an automobile. It almost made me want to take up driving myself, if I weren't so enamored of my carriage and horse, Maestro.

After bidding Oliver goodbye with promises of a proper visit with him and his family, we drove on to the *Messenger.* Having been away from the office for two days, I found an inbox stuffed to bursting with articles off the Associated

Press wire, as well as notices about upcoming events, political developments in Newport and farther afield, and proposed changes to our public school budget.

This last gave me pause. Derrick and I were still waiting for the go-ahead to purchase a plot of land beside our own. We planned to build a new home for ourselves on this property, while turning Gull Manor into a school for girls, where they could be fully educated in advanced mathematics and the sciences, as well as the usual curriculum of history, reading, art, and music. It had been well over two years now since we'd first conceived the plan, and as time passed, I began to feel more and more discouraged that we would ever see it come to fruition. We'd run into difficulty concerning the ownership of the property, which turned out not to be as straightforward as we had initially been led to believe. In short, we needed to find a certain individual, or evidence of his death.

I sighed, sliding my inbox directly in front of me. If I wished to continue dividing my days between the office and home, I needed to put my time here to good use. Knowing Annamarie was well cared for—if a bit spoiled—by Nanny and Katie certainly helped ease my mind and allowed me to concentrate all the better.

An entire hour passed before Harry Lehr crept back into my thoughts. He tried to blame Oliver's shop for the accident, which didn't surprise me—however much it disgusted me. One more example of the man's ability to cast aspersions wherever convenient for his purposes. But *why* had he taken the motorcar there in the first place? Yes, having it generally looked over to ensure its safety was sound reasoning, but why had Harry insisted on observing the entire inspection process? Had he been there to oversee . . . or to learn?

The notion so startled me, I let out a gasp.

"Deep in thought, I see."

I gasped again. I'd been *so* deep in thought, I hadn't noticed Derrick stick his head in the doorway. He offered me a lopsided grin, strolled into the room, and perched on a corner of my desk.

"Could Harry have been trying to learn how to tamper with his wife's motorcar the day he brought it to the Ocean House Garage?"

"Whoa, Emma." He crossed his arms. "That's a serious accusation, and I don't know that you have anything to back it."

"But Oliver said he practically breathed down his neck while he did the work. That's suspicious, isn't it? Why would a man like Harry—someone who's never done a serious day's work in his life, according to Bessie—want to know the particulars of an automobile?"

"Idle curiosity?"

"Perhaps. Perhaps not, especially when he then attempted to blame Oliver for the faulty brakes."

Derrick pressed his lips together, then said, "I agree that's suspicious. But again, according to what you've learned from his wife, he hasn't many scruples. Blaming Oliver for the accident could be simply another way to avoid paying his bills."

"But that's just it. I don't believe it was an accident."

"Based, my darling, on what? So far, we have no proof the brakes simply didn't fail due to a defect in the manufacturing. Something your friend might not have been able to predict."

I was shaking my head, only half listening. I needed to know what the other garage concluded when they inspected the automobile following the accident. Coming to my feet, I turned to grab my hat off the cloak rack beside the door.

Derrick hopped down from the desk. "Where are you going?"

"To the Newport Engineering Works."

"We can stop there on the way home tonight."

After pinning my hat in place, I took Derrick's two hands in my own. "I need answers."

"Why not telephone over to the police station and speak with Jesse?"

"My interference gets Jesse in enough trouble."

"Aha! So you admit you're interfering."

I swatted his arm. "Bessie Lehr asked for my help, discreetly, without police involvement, and I aim to oblige her as much as I'm able."

He grasped my shoulders, pulling me closer. "Emma, as you've learned countless times in the past, hunting for a killer is dangerous. How much more so if you're unwilling to involve Jesse in the matter?"

"Yes, I realize I've never investigated entirely on my own before, but I'm not this time, either."

"Aren't you?" He frowned, turning his head and gazing at me sideways.

"No." I stretched taller and pecked his lips. "I have you."

"The cable disconnected from the rear brake on the left side of the vehicle, sending it careening to the right when the driver tried to slow down." The mechanic at the Newport Engineering Works pointed to the motorcar presently occupying one of the maintenance bays. Using it as an example to illustrate his point, he bent lower and fingered the cable that ran from the foot pedal beneath the steering wheel to the rear axle. "There are two of these, one on either side, and when the driver presses the pedal, they cause the brakes to clamp around the axle, slowing the vehicle to a stop."

"Sounds simple," I commented.

"It is." The man straightened and regarded Derrick and me.

Derrick bent lower to inspect where the cable connected to the brake. "Had it been tampered with?"

The man scratched his head, then shoved hair back from

his brow. "Not necessarily. Could have just come loose. Cars jostle around on the road. Lots of things come loose. That's why it's so important to keep a constant eye on them."

"But *could* it have been tampered with?" I pressed him.

"Surely. But only by someone who knew what they were doing." When Derrick and I met this statement with puzzled expressions, he went on to explain, "There were no signs of the cable being sliced or yanked free from the brake. No fraying, no cut marks."

"So you're saying this could have been an accident, pure and simple?" I wanted to be as clear about the matter as possible.

"That's what I'm saying, ma'am, and as far as I know, the police agreed."

We left him shortly after and made our way back to the *Messenger.* On the way, I pondered Bessie's suspicions and the state of her marriage.

"I can understand *why* she might believe Harry wants her gone," I mused aloud while the carriage jolted over the pitted surface of Lower Thames Street. "But, my goodness, these streets truly do jostle one about."

Derrick took his eyes off the road long enough to cast me a puzzled expression. "I'm terribly sorry, darling, but I don't see how those two statements go together."

With a blink, I snapped out of my pensive state. "I was thinking about what the mechanic said about the roads jostling motorcars about and loosening their parts. Harry might leave much to be desired as a husband, but in the end, perhaps the cable merely came loose."

"Like the stair runner and the balcony railing Bessie also believes was caused by her husband." Derrick slowed the buggy to accommodate a carriage and a pony cart turning onto Thames from a side street.

"Exactly. There is nothing so far that can't be explained by happenstance."

"So far," Derrick repeated.

"Yes . . . and coincidence." I frowned. I hated coincidences in matters such as these. It nearly always turned out to be a distraction, a deception. I shook my head. "Harry Lehr isn't off the hook. He needs to be watched. Closely. And by someone whose presence won't put him off."

"Who would you suggest? Certainly not yourself. In the places Harry frequents, you'd stick out like a sore thumb."

"I've no doubt about that."

"Me, then?"

I studied him, lifting an eyebrow in judgment. "Are you telling me you frequent the types of establishments Harry does?" I knew for a fact he did not, for such a man would rarely be home in the evenings or on the weekends. Derrick had proven himself to be a devoted family man, for which I was grateful. But on occasion, I enjoyed teasing him.

"No, but perhaps it's time I branched out," he teased in return. "We wouldn't want me to stagnate, would we?"

"*Hmph.*"

He grinned as we drove on.

"Brady," I said suddenly, having been struck by an idea.

Derrick glanced up and down the sidewalk on both sides of the road. "Where?"

"No, silly. Brady is the perfect person to keep watch on Harry. He's here for the next few weeks before needing to get back to work at the New York Central."

"But your brother turned over a new leaf years ago. Won't it seem strange that he's suddenly gambling and drinking again?"

I waved this off with a flick of my wrist. "What difference if people think he's temporarily fallen back into his old ways? The point is, he won't have."

"Drat. Brady gets to have all the fun," Derrick murmured, and I knew he was teasing again.

Still, I experienced a moment's doubt. Was it a good idea to send Brady back into the very places where he had once nearly come to ruin? "Perhaps I should discuss it with Hannah first."

The reason Brady had started coming home more frequently in the past year was, in fact, Hannah Hanson, a young woman we had both known from our earliest days growing up on the Point. The two had taken a shine to each other years ago, but Hannah, like me, valued her career—in her case, as a nurse. It presented a difficulty for them, as Hannah's work was here, at Newport Hospital, while Brady's was in New York City, at the offices of my relatives' New York Central Railroad. But judging by how often Brady visited, I predicted a happy end to the distance between them.

"Actually, it shouldn't present a problem." Derrick turned the carriage onto Bath Road, then took another turn onto Spring Street. "Brady doesn't have to drink and gamble. He just has to stop by those places to make sure Harry is there, doing those very things."

"In other words, simply verify that Harry goes where he claims he's going."

Derrick nodded in concurrence. "Exactly. Supposing, of course, that Bessie knows where her husband goes at any given time."

"Quite frankly, his appointment diary gives the impression that he doesn't much care who knows where he is. Nor does he appear to feel in any way constrained by Bessie's disapproval."

"Unlike Hannah Hanson, perhaps." He and I traded a glance. He winked. "It might be better to ask Hannah's forgiveness—after the fact—than seek her permission now."

"Perhaps you're right." I blew out a sigh, not liking to

keep secrets from my friend, especially when they involved her, albeit indirectly. Then I had an idea. "I know. You can accompany him. You can both be seen to be sowing some wild oats together. But it will reassure Hannah that Brady will come to no harm."

"A capital idea. That way, Brady doesn't get to have *all* the fun."

I narrowed my eyes at him as he drew the carriage to a stop in front of the *Messenger.* "Just make sure those oats aren't *too* wild, sir, or it won't be Hannah you'll answer to."

Chapter 4

While Derrick and Brady set out on Harry Lehr's trail, I didn't sit idle. On Friday afternoon after working at home, I set out for Belcourt, the cottage owned by Alva Belmont, my erstwhile Vanderbilt relative. Although the rest of the family had shunned her after her divorce from Uncle William, I'd seen no reason to follow suit. She and I had maintained a cordial relationship ever since, and I found I could usually depend on her for small favors, such as the one I needed today.

Since Derrick and Brady had zoomed off in Derrick's Peugeot, I had Maestro and our carriage at my disposal. At Belcourt, I exited the vehicle in the courtyard and made my way to the interior door that led into the ground floor of the house. From there, led by a footman, I crossed a large, echoing space housing a banquet table that could accommodate a multitude, and climbed the darkly paneled grand staircase that led to the main, albeit second floor of the house. When Alva's husband, Oliver, originally built Belcourt, he'd reserved the entire ground floor for his horses and carriages. Alva's first order of business upon their marriage had been to reclaim that space for humans and create, in her view, more appropriate equine accommodations in an entirely new wing.

At the upper landing, we entered the salon, airier and brighter than the stair hall, and cozier and more inviting than the vaulted Gothic ballroom next door. "Mrs. Emmaline Andrews," the footman announced. The three ladies lounging on velvet sofas ceased a lively conversation and turned their heads. Aunt Alva pushed to her feet with a swish of azure silk. "Emma, darling, so good of you to join us."

I resisted an urge to laugh and merely offered a cordial smile. "Thank you for inviting me," I replied, but we both knew it had been I who had initiated today's informal tea. I hadn't informed Aunt Alva of the exact reason for it and, to her credit, she hadn't asked. I'd only said that I sought advice on a society matter and had let her do the rest. She had done exceedingly well, inviting exactly whom I had hoped.

"Come and sit with us, dear." Aunt Alva beckoned with an outstretched arm toward the sofa currently occupied by Theresa Fair Oelrichs, or Tessie as she was called by her friends. Aunt Alva resumed her place on the sofa opposite, beside Mamie Fish.

I had come to know Mrs. Fish well over the years. She and Aunt Alva were nearly the same age, Aunt Alva having been born in January and Mrs. Fish in June of the same year. But where Aunt Alva's figure had given way to stoutness, Mrs. Fish continued to hold her still-trim, albeit sturdy, frame with the stature of a much younger woman. I credited her sheer stubbornness, as well as her humor and mischievous nature, for keeping her young.

Tessie Oelrichs, on the other hand, was only a few years my senior, which made her nearly two decades younger than the other two. Still, one needn't wonder why they viewed her as a peer. Though of average figure and features, a spark of determination in her eyes warned against underestimating her. No, more than that. That spark foretold of dire consequences, should one attempt to thwart her. One of her more recent triumphs, besides the commissioning of her glorious Bellevue Avenue cottage, Rosecliff, completed a year ago, had been her success in orchestrating the marriage of her younger sister, Birdie, to Aunt Alva's older son, Willie. Alva hadn't wished for the match, and I suspect she had hoped for another connection to European nobility, as she had achieved with my cousin Consuelo. But Willie and Birdie had stood adamant that they would marry, and since Alva never cared to admit defeat, or even that someone had gotten the better of her, she had instead welcomed Tessie into her rarified inner circle.

And so, that day, I faced society's fierce and formidable Triumvirate, who were gradually replacing an aging Caroline Astor as the leaders of society—and in so doing, reshaping and redefining its boundaries.

We spent the first half hour pleasantly catching up. While I resided in Newport year-round, they had only just arrived following their spring cruises to Europe. I let the conversation amble where it would, biding my time and, in truth, enjoying myself. I had always addressed Mamie as Mrs. Fish, as doing any less had seemed woefully inadequate. Now she stopped me in midsentence.

"My dear, it's high time you started calling me Mamie. After all, you're one of us now."

By that, I knew she meant I had married into a wealthy family, which had elevated me in the eyes of the Four Hundred in ways my Vanderbilt heritage had never done. After all, I had been a relatively poor Vanderbilt, even after my uncle Cornelius had remembered me in his will. Never mind that marrying Derrick had failed to win me an esteemed place in the Andrews family. His father tolerated me kindly enough; his mother downright loathed me.

We moved into the dining room for tea, and there, in the bright sunlight pouring through a semicircular bank of floor-to-ceiling windows—which became mirrors when closed—I gently delved into the matter that had brought me to Belcourt.

Casually, as if remarking on nothing of great importance, I commented, "The Lehrs were in town early this year to host my cousin Reggie's wedding. It surprised me that they stayed on afterward. I had thought they'd leave and come back once summer Season began."

"They decided not to travel this spring," Tessie informed me. "Something about Harry helping your cousin fill his new stables with thoroughbreds."

"I see." This surprised me. Sandy Point, Reggie's new estate in Portsmouth, was a horse farm and I knew he meant to breed the finest racehorses money could buy. But I hadn't known he was collaborating with Harry Lehr. Was Harry only offering his advice, or did he mean to be a major investor? Could that explain his sudden need to control Bessie's money? "I didn't know Mr. Lehr to be an expert in racehorses."

"Harry is a man of many talents," Mamie said with a snort that suggested there was more to that statement than face value.

"He and Mrs. Lehr seem very happy together," I ventured.

"Indeed." Aunt Alva smoothed the lace at her neckline

before taking up her fork again. "And they have us to thank for it."

"Do they indeed?" My ignorance on the matter was entirely feigned. I knew the story, but I wished to hear it from the source, or, in this case, sources.

"Goodness, yes." Tessie Oelrichs slathered jam onto a scone she had just sliced in half. "Harry has long been a favorite of ours. Such a dear, and such fun. And always so attentive to his female friends. Harry Lehr is the sort of man who takes no shame in having women friends. He doesn't consider us in any way inferior to his male comrades. He even comes to us for advice. He respects our opinions. And we respect his." She emphasized this last point with a stab of her silver butter knife at the air.

"Alas, though, we found it unfortunate that a man Harry's age hadn't yet settled on a wife." Aunt Alva sighed.

"So we settled on one for him," Mamie announced as if delivering the conclusion of a joke.

The joke, unfortunately, was on Bessie Lehr.

Once again, I pretended innocence mingled with curiosity. "How did you settle on Bessie Drexel?"

"My dear," Tessie all but sang out, "she is simply perfect for him. Young, unworldly, yet having been married and widowed, not completely inexperienced. And of such docile temperament she would never give a man like Harry a moment's distress."

A man like Harry. I pondered all that implied: his greed, his selfishness, his utter indifference to his wife's needs. What about the distress he caused her daily?

"Let's be frank, ladies. Emma can be trusted, despite her little hobby." After winking at me as she referred to my newspaper work, Alva assumed one of her no-nonsense expressions. "Harry also needed a woman with money. Bessie is not only refined and sweet tempered, she is rich. Rich enough to satisfy the tastes of a sophisticated man like Harry."

Their enthusiasm led me to believe they didn't know the truth about the Lehrs' relationship. Apparently, the pair played their part so well in public they had everyone fooled. Bessie didn't wish me to alert the police about her suspicions because she knew that once out, within a day word of her failed marriage would reach the ear of every member of the Four Hundred.

Mamie sipped her tea, then stared contemplatively at the cup as she said, "She *can* be something of a flibbertigibbet at times, though."

"Can she?" My surprise here wasn't conrived. Yes, Bessie had been unsettled and distressed when she first came to see me, and I still questioned her suspicions, but she hadn't seemed the sort of woman to become overexcited or agitated without cause. Had I been wrong?

"Yes, that's true," Tessie agreed. "That polished exterior does hide a bit of a nervous constitution none of us noticed right away. Harry sometimes has reason to be concerned." She pressed her lips together, once more leaving one with the impression of significant things left unsaid.

Mamie, however, felt inclined to fill in a blank or two. "It's on account of her sheltered upbringing. We were all shielded as girls, of course, but Bessie's Catholic mother went about it rather more vigorously than the rest of society's mamas. And Bessie's first husband, I hear, was equally protective of her."

"Well, thank goodness she has Harry to bring her out of her shell," Aunt Alva concluded in a firm manner that put a halt to the gossip. "All in all, she's a dear, as is Harry. So all's well that ends well."

* * *

"You know it would be *highly* irregular for me to reveal whom our customers converse with, Emma." Gayla Prescott peered up at me from her seat before the switchboard at Newport's telephone exchange. "Oliver told me how you and Mr. Andrews were asking questions about Mr. Lehr. What's this all about, Emma? Some big article you're working on?"

I leaned a hip against the edge of her worktop and drew a breath. Just as she felt honor-bound not to reveal too much about who she connected to whom each day, I had made a promise to Bessie Lehr. How could I entice Gayla to help me without betraying Bessie's confidence? Then an idea struck me, thanks to my visit with Aunt Alva and her friends. "He and my cousin Reggie are partnering in a business endeavor, and I wish to make sure he doesn't lead Reggie astray."

Her eyes widened. "How so?"

"Can I count on you to be discreet?" I leaned down lower toward her, at the same time sliding a basket of Nanny's molasses cookies closer to her. She glanced down, flipped aside an edge of the cotton napkin covering them, and selected one as if choosing a diamond ring from a jeweler's tray.

"Of course you can. You know I'm the soul of discretion."

I bit back the laugh that sprang to my lips. "It appears Mr. Lehr will be helping Reggie assemble a stable of horses at his new farm in Portsmouth."

"Sandy Point, right?"

"Right. And I'm merely concerned that between the two of them, they might be induced to spend more than Reggie should, or perhaps do business with the wrong people."

"Goodness, Emma, you make it sound as though they're

dealing on the black market." She snapped a bite of cookie between her teeth and chewed. "Mmm . . . you'll thank Mrs. O'Neal for me, yes?"

"Of course, and no, nothing like that. But Reggie being the youngest son, my aunt Alice frets over him constantly. I don't want her to have to worry more than she already does. She's been through so much in recent years."

"To be certain, poor lady. Well . . ." She compressed her lips, then opened them for another bite. I felt almost guilty for having tempted her so, but I knew Gayla Prescott could never resist anything sweet, and that her gratitude for such a treat would loosen her tongue. "If you promise not to use the information for any other purpose . . ."

I pressed a hand over my heart. "Never. Perish the thought."

"Then I can tell you that Mr. Lehr's telephone calls have been fairly routine lately. He calls over to the Casino most days. He's called the Country Club and the Opera House several times in the past two weeks, and he's asked to be connected to a few private residences."

"And whose residences were those?"

She assumed a reluctant moue; then, eyeing the basket of cookies, she relented. "Mrs. Fish, Mrs. Belmont, and someone with whom I'm not familiar, a Mr. Noble. Ralph Noble."

"Noble." I pondered the name, hoping it might strike a bell. It didn't. "Do you know where this man resides?"

"Heavens, no. I connect according to numbers, not addresses. All I can tell you is that it was a local call somewhere in Newport."

"Noble," I repeated softly, committing it to memory. I hadn't learned much, but then my coming here had been a long shot. "Thank you, Gayla. You've been a help."

"I surely hope your cousin fares well in his endeavors." She patted the basket. "Would you like this back? I could empty the cookies onto a plate."

"Keep it for now, I'll pick it up another day. Enjoy the cookies."

Nearly a week later, Brady joined Derrick and me for dinner. He had solely taken over the task of shadowing Harry Lehr, which would have taken Derrick away from the *Messenger* and from home far too often. In that time, I had stayed in close touch with Bessie, and there had been no further occurrences threatening her well-being.

Yet.

Before the meal, the three of us—Derrick, Brady, and I—lounged in the parlor, along with Patch, who lay on the floor by Brady's chair, his chin on Brady's foot. I had given Annamarie her bath and we had tucked her in for the night.

"I'm afraid I'm not going to be any help at all, Em," Brady said, slinging one arm along the back of his chair. "I can honestly say Harry hasn't been anywhere he shouldn't have been, unless you consider that the man is almost never at home."

"I don't think his wife is complaining about that," Derrick murmured with a wry look.

"Not as I would," I assured him, resting my head on his shoulder for a moment. Then I returned to the subject by asking Brady, "Where *has* he been, then?"

"The Casino quite a lot, and at various times of day. He watches the tennis and sometimes plays himself, usually mixed doubles. He eats at the restaurant and attends shows at night. Sometimes with his wife, but just as often not. He's also been to the Opera House—without *Mrs.* Lehr—and he's lunched at Crossways and Rosecliff. Seems to me, he fills his days so that he's rarely if ever alone."

"This all confirms what Gayla told you about Harry's phone calls." Derrick threaded his fingers through mine.

As I nodded absently, thinking, Brady said, "Sorry, Em. I wish I had more information for you." He brushed a stray lock of sandy-blond hair back from his brow.

"No, this *has* helped," I said. "It suggests that perhaps Bessie is imagining things, or exaggerating coincidences in her mind until her suspicions have careened out of control. Aunt Alva and the others did tell me she can be a bit of a flibbertigibbet."

Brady held my gaze. "What do your instincts tell you?"

"That Bessie is neither flighty nor a bundle of nerves by nature. Brady, does the surname Noble mean anything to you?"

"Noble? Not particularly. It's not an uncommon name, but I can't think of a Noble I know personally."

"Well, Harry does. Gayla told me he's made telephone calls to someone by that name."

"Probably just a friend," Derrick said with a dismissive wave of a hand.

"Perhaps, but Harry is an opportunist, isn't he?" It wasn't a rhetorical question, and I waited for Brady and Derrick to respond.

"I'd say yes, given his ties to the Triumvirate," Brady agreed. "That he attached himself to Aunt Alva and the other two shows he likes to go straight to the top when it comes to society. The only question is, why do they accommodate him the way they do?"

Derrick chuckled. "I imagine he flatters them at every opportunity."

"I have no doubt." I drummed the fingertips of my free

hand on the arm of the sofa. "And he's attached himself to Reggie, I believe, because the others in the family won't have him. He certainly has nothing in common with Neily, and Alfred surely doesn't have time for his nonsense. As for Gertrude . . ." I laughed outright. "We all know she does not suffer fools."

"All right, so Harry likes to associate with people on the higher end of the ladder." Derrick shrugged a shoulder. "He's not alone in that. What are you getting at, my darling?"

"None of us knows who this Noble person is, which is unusual in a town like Newport at this time of year. It would suggest he's no one of note, but then what's Harry's business with him?"

Derrick hefted an eyebrow. "A good question."

"It sounds like I have my next challenge." Brady tapped a finger at the air. "Discover the identity of the mysterious Mr. Noble." He gazed at me and grinned. "How?"

"I don't know." I grinned back at him. "You'll think of something."

Nanny called us in to dinner, but on the way, Brady caught my arm and took me aside. "I want to show you something, Em."

Something about the look on his face made me wary. "Yes?"

He reached into his coat pocket and withdrew a small velvet box. When he lifted the lid, my jaw dropped and a gasp of surprise flew from my lips. Inside, nestled in black silk, was an emerald surrounded with small diamonds set on a gold band.

I searched his face. "Brady, are you . . . ?"

"I'm going to ask her tomorrow night, Em."

I threw my arms around his neck and squeezed. "It's about time. I was about to give up hope. I just hope Hannah hasn't."

"What do you think she'll say?" he asked after I released him, his voice endearingly unsteady.

"Brady, I'm not about to speak for Hannah. You'll just have to ask her. But I know what I'm hoping she'll say."

His lips curled in the same smile I remembered from Christmas mornings when we were children. "Me too."

Chapter 5

After settling Annamarie in her feeding chair in the kitchen, I lowered the wooden tray in front of her. "Don't wiggle like a worm, you, or you'll slide right out." I reached for her favorite mealtime toy, a painted wooden duck on wheels that she could roll back and forth on the tray. It had the advantage of being thoroughly washable.

I tied a fresh bib around her neck and donned an apron myself. Nanny handed me Annamarie's bowl of oatmeal porridge, sweetened with a drizzle of molasses. While my child rolled her duck back and forth, laughing and slapping the tray with her other hand, I managed to spoon the warmed cereal into her mouth without losing too much of it to spills. Once or twice, she reached for the spoon, but I floated it away like a tiny bird and distracted her with kisses. Only when I had deemed she had eaten enough would I relinquish the spoon and allow her to practice feeding herself.

Feeding time was always a challenge, but one I enjoyed.

That morning, however, my mind partly dwelled elsewhere, not that my daughter particularly noticed. But Nanny did. Nanny *always* did.

"You look lost in thought, lamb." She took a seat at the table across from us. We had installed a Dutch door leading out to the rear yard, and with the top half open, the fresh, sun-kissed breezes from the ocean gently bathed the room and stirred our hair. Annamarie's feathery curls, dark like her papa's, ruffled like the down of a baby chick.

We adults had eaten breakfast earlier and the tidying had been done. While Derrick prepared the buggy for our ride into town, Katie had gone out to the barn to tend to our retired carriage horse, Barney, whom I refused to sell despite our keeping another, much younger, horse, Maestro. Barney, a roan hack I'd inherited from my great-aunt Sadie, had faithfully transported her, and then me, all over Newport—and sometimes farther—for years. Didn't I owe him the same loyalty?

"Emma? Is something wrong?" Nanny's gaze bored into me, reminding me she wouldn't desist until I'd satisfied her curiosity.

"It's Mrs. Lehr."

"Ah, I might have guessed."

"Brady didn't report anything unusual in her husband's activities or whereabouts, leaving me to wonder again if Mrs. Lehr isn't mistaken in her suspicions."

"Perhaps she is, and the matter is best dropped." Annamarie turned her face in Nanny's direction, prompting Nanny to make a funny face, which made my girl giggle. "Mrs. Lehr wouldn't be the first woman to misunderstand her husband's intentions. From what you say, he's a cad, but there's a world of difference between a cad and a killer."

"I agree. But she seems so certain, and despite what Aunt

Alva and the others said about her, she simply doesn't strike me as being taken with flights of fancy."

"Could someone else be behind the incidents?" Before I could counter the notion, she held up a hand. "If you're so sure she isn't completely off the mark, then it could be someone other than her husband."

"But who else would profit from Bessie Lehr's death? Who could possibly hold such a grudge against that dear lady?"

Nanny tilted her head at me. "Why not look at it from another direction? You're considering motive, but maybe the motive is more complicated than a desire to control Mrs. Lehr's money. The problem you've come up against is finding when and how Mr. Lehr had the opportunity to threaten his wife's life."

"But he *did* bring the motorcar to the service station and then watched as Oliver performed the maintenance. Why would he do that if he wasn't planning to tamper with the vehicle himself?"

"As you know, and as I've learned from my servant acquaintances who have observed him closely, Harry Lehr is capricious and often illogical. Perhaps he genuinely believed the vehicle needed to be looked over, and perhaps watching Oliver Prescott amused him."

I fed Annamarie several spoonfuls while I mulled that over. "But if not Harry, who?"

"Who had the opportunity to tamper with the motorcar, loosen the balcony railing, and the other things that nearly injured or killed Mrs. Lehr?"

"Opportunity . . . well, Harry Lehr, of course. He lives with her, after all."

"Yes, but who *else*, Emma?" I could hear an edge of impatience creeping into Nanny's voice. It reminded me of years ago, when she would try to talk sense into me while I clung to my stubbornness.

For a moment, I wondered if it would be the same someday between Annamarie and myself. Would we butt heads, each of us entrenched in an opposing point of view? The notion sent a wave of dismay coursing through me. But as Nanny waited for my reply, I glimpsed the fondness in her gaze, the wholehearted acceptance of the person she had helped raise, and I didn't spend another moment fretting over my daughter's and my future contentions. Except for Derrick, I trusted no one more than Nanny. And to no one else, except him, did I turn instinctively when I needed solace. As long as I followed Nanny's example, Annamarie and I would be just fine.

Thus reassured, I gave her question serious consideration. And then it hit me.

"Her maid. Her lady's maid," I clarified. "What *is* her name?" I shook my head, unable to remember as my mind raced to recall exactly what Bessie had told me. "She . . . the maid . . . was there at each incident, ready to save Mrs. Lehr from what could have been a disaster each time. She prevented her from falling as the balcony railing broke away, steadied her when she tripped over the rumpled stair runner . . ." I paused, chewing my lip as I attempted to recollect what Bessie had told me about the morning they were to go shopping. I shook my head again, but this time to dismiss my theory. "No, it was the maid who discovered the motorcar wasn't behaving correctly, and that was why Mrs. Lehr had their man-of-all-work drive it into town, to the garage. Nanny, that doesn't at all sound like someone who wishes to harm her employer. If she bore ill will toward Mrs. Lehr, why did she save her each time?"

As I spoke, Katie came up the steps to the kitchen door.

Her light Irish brogue, tempered by her years in this country, made a gentle counterpoint to the sound of the breeze and the ocean waves. "Perhaps because it made her indispensable to Mrs. Lehr. Sorry," she added quickly as she opened the bottom half of the door and stepped in. "I couldn't help overhearin'."

I turned to stare at her as she went to the sink to wash her hands. Perhaps sensing my scrutiny, she met my gaze over her shoulder. "Pardon, Miss Emma," she said sheepishly. "I know I should mind my own business."

"Not at all, Katie," I replied. Annamarie seized that moment to reach for the spoon, suspended in midair in my hand. I let her take it. "That was a keen observation on your part. Perhaps no one wishes to harm Mrs. Lehr, but rather, as you say, to become indispensable to her. I'm not sure I would have thought of it."

"You would have, Miss Emma. But I've seen it before. Not with the mistress of the house, mind you. Nothin' as bold as that. But when I first started at The Breakers, there was a housemaid who hadn't been there very long, but went out of her way to be a help to the housekeeper. The thing is, she would hide things from her and then be the one to find them. She made the housekeeper think she was going daft, but then would reassure her anyone could mislay things."

Nanny tsked. "What happened to her? Was she found out?"

"To be sure, Mrs. O'Neal. She was let go before I was."

I rose, crossed to Katie, and put a hand on her shoulder. With a little squeeze, I acknowledged the courage it took for her to speak of her time at The Breakers at all. She had left under deplorable circumstances, her employers failing to protect her from the dangers all young maids faced in great houses. She smiled back at me, her gaze dipping for an instant before meeting my own again.

"My darling, are you ready to be off?" Derrick came in, holding his straw boater hat in one hand. He went to Annamarie's baby chair and chucked her beneath the chin. "Hello, you. Did you have a good breakfast?" Too late did he notice the spoon in her hand and the mess smeared not only across the tray in front of her, but all over her face and neck. He reclaimed his hand to discover his fingers covered to the second knuckle in porridge. "Ah. I see. I do hope you managed to get as much inside you as out."

"Don't worry, we did." After wetting a dishrag and rinsing it out, I went over to them. Derrick took my place at the sink, and while I cleaned up our daughter, he washed off his hand. "And yes, I'm ready to go."

Nanny had already gotten to her feet, and once I'd dislodged Annamarie from her chair, she reached with her steady, dependable arms to take charge of our girl until Derrick and I were home again.

I ruffled Annamarie's hair and gave her kisses on both chubby, dimpled cheeks. No matter how secure I was in the knowledge that she would be lovingly looked after, that initial moment of saying goodbye always produced a pang.

"Detour to Arleigh," I instructed Derrick once we'd started on our way.

To his credit, he didn't question why or groan at the prospect, but simply asked, "Do you think she'll be up this early?"

"I hope so. If not, I'll leave my card to let her know I need to speak with her. Katie made a rather eye-opening suggestion earlier. She told me about a maid at The Breakers who tried manipulating the housekeeper with the object of becoming indispensable to her."

"And you think something similar is happening to Bessie?"

"It could be." The wind tried to lift my own straw boater, testing the skill with which Nanny had pinned it down. I glanced at Derrick. How *did* men manage to keep their hats on their heads without such contrivances? I supposed that while theirs sat snug on their skulls, ladies' hats perched precariously on the curls and waves piled atop our heads. "On the off chance Harry isn't guilty, someone else could very well be."

"And you suspect one of the servants?"

"Not *suspect,* exactly. But I do feel the need to look into her lady's maid. Who she is, where she's from. That sort of thing."

"And whether she might know something about motorcars?"

I stared straight ahead at the road. "One never knows."

Bessie wasn't up and receiving when we arrived at Arleigh, but she came to me at the *Messenger* later that day. How incongruous the elegant Elizabeth Drexel Lehr looked in her sleek, cobalt-blue carriage ensemble against the drab gray walls, linoleum floors, and curtainless windows of our newspaper establishment.

And yet, she appeared oblivious to her surroundings, smiling as she entered my office as though she were entering my parlor for tea. "I'm so glad I caught you in. I'm terribly sorry I wasn't down yet when you called earlier."

"No matter." I wheeled over Ethan's swivel chair and bade her sit. "There was no great urgency"—I emphasized the word *great*—"but I do wish to speak with you about a matter that could prove important."

"By all means. What is it?"

"First, can I get you something? Coffee, tea? Or would you care to go elsewhere?" The absurdity of a woman like

Elizabeth Lehr sitting in an office chair amid reams of paper and bottles of ink—and the rumbling of the presses that vibrated the floor beneath our feet—continued to make me feel almost apologetic for her being there.

"I'm perfectly fine where we are," she said pleasantly. "And no, I'm coming straight from a luncheon at The Elms. Minnie was quite sorry you couldn't attend. Anyway, I couldn't consume another thing for hours yet."

"Did you . . . come here with your maid?"

"Miss Thorton? No, she's at home. Our driver brought me in our carriage. Why?"

"How long has Miss Thorton been in your employ?"

The question clearly puzzled her. A wariness entered her expression. "About a year now."

"And how did you find her, may I ask?"

"I see." She visibly relaxed. "You're looking for a maid for yourself. She came to me indirectly through Mamie Fish. Neddie—that is, Miss Thorton—was recommended by Mamie's housekeeper."

"Did she come with references?"

"No, not exactly. Only the housekeeper's word that she seemed a refined young woman of a good, if impoverished, family. She's from the South, you see." She added this last as if it explained everything, and in a way it did. Long before people like my relatives started vacationing here, Newport had been the summer haven of wealthy Southerners, until the war came and their fortunes were lost.

"Did she come North alone, or with her family?"

"Alone, I believe. Neddie—that's short for Edwina—doesn't like to speak of her past, and so we rarely do. Are you wondering if she might have a sister who would make a suitable maid? I could ask her, if you like."

"No." The answer came too quickly, and Bessie blinked.

"No, thank you," I amended. "I'd like to give it more thought first. I was merely curious about her, about how she came to be in your employ."

"I'm very lucky to have found her. She's been an asset in every way. Quite indispensable to me."

The word *indispensable* caused *me* to blink.

"If that's all for now, I must be going. Harry is forcing me to accompany him to the Opera House tonight and I'll need a lie-down first. Apparently, there will be a number of doyennes there for whom we must keep up appearances." She made a moue of distaste. "I tell you, Emma, this charade is terribly wearing. Especially knowing there is no end in sight." She came to her feet, prompting me to do the same. She held out her hand to grasp mine. "When Neddie brought me your message this morning, I thought perhaps you had something to tell me about Harry, that you'd found proof of his villainy."

"No, Bessie. If anything, I've only found proof of his innocence, with the exception of his odd behavior when he brought your motorcar to the garage for inspection. Did you know he stood by watching the mechanic do his work?"

"Did he?" She shrugged. "If Harry can annoy someone, he will. Especially if he deems that someone inferior—such as me."

She had clearly missed the point of my question, which suggested that Harry had wished to learn how to sabotage the vehicle by watching Oliver at work. I didn't elucidate it for her. Instead, another question, prompted by a remembered snippet of conversation with Tessie Oelrichs, popped into my mind. "Did you stay in Newport after Reggie's wedding because Harry is helping Reggie purchase horses for his new stables?"

She looked at me blankly, then said, "We stayed in Newport because I refused to lay out the money for a trip. I suppose Harry came up with that excuse to save face with his friends." She held out her hand. "Do let's have a proper visit soon."

"Let's do," I said, and gave her hand a squeeze. I saw her out, but the matter was far from over once the street door closed behind her. Perhaps Harry had been making excuses, or perhaps he'd been spending Bessie's money in ways she knew nothing about. And if anything, her defense of Neddie Thorton would send me in new directions for the express purpose of finding out more about the woman.

Though my days as a society reporter were well over, and through my marriage I had come to be welcome at the front doors of most of Newport's cottages, the next morning I bypassed the main drive of Crossways, Stuyvesant and Mamie Fish's columned, whitewashed Colonial-revival mansion set high on a hill on Ocean Avenue. I entered, instead, through the service area.

My sudden appearance caused a bit of a stir, with a footman stumbling over his feet to assist me, and the housekeeper hurrying over to ask if anything was amiss.

"Not at all, Mrs. . . ." I searched my memory for her name, but none came.

"Darvish, ma'am. Might I alert the mistress of the house that you are here?" She spoke with a Scottish brogue, though refined by an education that must have extended beyond grammar school. Her gaze subtly flicked the length of my carriage dress, which, though of serviceable, lightweight wool in a dependable shade of forest green, was of finer quality than any I had previously worn prior to my marriage. I could see her effort to smooth the alarm from her pleasantly lined features, the disapproval.

She obviously wished me gone from the delivery hall as soon as possible. Did she think I'd gotten lost on my way to visit Mrs. Fish? Funny, but years ago, the disapproval had typically come from the mistresses of the houses, not the servants.

Her discomfiture raised a smidgeon of guilt. "I am Mrs. Andrews. I'm terribly sorry to trouble you, Mrs. Darvish, and if you're dreadfully busy now, I'll return at a more convenient time."

If my presence here had startled her, these last words left her dumbfounded. "I . . . I . . . I suppose I have a few minutes to spare . . ."

Yes, I had guessed she might, given that at this time of the morning, the servants would already have completed their early chores and eaten their breakfasts. They had at least an hour yet before Mamie and Stuyvesant, along with any houseguests they might be entertaining, would rise from their beds.

"In that case," I said, "might we talk somewhere a bit quieter?" Behind me, the service doors had opened and two young men strode in, each carrying a crate brimming with produce. Before the doors had swung closed behind them, I spied another delivery wagon as it pulled up, its side advertising PHILIPS & SONS LTD., BREWERS AND WINE MERCHANTS

"Please follow me, ma'am." Mrs. Darvish turned on her heel and led the way past the kitchen and storerooms to her private parlor. It was a plain room, not much different from my office at the *Messenger,* but for a pair of faded floral easy chairs and a table that held a pretty porcelain tea service. To her, I must have been as out of place there as Bessie had seemed to me earlier.

The woman closed the door and gestured to a chair. "Won't you sit, Mrs. Andrews?"

"Thank you. I promise I won't keep you long. It's just that I understand you recommended Neddie Thorton to Mrs. Harry Lehr."

She had remained standing, and now her feet shuffled beneath her skirts. "I suppose I did, ma'am, although I recommended her to Mrs. Fish, who, in turn, mentioned her to Mrs. Lehr."

"I see." I crossed my fingers in the folds of my skirt and lied. "I'm looking for a dependable, skilled lady's maid, and I was wondering how you found Miss Thorton."

"I met her . . . in New York, ma'am."

"Under what circumstances? Are you acquainted with someone she worked with?"

"Uh . . . not exactly, ma'am. You see . . ." She clasped her hands at her waist. "I met her when she came to visit me at the Fishes' town house in the city."

"Came to visit you? I don't understand. Why would she visit you if you had never met her before?"

"On account of she was looking for work, ma'am, and I was in a position to help her."

"Excuse me?" My astonishment wasn't feigned. "You mean to tell me you recommended Miss Thorton to Mrs. Lehr without having prior knowledge of her?"

"She was . . . recommended to me, ma'am."

"By whom, might I ask?"

"By . . ." The woman's forehead puckered and she looked about to cry. She gazed down at her hems, drew in a breath, and met my gaze with her own fearful one. "Has there been trouble for Mrs. Lehr, ma'am?"

Determined not to break Bessie's confidence, I shook my head. "Not yet, no. But it does shock me, Mrs. Darvish, that you would have sent a lady's maid into the home of your employer's friend without having followed the proper channels. Did she come with references?"

"Not exactly." This came as a barely audible whisper.

I pushed to my feet, truly alarmed now. "Mrs. Darvish, what *can* you have been thinking?"

"I did it for Meredith, ma'am."

"And who is Meredith?" I swallowed. I had begun to raise my voice, but it wouldn't do to cause a scene. With more control, I repeated my query. "Who is Meredith?"

"She's head housemaid, ma'am, here and in the New York house. She told me Miss Thorton was a good friend of hers, that she had come upon hard times—dreadfully hard times, ma'am—and needed the work desperately. And Meredith has always been a good girl—dependable, a hard worker, always punctual—that I told her, against my better judgment, of course, to send Miss Thorton to me. And she seemed such an intelligent, gracious young woman, almost a lady herself, that I couldn't see the harm in helping her."

I studied the housekeeper during this lengthy explanation, and a niggling sensation came over me that there was more to this story. Why would a housekeeper risk her position to do a housemaid a favor? Even a head housemaid?

One logical answer seemed obvious: The housemaid held something over Mrs. Darvish's head. What that could be, I could only guess, but was it any business of mine? I didn't think so—at least, not beyond how it might affect the Lehr household. And to determine that, it looked as though I needed to speak to one other person before I left Crossways.

"Is this Meredith available to speak with me?"

"Must you, ma'am?"

"I believe I must, Mrs. Darvish." Would she suddenly remember that I had come seeking advice on finding my own lady's maid, and that I held no authority here, or would she remain so flustered at being caught out that she would continue to cooperate? To help set her mind at ease and ensure the latter, I said, "Mrs. Fish need not know about my visit today, provided I come away satisfied that her household is at no risk due to any lax protocol on the part of her staff."

"Goodness, no, ma'am. I assure you, I maintain the strictest household standards on the part of Mr. and Mrs. Fish."

Mmm. "Would you please send for Meredith."

The girl came a few minutes later, breathless and tucking strands of golden-brown hair back under her cap. "You asked to see me, ma'am?"

The housekeeper stepped into the room behind her. I held up a hand to her. "Mrs. Darvish, would you please leave us for a few minutes?"

Reluctance crept across her features, but she retreated into the corridor and closed the door.

"Now, then," I began, "I understand Neddie Thorton is a friend of yours?"

A frown immediately formed. "Is she in trouble, ma'am?"

"Not at all. I'm only wondering where you and she met. How do you know her? You see, I'm a friend of Mrs. Lehr, and it's come to my attention that Miss Thorton came into her employ without references. Can you explain that, Meredith?"

"Miss Thorton needed work, ma'am, and I thought she'd do well. She's ever such a nice young lady, ma'am."

"That's what Mrs. Darvish said. Then you've known Miss Thorton a good long while? Were you girlhood friends? Did you attend school together, something like that?"

Meredith's hands twisted in her snowy-white apron. "No, ma'am."

"I'm not here to get you in trouble. As long as you do

your best work for Mr. and Mrs. Fish, you have nothing to fear. But, Meredith, I need to know how you became acquainted with Neddie Thorton, and why you pressed Mrs. Darvish to furnish her with a recommendation."

In reply, the girl burst into tears.

Chapter 6

The door trembled from a fierce knocking on the other side. "Is everything all right in there?" Mrs. Darvish called through the thick oak.

Meredith stuffed her fist into her mouth to smother her sobs as I called back, "We're fine, thank you, Mrs. Darvish. Just another few minutes, please."

Would that prevent the housekeeper from rushing in? I cast a sharp look at Meredith. Now both hands covered her mouth, and she stared back at me from over them. I tilted my head at her in question. She nodded and slowly drew her hands away from her face.

Her breath trembled. "I met Neddie in the city at a tavern downtown, McCallum's, where some of us go when we have free time. Usually when the Fishes are away and haven't brought us all with them."

"What happened when you met Neddie?"

"She seemed so nice. Said she needed work. Needed *help* getting work, I should say. I saw her a couple more times, and the last time she asked if the Fishes were hiring. Said she'd make a fine lady's maid. I told her no, they weren't hiring, and she dropped it, or so I thought. The next thing I knew, she came uptown to visit me there and told me if I didn't help her, she'd let Mr. and Mrs. Fish know we'd been at McCallum's. We're not supposed to, especially us girls, and the Fishes wouldn't like it."

"What did you do?" I asked her.

She drew another deep breath and let it out in a whoosh. "All servants have their secrets, even the upper servants."

"I would imagine," I replied, then waited.

Reluctance filled her countenance, along with a silent plea that I not force her to continue. Instead, I merely waited. The silence stretched. Finally she said, "I know something about Mrs. Darvish. Please don't make me tell you what it is."

I shook my head. "I won't. Whatever it is has no bearing on why I'm here."

Her shoulders sagged with relief.

"I gather you threatened to reveal Mrs. Darvish's secret if she didn't help Neddie Thorton find placement as a lady's maid. Is that the long and the short of it?"

"It is, ma'am." She again sighed with relief, until my next words.

"Did it not occur to you that a woman like Neddie Thorton, someone who didn't hesitate to blackmail you, could be dangerous? That you might be putting her future employer at risk?"

Her features froze in horror. She whispered, "Has she done something terrible?"

I had spoken out of turn, I realized, said too much and risked betraying Bessie's trust. I shook my head. "No, not yet. And hopefully, she never will, especially if I caution Mrs. Lehr to find out more about Neddie. To keep a sharp eye on her."

"Honest, ma'am, I'd never have done it if I didn't believe

that, underneath it all, Neddie was a decent person. She was just desperate for a position, is all. You can understand that, can't you, ma'am? Being so frightened of having nothing to eat, nowhere to live, that you'll do anything to survive? I think that's all Neddie was doing. Trying to survive." She went quiet a moment, studying me, her lips compressed. Then, with a shake of her head, she murmured, "No, I don't suppose you can understand."

She was correct. Even at my poorest, I'd never been alone, never desperate. I'd never faced homelessness or hunger or wondered how I'd go on another day. My parents, though never wealthy from what my father made as an artist, had always managed to provide Brady and me with the essentials. Then I'd gone to live with Great-Aunt Sadie at Gull Manor, and I'd lacked for nothing I needed. Luxuries might have been few and far between, but we ate well and we sheltered beneath a sturdy roof. And when Great-Aunt Sadie died, she left me Gull Manor, a respectable savings to keep the house running, and I'd worked as a society reporter. I'd also had my Vanderbilt relatives, especially Cornelius and Alice, who not only offered help when I needed it, but were always more than happy to do so.

No. Who was I to judge any of these women—Mrs. Darvish, Meredith, even Neddie Thorton—for their secrets or their machinations?

And yet for Bessie's sake, I felt compelled to dig deeper, to discover if Neddie Thorton's secrets were those of a woman trying desperately to survive, or of a potential killer.

In the midst of my investigation, there also came a celebration. Brady had proposed to Hannah Hanson, and she had said yes.

With dizzying speed, her overjoyed parents threw together a fete that would have shocked the matrons of the

Four Hundred. Lucky for the Hansons, then, that none of them would be in attendance. But as Derrick and I approached their house in our carriage, it seemed the entire Point neighborhood had gathered in and around the modest saltbox home Hannah and her brother, Dale, had grown up in, very much like the one I'd lived in as a child. In addition, a good number of hospital staff—doctors and nurses—milled through the crowd, spilling from the open front door and the backyard. We had to drive around the corner and onto Second Street to find space to park our carriage. After Derrick set the brake and attached a feedbag to Maestro's harness, I looked at him with a touch of misgiving.

"Are you ready for this?" I asked him.

"For a shindig in your old neighborhood? Why wouldn't I be?"

"Because it's not what you're used to," I reminded him with a rueful smile.

He offered me his arm. "And what am I used to? Excruciating, endlessly boring affairs among people who have mastered the art of talking about nothing?"

I laughed as I wrapped my hand around his coat sleeve, feeling the solidness, the steadiness, beneath. Why should I feel nervous about bringing him here? He had dressed perfectly for such a gathering. Dark pin-striped trousers, a lighter vest, and a simple flannel suit coat cut straight at the bottom—no cutaway or tails for this occasion. To have worn a gentleman's evening attire would have been to throw his wealth in their faces, a condescension. He had known that instinctively, without needing to be reminded.

I did wear silk and chiffon, but in a simple style in pale yellows and greens, and I'd kept my jewelry to a minimum and wore my hair in a sleek upsweep without ornamentation other than my tortoiseshell combs. There would be women present tonight who owned perhaps a handful of dresses, the best one being reserved for church and occasions like these.

The air smelled of the harbor: salty, fishy, and slightly sooty from the coal-fed steamships. Not nearly as fresh and bracing as the clifftop properties lining the ocean; but to me, it was familiar and welcoming. It was still home in so many ways, though I hadn't lived on the Point in years.

The craggy brick sidewalks were familiar, too, so much so that I barely wobbled a step in my high-heeled boots. I could almost have said by rote where the paving stones dipped or buckled, where each crack and each chipped or missing block lay.

And then we were within the crush, but not the formal, well-choreographed crush of a ballroom, but rather one that heaved and swelled and swarmed and sometimes scattered, when someone laughed too loudly or moved too boisterously and tankards threatened to spill. This was not a crowd overly concerned with manners or decorum. My smile grew as we were enveloped and absorbed into it, exchanging greetings and introductions, and were directed to the food-laden tables along the fence. Hannah's parents alone could not have had time to prepare such a feast; the array of New England specialties, from shellfish to seafood chowders to roasted meats, potatoes, and corn, and—oh!—endless cakes and pies, had been brought by neighbors.

"Em!" Brady must have been watching for us. No sooner had we entered the back garden than he came striding toward us, wending his way in and out of islands of guests. Then he gathered me in a hug that all but suffocated me. "Em, can you believe it? She said *yes.* She didn't even hesitate. I thought she'd at least tell me she'd think about it, and then make me squirm for the next several days."

"I'm not surprised at all. Whatever made you think that?"

He pulled back, his hands still grasping my arms. "Because I don't deserve her."

"Nonsense. Derrick, tell him he's talking nonsense."

Derrick only extended his hand. "Congratulations, Brady. Where is the lucky woman? Lost her already, have you?"

Brady narrowed his eyes. Had they been two men alone, I'm sure he would have uttered something not suitable for mixed company, but only in jest. In the next moment, his grin—his joyful, exuberant grin—returned. "In the house with some of her nursing friends. Planning, as women do. She'll be out momentarily."

"Have you set a date? Made any wedding plans?" I asked, eager, as any journalist would be, for details.

"The fall, but no specific date yet. Soon, though. And, Em"—he leaned in closer as if to impart some astonishing secret—"even her parents are happy. Delighted, I think."

"Why shouldn't they be?"

His expression offered myriad reasons, but they were old ones, past history. Brady wasn't the same mischievous boy or the carousing young man he had once been, but his self-esteem had yet to catch up to the changes in his character.

Then, just as quickly as he had appeared in front of us, he was gone, swept up in a tide of friends who conveyed him to a newly tapped keg of beer. I knew I needn't worry about him, but even so, when Derrick questioned me with a look, I nodded and laughed. "Go keep an eye on him for me. I want to go in and see Hannah anyway."

He leaned to graze my lips with his own. "See you in a bit."

On the way to the house, I ran into Gayla Prescott. "Emma, isn't it wonderful?" she exclaimed as she caught me up in a hug. "I'm simply overjoyed for them, and I do so love weddings." She stole an instant to scan the yard behind us. "Oliver and my parents are here somewhere. If only your parents could be, too. Do you think they'll come for the wedding?"

"I'm afraid I couldn't say," I replied truthfully. "Paris is such a long way off."

"And it costs a bundle, I know, to make the voyage. Well, I'll say a little prayer they're able to."

After Gayla and I parted, I ran into Detective Jesse Whyte, my friend on the police force, coming down the kitchen steps. He wielded a pewter stein and a flushed look that said he had been enjoying himself. His high spirits prompted him to wrap me in a hug, which might not have happened if Derrick had been beside me. Jesse was another friend I had known all my life. For a short time, things had progressed a bit further, until I had come to discern the difference between deep friendship and passion. For Jesse, I felt the former; for Derrick, the latter—and so much more.

"How are things, Emma?" he asked after he released me. "I haven't seen you in a while. Which makes me suspicious as to what you're up to," he added with a wink.

He had good cause to be, though he didn't know it. I couldn't tell him about Bessie and the matters I was investigating on her behalf, not without breaking her confidence. So we talked about Annamarie, Derrick's and my plans for our school, and Jesse's own budding relationship with a young maid at Ochre Court.

"How is Nora?"

Jesse's smile blossomed. "Fine. She's here." He attempted to scan the crowd. "Somewhere . . ."

"You go find her. We'll talk more later."

With that, we continued in our respective directions. I found Hannah inside, in the parlor, surrounded by a host of young women I knew, and some I didn't. I assumed some were her fellow nurses at the hospital. As soon as she saw me, she jumped up from the settee and ran to throw her arms around me. "Here you are, my soon-to-be sister and my matron of honor. You will be, won't you, Emma?"

I laughed at her blunt way of asking me and nodded vigorously. "Of course I will. I'd be honored."

"Brady asked Dale to stand up for him, so it's perfect. What about Annamarie? We're planning a fall wedding. Do you think she might be old enough then to be a flower girl?"

I laughed again. "No, but if you want her to be, we'll manage it somehow. Is Brady asking any of our Newport relatives?"

Hannah compressed her lips, then replied, "Yes, but . . . that's the reason we're waiting until fall. Most of them will be gone by then and can easily decline the invitation. I don't want a Vanderbilt wedding, Emma. And neither does Brady, for that matter. Ours will be simple—much like yours was."

"I completely understand, and in all honesty, I believe Aunt Alice will understand as well. If she or any of them *do* decide to come, don't feel you have to do anything different for their sake. It's *your* wedding."

Mrs. Hanson stuck her head in from the kitchen. "Hannah, dear, it's time for a toast. Emma, lovely to see you. You must introduce us to your husband later."

"I've got to go," Hannah whispered to me. "Will you come back outside?"

"After you, my dear."

Exiting the house proved easier than entering, as now everyone headed in the same direction. Once outside, I located Derrick and took my place at his side. Hannah's father led us in raising a glass to the engaged couple, and while felicitations were exclaimed, a figure at the gate caught my attention.

I tapped Derrick's forearm. "Look there, but don't be obvious. Is that Harry Lehr?"

Derrick followed my gaze with a flick of his own. Then he sidestepped, putting his back toward Harry and, at the same time, shielding me from his view. "It is. Who's that with him, I wonder."

I peeked around his shoulder. "I don't know. Perhaps it's the elusive Mr. Noble."

I'd said it half in jest, but Derrick nodded solemnly. "Could be. What's he look like?"

"Light hair—blond, I think, though it's hard to tell in this light. He's got that heavy-lidded, bored look you see a lot on younger sons."

"Like Reggie?"

"Exactly like Reggie. He's also stout. If he isn't careful, his belly will come spilling out of his vest."

"Buttons everywhere."

"Weak chin," I concluded.

"Sounds like a charmer," Derrick murmured back.

"I'd better stop looking. I don't want Harry to recognize me. Not that he's seen a lot of me, but I'd prefer he not realize he'd been spotted here."

"What do you suppose they're doing?" Derrick craned to toss a glance over his shoulder. "They can't have been invited, surely."

"They probably heard all the noise and decided to investigate, see who was throwing the party."

"That would mean they were already in the neighborhood."

"Yes, and they seem to be making a decision. The bored one is tugging on Harry's sleeve. They're turning and leaving. We should follow them . . ." I started forward, but Derrick held me back. "What are you doing?"

His uncertainty penetrated the shadows of the maple branches overhead. "I'm not sure it's a good idea. If he sees us, he'll know we're curious about him, and if he *is* up to something, he'll be more careful from now on."

Compressing my lips in indecision, I thought this over. Then I started walking. "I left my wrap in the carriage, and it's growing chilly."

He caught up to me in a moment. "Have it your way."

I reached to give his hand a squeeze as we hurried along. By then, Harry and his companion were a block away, and nearly out of sight in the darkness. We were not the only people about. There were pairs, threesomes, and even larger groups out for strolls, walking their pets, or had spilled from the Hansons' property. Only when a match flared to light a cigarette was I certain we continued to follow Harry and his friend. They headed toward the harbor, passing Second Street. When they turned onto Washington Street, I hurried my steps, prompting Derrick to do the same. With others about, we needn't worry about the sound of our footsteps.

"You won't find your wrap down here," he reminded me as we traversed the sidewalk on the landward side of Washington Street. Harry and his mystery companion had crossed over to the harbor side of the road, where night mist crawled from between the houses.

"I've no intention of confronting them," I whispered. "I only want to see where they go."

That answer came only moments later, when they opened a gate in a honeysuckle hedge that bordered the front of the property. The house, a Colonial saltbox that had been added onto a couple of times through the ages, presented a modest façade beside its larger neighbors, and it was set farther back than the others, with a small front yard.

"The Sawyers lived here while I was growing up," I said, keeping my voice low as we watched from the corner. With the water so close, lapping against the seawall and caressing the hulls of small craft tied up at docks, there was very little chance of them hearing me. Harry's friend dug into a trouser pocket and procured a key. "I don't believe he's a Sawyer. None of them were built like that man."

The front door opened, and with a hand on Harry's shoulder, the friend guided him over the threshold. Their laughter reached our ears.

"Let's go back." Derrick took my hand and we turned to retrace our steps. "Brady's living close enough that he might be able to keep an eye out, now that we know Harry comes here."

I nodded. "It may be innocent enough."

A funny light entered Derrick's eyes. "Perhaps."

While I relied on Brady to find out more about Harry Lehr's acquaintance on the Point, I had inquiries of my own to make. Despite Bessie's obvious faith in her maid, Mrs. Darvish and Meredith had raised serious concerns in my mind. Neddie Thorton had been willing to make threats to obtain her position with the Lehrs. What else was she willing and able to do to further her interests?

And since I also wished to ask Bessie if she knew whether her husband frequented the Point, I decided to combine my fact-gathering mission the next time I visited her at Arleigh. I had sent my card ahead of time and she surprised me by telephoning—something ladies of the Four Hundred rarely did—as soon as she had read it.

"Yes, Emma, do come. Chef has made the most delectable pastries. I'll have tea ready for us at eleven, if that suits?"

"Perfect. I'll see you then."

I hadn't mentioned to Bessie that I'd be bringing Katie with me, but when we arrived, I sent her around to the back entrance with instructions to wait for Miss Thorton. Katie knew exactly what was expected of her. After I'd put Annamarie down for her nap, Katie and I had discussed our plan in detail at home and then on the way over in the carriage. Though I didn't like to be dishonest with Bessie, once we'd settled together in the parlor, I told her a lie—sort of.

"I hope you don't mind, but I brought my maid-of-all-work. I hoped she might be able to speak with Miss Thorton."

"With Neddie?" She seemed thoroughly surprised. "Do they know each other?"

"No, at least I don't think so." I chuckled. "I'd had a thought about promoting Katie from housemaid to lady's maid. She's been a wonderful addition to my household, and rather than hire someone who would then be above her, why not promote her and hire a new girl to assist my housekeeper."

"I see. Yes, that *is* a good idea." She rose and pushed a button on the wall. Barely a moment later, a footman appeared in the doorway—the very same who had found me fleeing Harry's office the day I'd searched his desk. He gave no sign of recognizing me. "Please tell Miss Thorton there is a young woman awaiting her downstairs," Bessie instructed him. She glanced at me.

"Her name is Katie Dillon," I supplied.

Bessie continued to the footman, "She is Mrs. Andrews's maid-of-all-work, but we'd like Miss Thorton to acquaint her with what she must learn to become a lady's maid."

"Very good, ma'am."

Once he had gone and Bessie returned to the sofa, she said, "You're awfully good to the people in your sphere, aren't you, Emma?"

"I try to be."

"It's because you understand them, and what their lives are like." She said this without the judgment I might have heard in other women's voices as they acknowledged, in so many words, that I hailed from a far less illustrious background than my relatives or any of them. Somehow, though, the way Bessie said it didn't sound like a veiled insult or an attempt to put me in my place.

"It's true, I do understand them," I replied. "I've known many of the servants at the cottages, as well as employees at the Casino, the Country Club, and other places all over town, all my life. I grew up with many of them. And I'm not at all ashamed to admit it."

"Why should you be?" Once again, the way she spoke left me believing she wasn't being condescending. "I envy you. Your independence—yes, even as a married woman. And your . . . how shall I put it . . . your ease with society, all levels of society . . ."

I couldn't help laughing, albeit softly and perhaps a bit ironically. "I may look at ease, but I'm not always so. Fitting into society hasn't been easy for me. There are those who would have shut all doors in my face, if they could have. If my Vanderbilt relatives had allowed it, and if my husband had. Why, his own mother—" I broke off, not wishing to dampen our time together with such dark thoughts. "Then there are those who have known me since childhood who believe I've gotten above myself." I shrugged. "I'm not complaining, truly, but in many ways, I'm neither here nor there."

"Well, I'm glad you're *here.* And I do understand something of your conundrum. I'm no typical society lady, either. Being Catholic, I'm often held in suspicion, although of what, I couldn't tell you." She, too, laughed.

Once tea had been served and we had enjoyed what proved to be some of the very best French puff pastry I had ever tasted, let alone the almonds, apricot, and custard cradled inside, I came to the point of my visit.

"Is your husband at home?"

She shook her head. "You may speak freely."

"The other night, Derrick and I attended a party on the Point. Are you familiar with the area?"

"Yes, of course. It's very quaint. My mother and I have driven through it a time or two, after shopping trips in town. The old houses are charming. It's where you grew up, isn't it?"

"It is. Do you know if your husband goes there often?"

"Harry? I can't imagine he goes there at all."

"He did the other night. Derrick and I saw him there, out strolling with another gentleman. They happened to walk by the home of my friend and lingered a moment, probably to see what all the noise was about, as there was a party. Derrick and I followed them when they continued on."

"Did you?" Surprise and a conspiratorial excitement lit her eyes. "Good. Did you learn anything?"

"Only that they went to a house on Washington Street. That's the last street before the harbor." I went on to describe the friend: the light hair, the paunch, the heavy-lidded and bored look.

"I'm afraid he doesn't sound at all familiar," she said with a shake of her head.

"Does the name Ralph Noble mean anything to you?"

"No, nothing at all. But Harry never tells me where he goes when he's not with me, nor with whom."

I had feared as much. We drank our tea, sampled more of her chef's French delicacies, and then I sent word belowstairs for Katie to meet me outside at the carriage.

"Did you and Miss Thorton have a good talk?" I asked her as I guided Maestro through the gates at the top of the drive. Across Bellevue Avenue, things were quiet at The Elms. I turned south, toward home.

"I don't know that I discovered anything you didn't already know, Miss Emma." Katie adjusted the ribbon tied beneath her chin and angled her straw hat to better block the sunlight. With her fair skin, she could never be too careful. "I got her to talk a little about her life before she entered service. She grew up in South Carolina, on her family's plantation. Only, in her lifetime, it's merely been a farm, and since their grand house fell to disrepair after the war, they lived in a much smaller house on the property."

"Did she tell you the name of this plantation?"

"She did, although I had a sense she didn't mean to. She called it Glenwood, and a wistfulness gripped her for a moment, though she coughed and tried to hide it."

"I would imagine she and others like her feel a great sense of loss about what happened to them."

"Yes, but, Miss Emma, they had *slaves,* didn't they?" Her summer-sky blue eyes widened in dismay.

"They did, Katie, much to this country's shame. Newport had a direct hand in it, too, though this city's involvement ended long before the war. Still . . ."

"Getting back to Miss Thorton," she said swiftly, guiding us away from the lamentable subject. I silently thanked her for doing so. "She traveled up to New York about three years ago to take a position as a governess."

"A governess? Then why wouldn't she have presented references to Mrs. Darvish at Crossways?"

"I couldn't say. When I asked her why she left being a governess to become a lady's maid, she said tending to ladies suited her better than trying to make children sit still and learn. Then, so she wouldn't get suspicious, I asked her a lot of questions about her duties, like where she learned to dress hair and take care of clothing. She said from the lady's maids where she worked as a governess."

"That does make sense. And none of it sounds particularly nefarious." We reached Ocean Avenue and I allowed Maestro his head. He knew the way home as well as Katie or I. "I don't suppose she mentioned the name of the family she worked for, or where, exactly, they lived."

Katie looked alarmed. "I didn't think to ask that."

"That's all right. She might have realized you were snooping if you had."

We drove past Bailey's Beach. The tide was out, and a strong brine tanged the air. At this time of day, with the sun almost directly overhead, there weren't many bathers in the water, nor dotting the sands. "I do wish I'd had more time with her," she mused, her hands entwined in her lap.

"What do you mean? I sat with Mrs. Lehr nearly an hour while you were downstairs with Miss Thorton."

"Aye, but after only about twenty minutes, a footman came and said Miss Thorton was needed elsewhere."

I frowned. "Where? As I said, Mrs. Lehr and I were together. Who else would have needed Miss Thorton's assistance?"

"I couldn't hear him. He'd beckoned her into the hall. When she excused herself, I didn't ask where she was going, though perhaps I should have?" She phrased this as a question, couched in uncertainty.

"No, Katie, you did right. Too much curiosity would certainly make her suspicious. We don't want to put her off at this point. But tell me, what was your impression of her? Did you like her?"

"I did, Miss Emma. She spoke to me kindly and seemed willing to help me learn. And she spoke highly of Mrs. Lehr. She seems happy with her position. I'm sorry. I wish I had more to tell you."

"Not at all, Katie. You did well." I spoke truthfully. I now had another piece of information I hadn't known before. I knew from where Miss Thorton hailed—a plantation called Glenwood in South Carolina.

After I dropped her at home, I turned around and went into town, to the *Messenger.* As soon as Derrick and I had a moment to ourselves, I told him about my visit to Arleigh.

"Could Miss Thorton have made up the name of this plantation?" he asked, sensibly enough. We stood out back, in the small, unpaved lot where our deliveries of paper, ink, and general supplies were delivered.

"I'd have suspected that, too, except Katie said she was overcome with a moment of wistfulness. That doesn't sound like someone who's lying. It sounds like someone who misses her home."

"So now you've got Katie spying." He gave me a lopsided smile.

"Believe me, it took no persuasion on my part." I blew out a rueful breath. "That's where it will end, though, I promise. I don't want Katie any more involved than this. And I don't like lying to Bessie."

"It's for a good cause and to her benefit, in the end."

"Yes, in the end, she'll know everything. But something tells me she won't thank me now for suspecting her lady's maid."

After I told Derrick what I had learned, he agreed to make inquiries through his contacts at his father's newspaper network. Though based in Providence, the family's business interests encompassed the entire New England region and, more recently, farther afield as his father bought up local newspapers, up and down the East Coast. I hoped that included towns in South Carolina.

In the afternoon, I walked over to Marlborough Street to visit Jesse Whyte. After being waved through the front office by another old friend in blue, I entered the large main room to spy Jesse at his desk on one side of the bustling space. Typewriters clacked, telephones jangled, and voices competed to be heard. Jesse sat with pen in hand, intently studying whatever missive sat on his blotter beneath his nose. Wisps of russet hair had slipped over his brow. He absently shoved them back.

"Have I caught you at a busy moment?"

I must have, for he started and drew back, darting a gaze up at me. Then he relaxed, though he came to his feet. "Emma, this is a surprise. I was just going over a spate of burglaries along the wharves. What brings you here?"

"May I?" I gestured to the chair in front of his desk, facing his.

He blinked and nodded. "Of course. Sorry."

"I've got something of a sensitive nature I'd like your help with, if you can manage it."

He drew a breath and regarded me much like a schoolmaster would a mischievous student. "What are you investigating now? I don't recall any recent murders."

"What about the Lehrs' man-of-all-work? The one who died driving their motorcar?"

"That was deemed an accident. Tragic, but not malicious."

"I beg to differ. We talked to the mechanic who examined the automobile after the accident. He said the brake cable had become disconnected from one of the rear wheels."

"Which could easily have been an accident. You know how these motorcars are, and the state of our roads. Things are shaken loose all the time. That's why they're constantly needing attention."

"Mrs. Lehr's motorcar had been inspected by Oliver Prescott, only a week or so before the accident."

"That doesn't mean the cable hadn't come loose after that." He stared down at his hands folded on his desktop, then back up at me. "Look, if I learn of anything that might point to it being deliberate, I'll be the first man on the investigation. But until that happens, I can't. The department won't allow me to open a case without hard evidence." He raised his eyebrows at me. "You know that."

I acquiesced with a reluctant nod. "I'm really here about Mrs. Lehr's lady's maid. I have reason to be worried about the woman's credentials and her intentions."

"Did Mrs. Lehr ask you to find out more about her?"

"Not exactly . . ."

"Emma, what are you onto?"

"I discovered she might have lied to Mrs. Lehr about her

former position, and I wouldn't like to see a nice woman like Elizabeth Lehr taken advantage of, or worse. The woman could be out to steal or swindle the Lehrs in some way."

"And have you spoken with Mrs. Lehr about this?"

I fought the urge to sigh in frustration. How could I enlist Jesse's help without breaking my promise and divulging everything Bessie had told me? Involving the police was exactly what she didn't wish me to do, and here I was. But Jesse wasn't merely a detective, he was someone I knew well and trusted. He had been my father's friend, albeit a much younger one, and he had become my friend after my parents moved away. He and I had solved more than a few crimes over the years: Jesse with his detecting skills and me with my ability to move among wealthy and ordinary Newporters alike, opening doors that would have been barred to the police and speaking to people who would have been resistant to him.

I decided to ignore his question and hoped he wouldn't notice. "I'd just like to trace her activities in New York right before she entered the Lehrs' employ. Her name is Edwina Thorton, although she goes by Neddie. I can give you a description, and even the name of a particular tavern she frequented. It appears Neddie ingratiated herself to one of Mrs. Fish's maids, and then threatened the girl if she didn't help find Neddie a position."

"Threatened, you say." When I nodded, Jessie pulled his notebook in front of him and opened it to a blank page. "Give me all the information you have."

I did, and he promised to cable the local police stations in downtown Manhattan. Before I left, he cautioned me that Neddie Thorton could be an assumed name.

"For now, I'm going to presume it isn't. Thank you, Jesse."

I started to walk away. Jesse's voice, half swallowed by the typewriters, telephones, and other voices, followed me.

"You never answered my question, Emma. Does Mrs. Lehr know you're checking up on her maid?"

I kept going.

"You were right, Em. His name is Ralph Noble. But it wasn't easy to find out." Brady joined us at home a couple of nights later. The moment he walked through our front door, my child practically launched herself out of my arms and into his. Only quick action on both our parts in passing her from one to the other kept her from falling. Still, my heart lodged in my throat while Annamarie, oblivious that she'd nearly tumbled to the floor, laughed heartily.

"It's a good thing you've always been a good catcher," I told him, leading him into the parlor.

"I have your father to thank for it. He practiced often enough with me."

I had reached the sofa, but before sitting, I turned and faced him. "He was your father, too, Brady."

He only smiled and ran his fingertips through Annamarie's dark curls. He took the armchair opposite me and snuggled her on his lap. Patch lumbered in and lay across his feet, canine and baby effectively pinning him in place. He took a moment to acknowledge my dog before turning his attention back to me. "No one in the neighborhood knows anything about him. He lives like a hermit, only venturing out when Harry's there."

He spoke of Harry Lehr's mysterious friend, whom Derrick and I had followed the night of Brady and Hannah's engagement party. That he turned out to be the very same man Gayla had mentioned didn't surprise me.

"So he holes up all alone, day and night, on Washington Street?"

"I didn't say he was alone."

Before Brady could elaborate, Derrick came into the room,

having just come down from changing into more comfortable clothes after our workday. "Who isn't alone?"

"Our mystery friend on the Point," I informed him. "He's still something of a mystery, but he *is* Ralph Noble. But Brady says his neighbors know nothing about him."

"That's odd, in a neighborhood like the Point." Derrick leaned to kiss Annamarie on the top of her head before crossing to sit beside me on the sofa. "I didn't think it was possible to remain anonymous there. I think I must have had five or six visitors drop by the first day I moved in, years ago. Most of them brought food."

"Perhaps the difference is, you let them." Brady jostled the baby on his knee, making her squeal for more. He kept it up, holding her hands to balance her while she bounced up and down as though on a pony. "They tell me he keeps entirely to himself, except for when he has company, which is often. But no one local. They're all unfamiliar faces, and all men."

"A gentleman's lair," Derrick murmured. "My guess is, there *are* women there, on the sly. Maybe they bring them in by boat."

I glanced at him sideways, raising an eyebrow. "Are you suggesting what I think you're suggesting?"

"It wouldn't be the first house of debauchery to spring up in Newport in the summer months," he replied with a shrug.

"But on the Point?" I shook my head. "Where families live?"

"It's not impossible." Brady finally stilled his knee, but distracted Annamarie with a key ring holding two keys, which he took from his pocket. "He has frequent deliveries, I'm told, which does suggest the man likes to entertain. I spoke to John Massey, who keeps in touch with the Sawyers, who still own the house. That's how I found out his name. You'll never guess who pays his rent."

"Who?" Derrick and I asked at the same time.

"I'll give you one guess and a hint. His initials are *HL.*"

We again spoke as one. "Harry Lehr?"

Brady flashed a significant look. "Got it."

"Oh!" I couldn't help exclaiming in disgust. "Bessie told me he hounds her for money constantly. What a cad, spending it on people she neither knows nor, I'd wager, would care to meet. But thank you, Brady. We'll take it from here."

Derrick crossed one leg over the other and slid his arm along the back of the sofa, his fingertips dangling against my shoulder. "How do you think this mystery friend could be connected to what's been happening to Bessie?"

"I'll answer that with another question," I replied. "Why is Harry paying his rent?"

"My guess is rent isn't the only thing Harry Lehr is paying for." Brady jingled the keys for Annamarie's benefit. "If he can't afford the house, how does he afford his frequent entertaining?"

"Makes me wonder if Mr. Noble is holding something over Harry's head," I mused. "If he's somehow blackmailing him."

Derrick inclined his head as he considered this. "They certainly didn't look to be at odds when we saw them."

"*Hmm,* no, you're right," I conceded. "They seemed to be on quite friendly terms. Could he be a relative? A ne'er-do-well cousin, perhaps?"

"Isn't Harry himself ne'er-do-well?" Brady moved Annamarie from one knee to the other. I reached out my arms.

"I'll take her if she's putting your legs to sleep."

He made a show of closing his arms around her. "Not on your life. I need to enjoy my fill of her before I'm off to New York again, or I'll have to take her with me. Won't I, little friend?"

"Over my dead body," I joked.

"And mine." Derrick made a threatening face, then took up where Brady had left off. "Harry *is* a ne'er-do-well, and isn't that the point? Slackers stick together and get what they want by taking advantage of someone else."

"Perhaps this person resents Bessie's attempts to curtail Harry's spending, and he's somehow to blame for her mishaps." I narrowed my eyes in anger on Bessie's behalf. "Even if neither of them is threatening Bessie's life, they may be doing their best to make her life a misery. And I won't stand for it."

Chapter 7

The next time I met with Bessie, it was in town, at the tea-room at the Perry House Hotel in Washington Square. Though a public place, I felt more at ease discussing her situation there than at Arleigh, where any servant—or Harry himself—might be lingering outside a doorway. I also wished to put distance between Bessie and the main topic of our conversation.

Namely, Miss Thorton. Derrick's and Jesse's inquiries had yielded results about her Southern origins and her activities when she had first arrived in New York.

We ordered afternoon tea and were soon served tiered trays of delicate sandwiches, warm scones, and colorful cakes. I waited until we'd started the scone course to begin.

"I have news."

She looked up and nodded. "I thought you must. Is it about Harry?"

I regarded the blueberry jam and the lemon curd, chose the latter, and cut my scone in half. "No. It's about Miss Thorton."

"Neddie? What about her? She's been an angel. A treasure."

"I'm sure she seems so to you."

"Are you implying she's been deceiving me?"

After smoothing lemon curd on both sides of my scone, I placed both scone and knife on my plate. "No, Bessie. I'm not implying it. I'm telling you. Neddie Thorton isn't what she appears."

She fingered the handle of her teacup even as she pinned me with her disapproving stare. "Tell me who and what she is, then."

I let go a sigh. "She *is* from the South, as she told you. But as far as we can discover, there was no governess position that brought her North."

"What do you mean by 'we'?" A look of alarm crossed her features.

I nearly bit my tongue at my mistake. "I'm sorry, I took Derrick into my confidence. You can be assured of his discretion, I promise." It wasn't a lie. It simply wasn't the *whole* truth, and I believed she didn't need to know of Jesse's involvement.

"All right." She drained her tea, then refilled her cup, as if settling in for an unpleasant duration. "Tell me everything."

"She *is* from a plantation called Glenwood, which had fallen on hard times after the war. But the family had no daughters, only sons. Neddie's family were sharecroppers on the land." Katie's description of Neddie's wistfulness when speaking of Glenwood flashed in my mind; now I believed the woman's sentiment hadn't been one of homesickness, but of regret that her family had been merely poor farmers on the estate. But I didn't see the point of mentioning that to Bessie. "Whatever she did when she first arrived in New York, we don't know. But . . ."

I leaned and pressed my hand over hers where it lay on the

table. "She has been arrested more than once . . ." I trailed off again as Bessie's eyes darkened. How I loathed delivering such news about someone she trusted. "For fleecing gentlemen whom she met at various taverns."

"Did she . . ." The way Bessie drew herself up led me to believe she was about to ask if Neddie had resorted to prostitution. In this, at least, I could reassure her.

"No. Not that we know of. She would meet these gentlemen, persuade them to buy her dinner or a drink, and once they were comfortable and not on their guard, she would find a way to steal their money. Like a pickpocket."

"Were charges brought? Did she spend time in jail?"

"No, to both questions. None of the men were ever willing to testify against her, in the end. Once their indignation abated, they'd inform the police they wanted the matter dropped to avoid the scandal and the wrath of their wives. That was another thing. It seemed she only targeted married men. Then she met a girl named Meredith, who works as a maid for Mrs. Fish. She . . . *convinced* . . . Meredith to help her find a position."

She cleared her throat. "Is that the whole of it?"

"As far as we've been able to find out."

"I see." She leaned back in her chair as far as her corset allowed, which merely meant she no longer sat as severely upright as she had been. Lowering her gaze, while raising her eyebrows in a show of dignity, she said, "I knew most of this."

"*What?*"

Her lashes fluttered as she raised her eyes to me. "Neddie told me much of this. Not the part about Mrs. Fish's maid, or the specifics of how she made her way once she arrived in New York. But she did explain about her origins in South Carolina, and went so far as to tell me she had done things she's ashamed of when she arrived in New York. It was several months after she came to work for me, once she felt she could trust me. She knew the risk she was taking, but she wanted me to know the truth."

"Why didn't you tell me?"

"Quite simply because I will not entertain the notion that Neddie is guilty of any wrongdoing when it comes to me. She swore to me she has turned over a new leaf and I believe her."

"Bessie—"

"I won't hear another word against her, Emma."

I nodded. But that didn't mean I would drop the matter entirely.

"I *can* tell you something, though." Bessie suddenly took on a sheepish expression. "It's about something that happened at Reggie and Cathleen's wedding. I should have told you before this, but I've been so sure it's Harry trying to be rid of me. But now . . ."

"Whatever it is, please tell me." A suspicion crept over me as I remembered following Bessie after her argument with Harry. "Does it have to do with Reggie and his friend Ely Forrester?"

"It does. I should have told you then, but I was afraid to. And Reggie's your cousin, after all. I didn't like to speak ill of him to you."

As I had just spoken ill of Neddie Thorton. She didn't have to say it for me to experience a pang of guilt. I shook it off and said, "I'm quite used to Reggie and his ways. You can't shock me, whatever it is."

"I hope not, because it shocked me. So much so, I vowed never to speak of it. Especially since I never thought it would have any bearing on my life."

"Good heavens, Bessie, you must tell me."

"Ladies, will that be all?" The waiter's query startled me; I hadn't noticed his approach. With our tiers cleared of treats and our teapot empty, there remained no reason to prolong our stay. We paid the bill, collected our handbags, and exited the building.

Outside in sun-drenched Washington Square, I beckoned for her to join me in the park between the thoroughfares. Her manner left me with the impression that walking would not be conducive to this conversation. Rather, we needed a quiet place that ensured our continued privacy. There were others scattered about the lawn and walkways—nannies with prams, elderly men sitting on benches and chatting, workers eating the lunch they'd brought from home—each minding his or her own business. We chose a bench near the monument to Commodore Oliver Hazard Perry, his arm outstretched and his hand pointing toward the heavens, perhaps toward some dream of what Newport could and should be. Only the birds roosting in the branches over our heads would be privy to our conversation.

Bessie hesitated, seeming unable to meet my eye. I patted her hand. "You can tell me anything, truly. It's quite hard to shock me." I gave a little laugh to lighten the mood.

She didn't join in. "Perhaps I've been wrong about Harry. He's a scoundrel, all right, but perhaps he's not trying to be rid of me. Do you remember at the wedding, when you followed me into the morning room?"

"I saw that you and Harry had exchanged words, and I wished to see if you were all right."

She nodded absently. "You waited before following me into the morning room. In those moments before you did, I overheard your cousin and his groomsman talking about . . ." She left off, frowning. "Have you read about the case against a gambling ring in Saratoga?"

"The Canfield case?" A sense of unease closed around me. Back in the winter, one Richard Canfield, along with several associates, was accused of running private gambling rooms at his popular gentlemen's club for the express purpose of fleecing his customers. There had been large sums involved, often tens of thousands of dollars. The *Messenger* had covered the story. All the newspapers had covered it.

What did this have to do with Reggie?

"Of course you have. You're a reporter." She shook her head as if at her own silliness. "It seems your cousin and this other young man, Ely Forrester, are involved."

My stomach dropped.

"That's what they were talking about when I entered the morning room," she went on before I could utter a word. "Reggie was telling Ely he had no intention of returning to New York State anytime soon, not with a summons hanging over his head, because he'd be forced to testify. I already knew about that because Reggie had confided in Harry. That's why the wedding was held in Newport, and *not* Manhattan."

"*That's* why!" I exclaimed, having had no idea of the truth. "And Mr. Forrester?"

"Is also involved, apparently, but the authorities don't know it. *Yet.* He was threatening Reggie when I walked in, telling him under no uncertain terms that if Reggie reveals his secret, he, Ely, will drag not only Reggie, but his whole family, into the scandal—not to mention Reggie incurring the wrath of the thugs running the gambling ring. Before Ely stormed out of the pantry, he suggested that even Cathleen's life could be at risk."

I sucked in a breath. "Bessie, why didn't you tell me this sooner? Right away, in fact."

"I was so certain it was Harry and that this other matter had nothing to do with me."

No wonder she had looked so shaken in the morning room. It had had nothing to do with her argument with Harry. But then something she *had* told me made me pause.

"Wait. You said the balcony railing broke at your Long Island home, not here at Arleigh. Ely Forrester would have had no reason to harm you then."

"Perhaps that was only an accident. But the other mishaps—the loose stair runner, the automobile. Those couldn't have been accidents, and Ely could have been responsible."

"The automobile, perhaps. But the runner? That, too, could have been an accident. When would Ely have had access to the staircase after the wedding?"

"Don't you remember? I nearly tripped and fell the very next morning after the wedding. He could have done it right before leaving. Some of the wedding party were there rather late, after most of the other guests had gone home. Harry egged them on to stay and keep drinking." She suddenly sat up straighter. "Perhaps he and Ely are in on it together."

I didn't reply to that, for Mamie Fish's description of Bessie flashed in my mind.

Flibbertigibbet.

No, I refused to believe it. Bessie was frightened, not irrational.

"In that case, Ely would have been taking a risk that someone other than you might trip on the stairs."

"But who? A man wears trousers and flat-heeled shoes. He is much more likely to catch his balance and not fall. And none of the servants use those stairs."

"Except Miss Thorton."

"But Ely couldn't have known that. A woman having her maid accompany her down the main stairs in the morning is unusual. Believe me, Harry tells me often enough that I'm breaking protocol."

And there, once again, we had arrived at the one fact that continually plagued me: Miss Thorton, a woman with a dubious past, always there, always on hand when needed most. A lucky coincidence, or a carefully contrived plan?

Despite what Bessie had just confided, I couldn't cross Neddie Thorton off the list of suspects. I could only add Ely Forrester, along with Harry Lehr himself and possibly even his friend on the Point.

I met Bessie's troubled gaze with an unflinching one of my own. "It's time to consult the police."

"No! Emma, you promised to do this my way. If you wish to have nothing more to do with the matter, I'll understand, but—"

"Bessie, in light of what you just told me about Reggie and Mr. Forrester, your life could very well be in danger. I can no longer do this alone." In fact, I hadn't been, but I saw no reason to divulge that to Bessie. "I have a friend on the force. Detective Whyte."

"Yes, you mentioned him, I believe." She assumed a miserable expression, as if her very life was about to unravel. Perhaps it already had.

"He will be discreet, Bessie, I promise you. You can trust him to keep your confidence." In the pinching of her lips, I sensed her resistance and added, "Think of this, if Ely Forrester is responsible for the attempts on your life, and if he not only threatened my cousin but his wife as well, who else might fall victim at his hands? Who else knows about his connection to the Canfield case?"

"I hadn't thought about it that way . . . No, you're right. If it's him, he must be stopped." She looked up at Commodore Perry, immortalized in bronze, his arms and head now playing host to several birds, then nodded. "All right. Shall we go there now?"

"No. I'll ask him to come to Gull Manor tomorrow. You can meet with us there. You'll be safe."

"All right, Emma. I'll trust you."

* * *

"She's here." Nanny poked her head into my bedroom the next day and spoke in a hurried whisper. "She's waiting in the parlor."

I turned away from the dressing table mirror after smoothing my hair and adjusting the bow tie that held the collar of my shirtwaist closed. "Bessie Lehr? It's too early."

Nanny shrugged. "She's here, all the same."

I came to my feet. "Is Annamarie down for her nap?" My daughter had had a busy morning playing with both her parents, as Derrick had gone into town later than usual. I would be joining him at the *Messenger* after meeting with Bessie and Jesse.

"I left her lying on her back, playing with her pony. Her little eyelids were very heavy, though, so she's probably already asleep."

"Good." I joined her in the hallway. "I'll go greet our guest then."

In the parlor, Bessie stood before the bookcase, bending at the waist as she scanned the volumes on the lower shelves. As I entered, she straightened as if caught at something forbidden. She held only her handbag; she had not brought Hippodale this time. I smiled at her. "How are you this morning? Is everything all right at home?"

"If by 'all right,' you mean did Harry spend half an hour berating me for agreeing to host a benefit meeting for Newport's Working Women's Resource Center before storming off, then yes, everything is fine."

Her wry humor made me smile again. "Please have a seat." I gestured toward the sofa. "And you can count on me for a donation. Tea?"

"Please."

Instead of ringing a bell, as Bessie might have done had we been at Arleigh, I crossed to the hallway and called out, "Katie, tea, please. And include a third cup for Detective Whyte."

"Yes, Miss Emma!"

Bessie shook her head at me when I rejoined her, taking one of the armchairs opposite the sofa. "Your aunt Alice must be horrified with you at times."

I took no offense. "Believe me, she is. But only at times. Now, it hasn't escaped my notice that you're here rather early—no, very early. May I deduce that you'd like to speak to me before Detective Whyte arrives?"

"I would." After setting her handbag on the side table, she folded her hands primly on her lap. "I'd like to establish certain boundaries."

As she paused, apprehensions took hold of me. I guessed she was not going to make this interview with Jesse easy.

"I don't wish to discuss Harry with him."

"Even if he's guilty?"

"We'll cross that bridge when we come to it. For now, I wish to preserve my privacy. It's of the utmost importance to me, Emma."

"All right." I schooled my features to hide my disapproval.

"And Neddie is innocent, so there is no reason to bring up her name, either."

"Bessie—"

She held up a hand to silence me. "She is innocent, and there's an end to the matter. I'm here to discuss what I heard at the wedding—and nothing more."

I nodded, and while I might have pointed out that bringing *that* matter to the attention of the police might endanger Reggie, I kept quiet. Reggie had, after all, chosen to involve himself with unsavory characters—again. When would he ever learn that being a rich man's son didn't make him immune to the consequences of his actions?

Katie brought our tea, and soon a knock at the front door heralded Jesse's arrival. I answered it myself and led him into the parlor, but not before his eyebrows surged and the corners of his mouth pulled in mock astonishment. I understood. It wasn't every day a member of the Four Hundred willingly met with the police.

I made the introductions, noticing that Bessie barely met Jesse's gaze. After I'd poured Jesse a cup of tea and refreshed Bessie's and my own, he cleared his throat.

"Mrs. Lehr, I understand you have reason to fear for your well-being, and that you and Emma—uh—Mrs. Andrews—have a suspect in mind."

"You are correct, Detective."

Jesse and I both waited for Bessie to continue, but the silence grew. Certainly, this felt as awkward for her as it did for Jesse, and she appeared at a loss as to how to continue. Which left me with no choice but to play the mediator.

I said to Jesse, "You remember that my cousin Reggie married Cathleen Neilson at Arleigh in April?"

"Who could forget?" His tone conveyed his sentiments concerning the excesses of the Four Hundred. He caught himself, cleared his throat again, and said more seriously, "The police department was on alert to ensure there were no incidents to interfere with your cousin's big day."

"Yes, well, during the course of that day, Mrs. Lehr and I happened to separate ourselves from the general festivities. To take a short break." I looked to her for concurrence. She held my gaze, hers conveying her thanks that I didn't mention her argument with Harry. "Mrs. Lehr went ahead of me into the morning room for a bit of quiet, but it wasn't to be. She overheard something rather alarming."

Jesse stopped me with a wave of his hand. "Did you overhear this as well, Mrs. Andrews?"

"I did not. As I said, Mrs. Lehr went in ahead of me."

"Then I must hear what was said from Mrs. Lehr's own lips." He pulled out his small notebook and a pencil. "Ma'am, if you would, please."

Her gaze darted back and forth between Jesse and me, making it quite clear she would have been happy to let me do all the talking. Then she nodded in resignation. "I could hear Mr. Vanderbilt—Reginald—speaking with one of his groomsmen, a young man named Ely Forrester."

"And where were they at the time?"

"In the pantry that connects the morning room to the dining room and kitchen."

"Could you see them?"

"Not then, no. The swinging door was closed. But I could hear them quite clearly."

"And you're certain the two men speaking were those you just identified?"

"Quite."

Jesse wrote in his notebook. "You say the pantry connects to two other rooms. Could there have been someone else with them who exited the pantry another way, without your seeing him?"

"I don't believe so. I know their voices, especially since we spent so much time among them during much of the wedding planning and pre-festivities."

Bessie went on to tell Jesse about Ely Forrester's threats toward Reggie, but, most importantly, the venomous look he cast Bessie on his way across the morning room. He clearly viewed her, she said, as someone who could incriminate him due to what she had overheard. Bessie stressed that although Reggie's connection to the Canfield case had been established by the authorities, Mr. Forrester's had not. Neither the police nor his family knew anything about his involvement and he intended to ensure it stayed that way.

Jesse listened calmly, taking notes, his gaze occasionally connecting with mine, sometimes questioning, sometimes resigned, but never, I judged, surprised. At least, not when it came to Reggie's antics.

When Bessie had finished, Jesse asked me, "Can you corroborate this?"

"As I said, I didn't hear everything that was said, but I did see how Mr. Forrester regarded Mrs. Lehr when he strode out of the pantry. Next came Reggie, who seemed about to explain, but merely shrugged and sauntered off. I can tell you he appeared shaken."

"I might add," said Bessie, "that Mr. Forrester went so far as to extend his threats to the new Mrs. Vanderbilt. Not that he threatened to harm her himself, but implied that certain individuals from Saratoga might exact their revenge on both Mr. Vanderbilt and his bride."

Jesse, nodding, made a few more notations in his book. Then he looked up. "Has anything happened to convince you your life might be in danger, Mrs. Lehr? That this Mr. Forrester wishes to silence you?"

She nodded tersely. "The incident with my automobile that claimed the life of Ellis Jackson, my man-of-all-work. I should have been in that motorcar that day, along with my maid. It was my maid's knowledge of motorcars that saved us, but resulted in his death."

"He was driving it to the service garage," Jesse supplied, and Bessie nodded. "Had you seen Mr. Forrester on your property around that time?"

She looked disconcerted for an instant, then raised her chin and said in an admonishing tone, "No, but that doesn't mean he hadn't sneaked in and tampered with my automobile, Detective."

"Does anyone know where this Mr. Forrester is these days?"

"I'm sure I've no idea," Bessie replied with a tinge of impatience. "He could still be somewhere in Newport, one supposes. Perhaps staying at The Breakers?" She shrugged.

Jesse closed his notebook and tucked it away in a coat pocket, along with his pencil. "I promise I'll look into his whereabouts, and once we find him, he'll be questioned. He'll also be watched." He looked at me. "Your cousin, as well, as soon as he returns from his wedding trip."

A burst of pique had me drawing up taller. "Surely, you don't think Reggie would threaten anyone's life? Especially not when his role in the matter is already known by the authorities. Hence his refusal to return to New York."

"I only meant he'll be questioned in regard to this friend of his, this Mr. Forrester."

His answer satisfied me, though I wondered how I could spring to Reggie's defense, knowing him as well as I did. But I'd always had a soft spot for him—little Reggie, Alice and Cornelius's youngest son, mischievous yet charming, infuriating and endearing by turns.

"I have one more question for Mrs. Lehr," Jesse said as he pushed to his feet. "Does your husband know about any of this? Could he be in danger as well?"

"No, Detective, to both questions. I didn't share what I overheard with him. I don't want him to worry. Mr. Lehr can be . . . overprotective. I hope you'll keep my confidence, at least while you look into the matter." Bessie also rose, slipping the strap of her handbag onto her wrist.

"As you wish, ma'am."

"Thank you." She turned to me. "My thanks to you as well, Emma."

I walked them out. Jesse climbed into his police buggy, while I saw Bessie to her waiting carriage. The footman assisted her in, and she extended her hand to me out the open window. "We'll keep in touch, yes?"

"Of course. You mustn't worry. We'll get to the bottom of this."

She knocked on the roof of the carriage and they started off. Only when they'd turned onto Ocean Avenue did Jesse spring down from his buggy and rejoin me by the front door.

"I suppose you'd like to share the rest of the story with me now?"

I grinned at his perceptiveness. "Come back inside."

Chapter 8

Before Jesse left me that morning, he had filled another two pages in his notebook. I told him about Ralph Noble, Harry Lehr's friend on the Point, and explained about Harry's recent spending—careful not to divulge the full state of Bessie and Harry's marriage—as well as his friend's mysterious entertaining. Not fully convinced, Jesse guardedly agreed the fellow might have a reason to want to do away with Bessie, thus giving Harry—and, by association, himself—greater access to her money.

Then Jesse brought up Neddie Thorton. "When you came to me about her, you were merely concerned about her lack of references and that she could be out to swindle the Lehrs." His gaze became probing. "You think she could be behind these incidents, don't you?"

"Bessie is adamant that Neddie is innocent," I said with a shrug.

"But you're not so sure about that."

"No." I felt relieved to admit it to him after keeping Bessie's secret for so long. "Of anyone, Neddie Thorton has had nearly unlimited access to Mrs. Lehr and her possessions, including the railing on her balcony on Long Island and her automobile. Ely Forrester might wish ill on Mrs. Lehr, but he could never move as freely about Arleigh as Miss Thorton can."

Jesse considered this, then said, "I understand your concerns about this Miss Thorton. To be sure, her background isn't what she claimed, and yes, she lied to the Lehrs, but this is a serious accusation. I need more than her simply having access to Mrs. Lehr to hold her in suspicion."

"I know. But Mrs. Lehr told me it was Miss Thorton who realized the motorcar wasn't running up to snuff. She might have tampered with the brakes herself."

"Why sabotage the vehicle, only to warn her mistress away from it?"

I explained my theory about Neddie possibly wanting to ingratiate herself to Bessie to make herself indispensable and thus guarantee her position in the Lehr household. "She hails from a family of poor sharecroppers renting land on a plantation. The fear of falling once again into that kind of poverty could surely motivate someone to take drastic measures."

"Does Mrs. Lehr know about Miss Thorton's background?"

"She does," I replied after a hesitation, easily guessing what his next comment would be.

"Seeing as she never mentioned Miss Thorton once this morning, she obviously trusts her, no matter her background."

"She *clings* to her trust in Neddie Thorton," I said with emphasis.

"An interesting way to put it."

"Which puts Miss Thorton in a position to take advantage of Bessie's . . ."

"Gullibility?" Jesse supplied when I hesitated to say it.

I nodded, then added, "And good nature."

He held me in his gaze a long moment before asking, "What about the husband? I've heard he's an eccentric. Could he have any motive to do away with his wife?"

It had only been a matter of time before Jesse lighted on such a possibility. I averted my gaze, sure he would know I wasn't being forthright. I also crossed my fingers. "Bessie would have told me if she believed it to be him."

"If this other fellow, this Ralph Noble, wants her money, perhaps her husband wants it just as badly. The money is hers in her own right, yes?"

"Yes, but . . ."

"After hearing everything the two of you had to say, my money is still on these incidents being happenstance." He flashed me a placating look when I started to protest. "And if not that, I'll wager the husband is involved. This Ely Forrester does worry me somewhat, though. If he's so keen on keeping his secret, he might wish to frighten Mrs. Lehr into remaining silent, if not out-and-out kill her. I'll see if I can discover his whereabouts. When is your cousin due back?"

"In a week or so, I believe. Do me one favor, Jesse. Search for Mr. Forrester, but leave Reggie to me. He'll talk to me, whereas if he hears you're looking for him, he's likely to bolt again."

"*Hmph.* I'd have thought he had run out of states by now."

"I'd also like to have a look at Miss Thorton's room at Arleigh. Something else I might manage, whereas you're not supposed to know her name ever came up."

"What are you hoping to find?"

I shrugged. "I'm not sure. Perhaps a manual on automobile brakes."

* * *

Word came that Reggie and Cathleen returned from Europe and had gone straight to Sandy Point, Reggie's horse farm in Portsmouth. I decided to give them a few days to settle in before barging in on them. In the meantime, I chose Sunday afternoon to pay Bessie a visit. Traditionally, the servants were given time off after church, and I hoped that would be the case with Neddie Thorton. I telephoned ahead of time and, as luck would have it, Bessie didn't have plans until later that evening. I didn't mention Neddie.

As I had expected—and hoped—the house was unusually quiet when I arrived, the front door being opened by a housemaid, probably a lower one. Often the lower servants alternated their time off so the family wouldn't have to fend completely for themselves.

She escorted me into the small parlor, where Bessie awaited me, with Hippodale in her arms. From several rooms away, I heard male voices. Harry must be home, then, with company. My pulse raced a few beats. Was his mystery friend here? Could I manage to gain entry to Neddie's room *and* peek into Harry's office? I wondered how many times I could falsely claim to be lost on my way to the lavatory.

"Shall I ring for tea?"

"No, thank you, Bessie. I've come for a reason."

Her eyes widened with eagerness. "You've learned something."

"I'm sorry to disappoint you, but no. I'm here to put my mind at rest. You're so sure of Miss Thorton—"

"I *am* sure." She ran a hand down the ebony fur on Hippodale's back.

I drew a breath, searching for patience. "Can you not see that by tying my hands, not to mention Detective Whyte's, you could be obscuring something vitally important. Perhaps Miss Thorton is innocent—I truly hope she is—but would it not be better to vindicate her beyond all doubt? This way, there is no question."

"How can you do that?"

"Is she here at present?" I held my breath as I awaited the answer.

"No, she and some of the others have gone into town. It's their half day."

I discreetly exhaled. "Would you allow me to see her room?"

"You wish to search Neddie's room?" Hippodale whined at his mistress's sudden agitation. She soothed him with more petting and a kiss on his sleek head.

"I wish to make sure there is nothing incriminating hidden there."

"I don't think . . ."

"Bessie, if I find nothing, I'll never speak another word against her. You asked for my help. I can't help you properly if you refuse to let me."

She surprised me by coming to her feet. "All right. We'll go up the back way. I don't want Harry to see what we're up to. It would involve awkward explanations."

With Hippodale in her arms, she led me through the morning room corridor and to the back of the house. From there, we accessed the backstairs, which took us up to the third floor. Bessie attempted to muffle her footsteps on each tread, not for fear of being heard, I surmised, but because she was unused to the sound of her own footsteps on uncarpeted wooden stairs. I wondered what excuse she would give for us being in this part of the house if we were seen, but we passed no one along the way.

As befitting an upper servant, Neddie Thorton's room was small but well appointed: a roomy bed in a decorative brass frame, an ample dresser, a wardrobe, even a dressing table, and a comfortable chair, which occupied a corner. A rug woven with colorful flowers and vines covered most of the wooden floor.

My gaze returned to the chair. A bouquet of flowers lay strewn across the seat as if tossed there. I crossed the room to more closely examine the single pink dahlia surrounded by purple asters and a spray of blue hydrangea. The petals drooped, browned around the edges. How long had these flowers lain there, neglected and starved for water?

"She clips flowers from the hothouse for my bedroom every morning," Bessie explained, though I hadn't asked. "And she's permitted to take some for herself. Odd that she left them there. She must have forgotten about them."

I turned and gestured to the dresser. "Especially when she has a vase right there." A brass vase with an enameled design stood beside the mirror.

As I began my search, Bessie backed into the doorway, as if not wanting to play any part in it. She merely watched me, one hand stroking Hippodale's head.

I began by sliding my hands beneath the mattress on both sides. Then I hunkered down and peered beneath the bed. When I came up empty-handed, I saw that Bessie had averted her gaze from my undignified position. I moved to the wardrobe and once again found no reward for my pains. Neddie Thorton owned the requisite conservative wardrobe of a lady's maid—nothing flashy or overly delicate, but, rather, sturdy cottons and serges in dark colors that would allow her to blend into the background. A sensible pair of lace-up boots sat below the dresses. If she owned a nicer pair, perhaps with heels, she had probably worn them into town.

"Please finish up," Bessie implored me. She shifted Hippodale in her arms.

"Almost finished." I went to the dresser next, and in one

of the topmost drawers, I discovered a package of Duke's Cameo Cigarettes. "Miss Thorton smokes," I commented.

"Occasionally. I won't deny her the pleasure."

I kept searching and in the lowest drawer, beside a stack of flannel underthings, found a small cardboard box. Its lid lay partially askew, making it appear as if Miss Thorton had tossed the box in haphazardly. I slid the cover completely off. Nestled in wrinkled tissue paper were two pieces of jewelry that appeared to be handmade: a bracelet strung from wooden beads and a ring woven from dark brown hair.

"Have you ever seen these?" I lifted the box and showed it to Bessie.

She came closer. "No, I've never seen her wear either."

"This ring—it could be mourning jewelry. Has she ever mentioned losing a loved one?"

"Not to me. Perhaps they're tokens from a former sweetheart, someone from her days in South Carolina. They don't appear to have any monetary value."

"No." I studied them closely. Bessie was right. These were sentimental pieces, perhaps from her life before entering service. But then, why did they appear to have been abandoned in the bottom drawer?

I placed the box back as I had found it and moved to the dressing table, where I found nothing more of interest. If anything, Miss Thorton seemed to have a distinct lack of personal items. Almost as if her life had begun here, in Bessie's employ.

"Are we finished?" Bessie's voice carried a note of defiance.

"Quite finished." I offered an apologetic smile.

She entered the room fully, as if previously she hadn't wished to sully herself with too-close proximity to my search. Now she tucked Hippodale under one arm and retrieved the flowers from the chair, holding them away from the dog's inquisitive nose. "Let's be going, then."

I followed her out, nearly bumping into her when she stopped short in the corridor. "Fullerman! Goodness, you startled me. What are you doing here? You should be in town."

The footman's face flamed, and I recognized him from the day I'd searched Harry's office. He had blushed just as fiercely then, too. "Sorry, ma'am. I'll be going in a bit, when Simpson returns. Is there something I might assist you with?" He undoubtedly wished to know what his mistress and her guest were doing on the third floor, but he would never dare question her outright.

"Actually, there is, Fullerman." She thrust the bouquet into his arms. "Please see that these are properly disposed of."

With no word as to the whereabouts of Ely Forrester, I decided to visit Reggie two days later. I cabled ahead of time, as the telephone lines to his new house were not yet installed, and let Reggie know I needed to speak with him privately. I saw no reason to burden Cathleen at this point. She must certainly know about Reggie's connection to the gambling ring, since it was the reason they had been married in Newport. She might not, however, have the faintest notion of there being any lingering danger associated with the matter, and I had no wish to be the person to enlighten her. When Reggie replied to my wire, he indicated she would be tied up all morning with a decorator, as there were still rooms in the house to be completed. He would give me a tour of his stables, where we would have all the privacy we needed.

That morning, I took the train from Long Wharf out to Portsmouth, enjoying the scenic half hour ride along the coast. Reggie met me at the train station in a two-seater motorcar painted a bright, shiny red, with gold and brass accents. My stomach clenched at the prospect of riding with him. The newspapers were always full of his exploits as he raced around Aquidneck Island.

Standing beside the motorcar when he saw me, he flashed a delighted smile and hurried over to me. "Em, so good to see you."

"And you, Reggie. I trust you and Cathleen enjoyed your time in Europe?" Though I greeted him as if I hadn't a care, I continued to contemplate the motorcar from over his shoulder.

"We did, we did, but it's good to be home. Especially since this lovely lady greeted me upon our arrival." He pointed to the vehicle. "It's a Daimler. Bought her in London and had her shipped over. Isn't she a beaut?"

"That, she is." I forced a smile. "Are we . . . motoring over to Sandy Point, then?"

"Of course we're motoring, Em. You don't think I'm about to leave my new baby here, do you?"

"Of course not," I replied faintly, and allowed him to escort me to the passenger side and hand me in.

True to form, Reggie raced around corners, gunned the engine on straightaways, and sent a flock of sheep scattering along the roadside. At this last, he turned his head and yelled out, "Farmers should keep their livestock contained, dash it! Damned nuisance, running around free like that."

"You know, the farmers have been here a long time. Generations," I shouted to be heard over the wind rushing around us in the open vehicle. Derrick never drove this fast—at least, not with me in the car with him. And true, my carriage was of the open variety with only a roof above my head, but not even Maestro, our young and lively carriage horse, could travel at speeds such as this.

"The automobile is here to stay, Em," he shouted back,

his voice ringing with laughter. "And people have to learn to adapt. As do sheep!"

Sandy Point didn't come soon enough for me. A pair of stone pillars marked the entrance to a long and winding drive that led to a Federal-revival house of many wings, so large I found it startling. A lengthy porte cochere thrust outward above the front door, allowing carriages, two deep, to stop beneath its roof and drop its passengers at the foot of the entry steps without being exposed to the weather. Upper verandas, rooftop balustrades, and large, endless windows assured me Reggie had spared no expense.

We continued past the house to another structure close by—much closer than most people built their stables to their homes. This didn't surprise me, given Reggie's passion for all things equestrian. The building was massive, sprawling nearly as large as the house itself. Clad in carefully weathered clapboard trimmed in hunter green, the structure didn't only rival the house in size, but in design as well. Clerestory windows, dormers, and, most surprising, a soaring clock tower reminded me of the Newport Casino, and I wondered if that establishment had served as Reggie's inspiration.

The scope of Sandy Point Farm, which I knew to encompass acreage from East Main Road down to the banks of the Sakonnet River, had already caused my chin to drop several times. Entering the interior of the stables and riding ring unhinged my jaw yet again. I had nothing to compare such an enormous indoor space with. It far outsized any ballroom I'd ever set foot in, and its vaulted ceilings, supported by countless wooden timbers, only made it appear more vast. There seemed enough room here to host a derby.

"The riding arena alone is 15,000 square feet, Em. Well, what do you think?"

"I'm . . . stunned, Reggie." I took in the jumps of varying

heights set up at intervals along the riding course. "I had no idea what you were up to when you announced you were building this place."

"I didn't build it from scratch. It already existed, but let's just say I improved upon it." His grin was infectious. "I don't do these things by half."

No, I silently agreed, but I wondered how many more such projects he would embark upon before his inheritance ran out.

"Want to see the horses?"

The question snapped me out of my bemusement. For the first time, I noticed the stalls lining two sides of the riding arena, their doors facing inward, toward the ring, while light streamed in from windows on their outside walls. There looked to be more than twenty stalls in all. "Good heavens, they aren't all filled, are they?"

"Not yet, but they will be." He led me around the fenced area and to one side, which formed a kind of open corridor pleasantly redolent of fresh timber, leather, hay, and horse. Two grooms were presently tending to the horses. They tipped their hats when they noticed us and acknowledged Reggie with, "Sir."

My bewilderment escalated as he walked me past one thoroughbred after another, each more magnificent than the last, each with an impressive pedigree "This is extraordinary, Reggie," I commented as we reached the end of the row. With an inner and somewhat self-deprecating chuckle, I compared the place with Gull Manor's two-stall barn, and these prized thoroughbreds to my carriage horses, albeit Maestro did possess a lively step.

"It's more than that. Sandy Point will be one of the world's greatest breeding farms, Em. That's my dream for it. People will come from far and wide to purchase my legendary horses, see if they don't."

"I believe you," I replied earnestly, then asked, "Is Harry Lehr helping you find your horses?"

"Harry? He's given me an opinion or two, but I know not to take anything he says seriously. Why?"

Perhaps Harry's claims to Tessie Oelrichs had merely been idle boasting, then. I swept the row of stalls with another appreciative look, then met Reggie's gaze. "Thank you for showing it to me. But I did come here for another reason."

"Yes, yes." He looked disappointed, but only for a moment. "Come with me. We'll talk in the lounge. It's just through here."

We left the stables and entered a large, comfortable room, which might have been part of a hunting lodge. Leather and mahogany furnishings, bookcases, and a bar with an extensive liquor cabinet—not to mention the large, safelike humidor beside it—declared this a man's refuge. I didn't doubt Reggie would spend quite a lot of time here, sometimes entertaining his male friends, at other times alone. For years now, that had been something about Reggie that worried me: his penchant for sneaking off alone to indulge in his brandy.

"What is it you wish to speak to me about?" he casually asked as he walked us to one of the leather sofas.

"Saratoga . . . and Ely Forrester."

The jovial light faded from his eyes. "What do you know about any of that?"

"I know you were summoned to testify against the leaders of the Canfield gambling ring."

He stared sullenly across the room. "Are you writing an article for your newspaper?"

"You know better than that. I simply want to know about Ely Forrester's role in the matter."

Reggie suddenly sprang to his feet and crossed to the bar. He yanked a bottle off the shelf, tugged out its stopper with a squeak, and sloshed spirits into a cut crystal glass. When he returned, he was scowling. "You should leave it alone, Em."

"Are you in danger, Reggie?"

"Not if you leave it alone."

"Is Mrs. Lehr in danger because of what she overheard at Arleigh the day of your wedding?"

He gulped down a draft of his brandy. "You're not going to leave it alone, are you, Em?"

"Is she?" I persisted.

"Not if she keeps her yap shut."

"Where is Ely Forrester?"

Another swallow slid audibly down his throat. "I don't know. Haven't seen him since before Cathleen and I went to Europe."

"I understand he has a lot to lose, should his family learn of his connection to those men. Some of them have already gone to prison, but others have yet to be indicted. How far will Mr. Forrester go to protect them and himself?"

"I wouldn't want to put it to the test," he admitted.

"How far will you go to protect yourself?" I asked softly. "And Cathleen?"

"Protect myself from what? If the police wanted to arrest me, they would have. And since I already have my inheritance, my family isn't a concern. And don't bring Cathleen into this."

"I understand Mr. Forrester already has. He made threats against you both."

He shook his head. "Mrs. Lehr should forget what she overheard."

"Perhaps, but has Mr. Forrester forgotten?"

"Blast it, Em, you're not going to give up, are you?"

"Not until I know where he is."

"I tell you, I don't know."

We sat glaring at each other for several moments, both of

us stubborn, unwilling to give in. Finally, when I thought I would get no more out of him, I came to my feet. Reggie surged to his as well.

"Shall I drive you back to the train station now?"

"Not just yet. The train back to Newport isn't for another forty minutes or so." I checked my watch, secured to my wrist by a delicate satin band. Then I showed him a cordial smile. "Besides, I must pay my respects to the new bride."

"What?"

"You heard me." My feet were in motion.

"You said you'd leave Cathleen out of this."

"Don't worry, I won't stay to tea and certainly not dinner, but a few moments just to reiterate to Cathleen how happy I am for you both."

He caught up to me as I opened the door to the outside. "I'm sure she's still busy with the decorator."

"Perhaps she'd like another opinion."

He caught me by the arm. "Too many opinions will only muddle things."

I faced him, suspicion brimming inside me. "Are you hiding something—or someone—in the house?"

"Of course not. Don't be daft."

"Good. Then escort me inside. I can't come all the way out here without having a glimpse of the place. Nanny is going to ask all sorts of questions about it. She'll be out here herself if I don't satisfy her curiosity."

He blew out a frustrated breath. "You win."

The inside of the house proved as impressive as the exterior, its proportions and design as ornate as one could wish. Yet, I had to hand it to Reggie and Cathleen. Somehow, even amid the gilding and carving and the array of priceless objects, there remained something inviting, something of warmth and relaxation that made this showplace a home.

Reggie again asked me what I thought.

I reached for his hand and gave it a squeeze. "It's wonderful. You've got quite a treasure here."

Light footsteps drew our attention to Cathleen, descending the grand staircase. She wore a tea gown of yellow silk chiffon embroidered with pink roses, which floated around her as she came down the steps. Her pretty features, always so serene, were framed by the dark upsweep of her hair, which left a few curling tendrils to tease her neck. How young she looked, how trusting and ingenuous. At the tender age of eighteen, she was far too inexperienced to envision all that could go awry in life. Suddenly I wished to grasp Reggie by the lapels, shake him thoroughly, and make him promise to always do right by his bride.

She smiled earnestly as she reached us and extended her hand. "Mrs. Andrews, how lovely—"

"No, dearest, this is our Emma," Reggie scolded lightly. "You must call her that."

"May I?" she inquired, still holding my hand.

"I do hope so," I replied with a laugh. "If I may call you Cathleen."

"You're certainly not to call her Mrs. Vanderbilt," Reggie said with a shudder. "I'll think you're addressing my mother." He looked about us in mock horror. "She's not here, is she?"

Cathleen released me and swatted Reggie's arm. "You know you don't mean that." To me, she added, "He adores his mama, and she him."

I nodded. Well did I know their affection for each other, which had resulted in Reggie becoming the indulged youngest son, his transgressions continually overlooked by my doting aunt Alice.

Cathleen remembered her duties as hostess. "Shall we adjourn to the conservatory for tea? It's lovely there at this time of day."

From the corner of my eye, I noted Reggie's look of impatience—or was it something more emphatic? I shook my head. "I'm sorry, but I should catch the midmorning train back to Newport. I couldn't resist a peek inside before leaving, though."

Before I could elaborate, Reggie put in, "The *Messenger* calls, doesn't it, Em?"

"It does. But perhaps another time?"

"Most certainly," Cathleen readily agreed. "But it's still early. Before you run off, do let me show you some of our new home."

"She really hasn't the time, Cathy—"

"I'd love to see it," I said, cutting my cousin off. "I have time for at least a few rooms. Who is your decorator?"

"For the most part, we've consulted with Georges Allard, Jules's son. I was just upstairs with one of his assistants. We're doing a sitting room up there. But Reggie and I have had our own ideas as well. Let me show you . . ." She drew me into the drawing room, showing me various features of both the furnishings and the room's architectural adornment. Reggie followed at our heels, almost breathing down my neck. I could all but feel him pushing me toward the door, at least with his thoughts.

Cathleen, seemingly oblivious to her husband's eagerness to have me gone, showed me the ballroom, dining room, and finally the conservatory, where we would have had tea, had I agreed to stay long enough. I began to take pity on Reggie, although why I didn't know, and finally announced that I must be getting back to the train station.

"I'll drive you," Reggie volunteered over his wife's regrets that my visit must be cut short.

"You and Mr. Andrews will join us for dinner soon," she said. "We'll make a party of it, won't we, Reggie?"

"We most certainly will, my love. Come, Em, we wouldn't

want you to miss your train." Reggie went so far as to give my arm a tug. Even at that, Cathleen and I spent another several minutes in conversation. She wished to know about my charity work in Newport and how she might become involved.

In the motorcar, Reggie immediately relaxed. I stole glances at him, noting the brackets around his mouth had eased considerably from when we were in the house. He clearly hadn't wanted me there; he just as clearly didn't wish to tell me why.

I'd try anyway. "You were awfully eager for me to leave."

"Not true."

"You can't fool me, Reggie. Tell me the truth. Has Mr. Forrester been staying with you?"

A blush climbed the cheek visible to me in profile. "Only for a little while, just after the wedding. Cathleen and I weren't even there. We'd already left on our honeymoon. Look, maybe he's gone back to The Elms."

"*The Elms?*" I couldn't hide my surprise.

"Sure. He stayed there a couple of days before the wedding. His parents and the Berwinds are great friends. Didn't you know?"

I hadn't. I made a mental note to pay a call on Minnie Berwind.

At the station, he jumped out and helped me down, then pecked my cheek and said, "It was splendid seeing you today. Thanks for letting me show off a bit. Cathleen too. She's proud of the old pile. Or new pile, I should say. Anyway, next time we'll have it all planned and show you and Derrick a right good time. Promise."

"We'll look forward to it, Reggie."

I thought he'd walk away, but he held my gaze, looking as uncertain as he often had as a boy when he was trying to decide between lying and telling the truth. I waited, wondering which it would be.

"Look, Em, I know Ely said some things that day. But it was just talk. He's harmless, I assure you."

"But—"

"If there's someone you should be looking into, it's a friend of Harry Lehr's. Name of Ralph Noble. He's always pestering Harry to gain better control of Bessie's finances."

"How do you know this?"

He shook his head and shrugged. "I hear things."

"This Ralph Noble—does he rent a house on the Point?"

"I have no idea. It's not like I ever visit the man or ever will. He's got a nasty reputation among . . ."

"Among whom, Reggie?"

He shrugged again. "Men you've no business knowing anything about, Em, and that's all I'm going to say on the matter." With that, he turned on his heel and was gone.

Chapter 9

Reggie's final words to me echoed in my head in rhythm to the train's chugging. I tried to relax in my seat, but a strange sensation kept my gaze darting about the car. The seats were about half full, and while some passengers were speaking in low tones, others read newspapers or simply stared out the window at the passing scenery. No one seemed to be paying any attention to me, yet an odd apprehension kept me vigilant.

Ralph Noble and Ely Forrester—was one of them on the train with me? It was a silly notion, one I attempted to shake off as illogical, however much the hair at my nape bristled. How would either of them have known I was traveling out to Sandy Point today? Then again, Reggie had been so eager to have me out of the house. If he had had his way, he would never have allowed me inside, to begin with. What had he been hiding? Or whom?

Could he have merely feared I might say something he didn't wish Cathleen to hear? That I might bring up his Saratoga connections again? Reggie should know me better than that. I wondered how much Cathleen knew, if he had discussed it with her at all. If he had, would it have made a difference to her? Would she have married him anyway? I knew very little about her, about the kind of young woman she was. Today she had seemed genuinely pleased to see me, had welcomed me warmly despite my being an uninvited guest. I'd like to think she saw qualities in Reggie that ran deeper than the happy-go-lucky bon vivant he appeared to be. Or had she married him solely for the Vanderbilt name and fortune?

I sighed aloud. Cathleen and her marriage to my cousin were not my concern, other than my wishing them well.

The back of my neck prickled again, scattering thoughts of the newlyweds and reminding me of Reggie's haste in returning me to the station. My heart raced as I glanced around, straining to make myself taller against the back of my seat so I could better view the car. Was Ely Forrester on the train? Had he overheard Reggie's intention to drive me back to the station and made his own way over? Reggie and I hadn't left Sandy Point right away. Mr. Forrester would have had time to arrive and board the train ahead of me.

But to what end? He could hardly accost me here, surrounded by other passengers. I told myself I was safe enough for the time being.

When the train pulled into the station at Long Wharf, I made sure to stay among the other disembarking passengers as I made my way toward town. With a brisk stride, I trekked up to Washington Square, though I admit I stole glances over my shoulder every few steps. At Spring Street, I hurried along, attempting to blend into the afternoon bustle. When I finally spied the *Messenger*'s sign above the street door, I broke into a trot that sent me bursting into the front office.

Both Derrick and Stanley Sheppard were sitting at their

desks. Both looked up sharply, clearly startled by my unseemly entrance. In another moment, they both came to their feet. I gestured Mr. Sheppard back into his chair, but nearly flung myself into Derrick's arms and buried my face against his shoulder.

"What happened?" I heard no placating tones in his voice, no attempt to comfort. He was demanding to know who and what had put me in such a state, so he could make whatever retribution might be warranted. I felt the fight enter his very bones and radiate outward to his limbs, reminding me he had trained as a boxer in his university days. "Emma, tell me what happened."

I eased away from him, letting my arms fall to my sides. "I'm sorry, I'm being silly. I thought . . . but I wasn't, I'm sure it was nothing . . ."

Mr. Sheppard came to his feet. "There's something in the back that needs my attention."

He started to go, but Derrick waved him back to his desk. "You stay. We'll talk in Emma's office."

Ethan was there when we arrived, but he quickly gauged our mood—my flushed cheeks and rapid breathing, Derrick's stern expression—and excused himself. Derrick backed up against the edge of my desk and drew me into the circle of his arms.

"Now, tell me what has gotten you in such a state. This isn't like you at all. Did something happen out at Reggie's?"

"You're right, it's not like me and I'm sorry. And no, nothing happened at Reggie's. Or . . . I'm not completely certain. I thought they were alone in the house, he and Cathleen. They've only just come home from their wedding trip, after all. But he was *so* keen on my leaving it seemed suspicious. And then, on the train, I had the eeriest sensation someone was watching me."

"Who do you think it could have been? Ely Forrester?"

I nodded. "But I never actually saw him. Not at Reggie's and not on the train. Reggie claimed he wasn't at Sandy Point and suggested he might be staying at The Elms. I'll check with Minnie, but I doubt it." I paused a moment to catch my breath. "I could have been imagining the whole thing."

He studied me, then peered deeply into my eyes. "Whatever happened, it spooked you. And that's a rare thing, which makes me inclined to believe you didn't imagine anything. Come. I'm taking you home."

"It's still early."

"I don't care."

"But I'm sure you have work yet to do. I do as well."

"We'll take it home with us. We're going."

Despite my protestations, we were on our way within the half hour. Guilt plagued me, along with a sense of foolishness. I typically prided myself on being levelheaded and not falling prey to what men liked to term feminine sensibilities. We did indeed have work to do and I had taken us both away from that work, and for what? For having let my imagination run wild.

Yet, once the ocean came into view along the side of the road, with the sunlight making diamonds to rival anything Aunt Alice owned, and the salty breeze caressed me, I began to release my misgivings. Derrick had been right to bring me home. Not that I needed to hide away. I wasn't as delicate as that and he knew it. But I needed this—the wide-open ocean framed by the rocky coastline. This is where I gained my perspective, my steadiness, my strength.

That, and the little arms that circled my neck as soon as Katie handed Annamarie to me. I still wore my hat, but Katie reached around to pull out the pin and plucked it from my head. I held out each of my hands and she relieved me of my gloves as well, while I buried my nose in Annamarie's hair, in the soft, powdery smell of her. The last of the tension inside me dissipated like a wisp of smoke.

"Emma, Derrick, you're home early." Nanny came shuffling out from the kitchen, delight plain on her face and in the flashing of her half-moon spectacles. "Shall we eat early tonight?"

"No need for that, Nanny. We'll have more time to spend with Annamarie." Derrick removed his own straw boater and tossed it beside mine on the hall table. "Any post?"

"Something from Amity Carter's lawyer, I believe." She didn't try to hide her excitement or her curiosity. Amity Carter owned the property next door, where we wished to build our new home. She—and we—had believed she owned the property outright, but when she attempted to sell it to us, our lawyer discovered she had a cousin who owned the lot jointly with her, and whose cooperation she needed.

Derrick and I traded glances. We both knew Nanny took an inordinate interest in our correspondence; to the point, I didn't doubt, that she might occasionally hold a letter up to a lamp. I didn't begrudge her, nor did I ever challenge her about it. At Nanny's age, she had earned the right to be a bit of a snoop. I knew it came from a place of love.

Derrick lifted the envelope from the tray. "It does appear to be from Miss Carter's attorney."

Annamarie babbled a baby word and reached out a pudgy arm to snatch the letter from him. He grinned and handed her a calling card from the inner pocket of his linen coat. Then, again meeting my gaze, he led the way into the parlor. I'd barely settled with Annamarie on my lap before he tore open the seal and began to read.

I pressed forward. "Don't keep me in suspense."

He slapped the letter to his knee and reached over to cup our daughter's cheek in his palm. "Well, little one, we might soon be living next to a school—the very school you might someday attend."

"What? Let me see!" He handed me the letter and took Annamarie onto his knee. "Good heavens, they've found Amity's cousin, Rodney Briarton! And to think, Amity believed him to be dead."

"He's very much alive, according to this. And it seems he's inclined to sell his share of the property."

I had continued skimming, my excitement growing. "Do you realize what this means?"

"Yes, it means we'll be busier than ever soon."

The hand holding the letter fell to my lap. "Not too busy to spend time together as a family. I promise we'll make time for that. Won't we, darling girl?" I reached over to our daughter. She seized my hand and, all smiles, tried to take the wedding ring off my finger. "Oh, no you don't, little one. You're much too young for one of those."

"That's right, my dearest," Derrick said, addressing Annamarie. "Who needs a ring when you can have a horsey?" With that, he shrugged out of his coat and got down on all fours. When I balanced Annamarie on his back, she shrieked with laughter and urged him to a trot. The ruckus must have drawn Patch's attention, for he streamed in and added his barking to Annamarie's laughter. It was thus Nanny found us when she came to announce that Annamarie's meal of mashed carrots with bits of shredded chicken was ready.

"Sometimes I have trouble remembering who the child in this house is." She clucked her tongue and shook her head at us, but those half-moon spectacles flashed with humor.

After feeding Annamarie, I brought her upstairs, readied her for bed, and read to her from *A Child's Garden of Verses* by Robert Louis Stevenson. The poems never failed to lull her to sleep. Then I changed my frock, although unlike my relatives and others like them who dressed for dinner, Derrick's and my practice was to change into more comfortable clothes than we had spent the workday in. Yet another breach in etiquette that would shock my aunt Alice.

Our lawyer's letter and our time spent with our daughter had soothed my raw nerves, but after dinner I once again fell to fretting. When Katie announced she was going out to the barn to settle Maestro and Barney for the night, I came to my feet and said I'd go, instead. I took the lantern off its hook beside the kitchen door and lit the flame.

"Are you sure?" Derrick asked me, ready to vacate his chair. "I could go."

"No, I want to. I find it soothing." Odd how being in the warm quiet of the barn, tossing a bit of hay with a pitchfork, filling the troughs with fresh water and the feed boxes with fresh grain, and simply giving our horses a reassuring pat good night could help steady me. But it rarely failed.

"Still thinking about earlier?" He searched my expression.

"I haven't been, until now. But doing something useful will help." I gave a shrug. "I won't be long."

I went out through the kitchen, Patch a few paces behind me. Hazy clouds silvered a half-moon and obscured the last outline of sunlight far to the southwest. The air smelled of summer, of burgeoning plant life on both land and sea, made heavily pungent by the night moisture. I breathed it in deeply, exhaled slowly, and savored its flavors on my tongue. Patch lumbered over to me, his nose working furiously, then trotted away, this being repeated several times before I reached the barn door.

He followed me in, nosed at the horses, and then sauntered out, while I secured the lantern on its shelf and found the pitchfork. After stirring the hay already covering the floors of the stalls, I added more. When I came up beside Barney, he turned his head to me and gently nudged my shoulder. It seemed a gesture of thanks. By rights, my retired carriage horse should have been long gone from Gull Manor. But I hadn't been able to part with him, especially knowing that once he left, his life would have ended shortly thereafter. I stroked his neck.

"You're very welcome, old friend. You served Great-Aunt Sadie well, and then me. We'll take care of you as long as you need us."

Patch sauntered back inside, watching me in the dim lantern light as I finished up. "That's about it, gentlemen," I said to my equine friends. "You might not be prized thoroughbreds, but to me, you're every bit as valuable."

As I placed the pitchfork in its place against the wall and returned the bucket to its shelf, Patch emitted a low whine. His attention had turned to the open barn door. A night creature, perhaps a raccoon must have been prowling about the yard. I hoped it wasn't a skunk, or if it was, that Patch would keep his distance.

I retrieved the lantern and turned down the flame. I knew the way back to the kitchen door well enough. "Come on, boy, let's go in."

I was nearly to the barn door when he growled. It stopped me cold. I lingered, motionless and listening, and put out my hand to bring Patch to my side. He came, his hackles spiked, his ears back, and his breathing audible. Had I not experienced the sensation on the train of being watched, I would have dismissed my companion's unease as perhaps hypervigilance, but tonight my own hackles rose as my senses went on high alert.

In the next moment, he relaxed, and I blew out a breath, shaking my head at my own foolishness. It must have been an animal, after all, perhaps even a fox, searching the night terrain for a meal. I crossed the threshold and was about to grasp the heavy handle and slide the door closed, when Patch let out a growl. Then a chorus of barks.

"Is someone there?" I demanded of the darkness. A hand closed over my shoulder from behind, and I felt myself propelled face-first against the barn wall. My chin hit the wooden slats and my teeth clacked together painfully, leaving me instantly dazed. The lantern fell from my hand and clattered to the ground. Patch, in a frenzy now, barked and leaped, but whoever held me immobile, his weight pressed against me, paid him no mind. Fear rose to choke me, squeezing so tight I couldn't gather enough breath to cry out.

In another instant, I was on the ground, facedown in the weeds. "Harry Lehr says stop meddling, or you'll be sorry."

Chapter 10

"Emma? Where are you? What's going on out here?" The shouts were Derrick's. His footsteps pounded across the yard. He reached me in seconds, but by then my attacker had vanished, leaving me lying on the ground as Patch howled and lurched, searching the empty air for our foe.

I rolled over and somehow managed to sit up. Fear threatened to choke me. "Patch? Is he hurt?"

"He's all right. Are *you* hurt?" Derrick put a supporting arm around me, then both arms as I began to shake uncontrollably. Patch proved his words true by attempting to nose his way into our embrace. I reached out and drew him in, gaining courage from both his warmth and Derrick's against me.

Nanny and Katie hurried through the grass to us. "What on earth . . . ?" With surprising youthfulness, Nanny sank to the ground beside us and added her arms to Derrick's around me.

Katie stood over us, her hands clenched in front of her. "Are you all right, Miss Emma? What can I do?"

"Go back inside and telephone the police," Derrick told her, and then, in a less commanding tone, said to me, "Let's get you inside."

I soon found myself in the warmth of the kitchen, wrapped in a blanket and sipping some of Nanny's strong tea with a wee splash of brandy. She insisted it would do me good.

After refilling my cup, she set the teapot on the table and took the seat next to mine. "Can you tell us what happened, lamb?"

Derrick had only just come back inside after walking the property. We hadn't expected him to find anyone lingering, but he had to be sure. Slowly I told them everything and left nothing out. Though it had happened so quickly, I remembered every bit of it, right down to the taste of the wild sea oats growing along the side of the barn where the intruder had forced me down. Derrick held my hand as I spoke. When I got to the part about being shoved to the ground, his hold tightened.

"Did you recognize his voice?"

I shook my head. "It was raspy and hurried, and he might have been wearing something over his face that muffled it."

"Could you see any part of his face?"

"I didn't see anything of him at all. It all happened so fast."

"Think," he urged me. "Could it have been anyone we've suspected of trying to harm Bessie Lehr? Could it have been . . ."

In his pause, Nanny supplied, "Ely Forrester? Maybe he *did* follow you back on the train."

Yes, he very well might have. Except that . . . "I don't even know for sure he was at Sandy Point today."

"But Reggie was eager for you to leave."

"Yes, but Reggie is always up to something. It could have been one of a half-dozen different things. And . . ." An important point only just occurred to me. "If it had been Ely Forrester who attacked me, why would he bring Harry's name into it?"

"To throw suspicion on someone else," Nanny suggested.

"But why Harry?" I persisted. "No one, except the three of you and Jesse, knows I'm looking into Bessie's fears concerning her husband. Ely Forrester certainly wouldn't know of it, nor would Reggie. The more I think about it, the more convinced I am it was someone associated with Harry and Bessie, who now believes I might be getting close to discovering them. Not that I am," I added with a shake of my head.

Katie laid some meat scraps in Patch's bowl, set down another with fresh water, and came to the table. "Could it have been Mr. Lehr himself?"

Derrick looked as eager as Katie for my reply. Once again, I tried to remember the voice, tried to find a familiar quality in it that could help me identify my attacker. I shook my head. "I truly couldn't say."

From the front hall, the ringing of the telephone startled us. Derrick rose and headed down the corridor. "Who on earth can that be?"

Moments later, his voice drifted back to us. He sounded puzzled, vaguely alarmed. When he returned, his brows were tightly knotted. "It's Bessie. She wishes to speak to you, Emma. I told her you were indisposed, but she's insistent. She sounds quite upset."

I was already on my feet, impelled by a sense of alarm. "Good heavens, it must be urgent for her to use the telephone at this time of night." Ladies of the Four Hundred generally avoided what they considered a gauche invention. Telephones, other than the in-house ones used to communicate with the servants, were typically kept below stairs, a device used by butlers to order supplies from town. The lines were also notoriously lacking in privacy, often with multiple people attempting to converse at the same time. Bessie had telephoned me before, but only in response to my request to visit her that day.

Derrick shadowed me down the corridor to the alcove beneath our staircase. When I spoke into the mouthpiece, words tumbled from the receiver in a breathless rush.

"Emma, it's happened again. Someone has tried to kill me. Can you come? I'm sorry to ask it, but I don't know what else to do. There's been a fire and I believe it was deliberate. It was so terribly frightening . . ."

"Bessie, please slow down. Are you safe at the moment?"

"I don't know. I think so. Yes. I'm in the butler's pantry. He's here with me. So is my housekeeper. I'm not alone."

"Good. Stay with them. I'll be there directly."

"*We'll* be there directly," Derrick corrected me as soon as I'd disconnected.

I was of no mind to contradict him. After placing the earpiece in its cradle, I turned and walked into his arms.

Before we left the house, I telephoned the police station, hoping to get a message to Jesse to meet us at Arleigh, and not Gull Manor. He had already set out, but they would send an officer after him.

The ride to Arleigh was tense. We motored over, wishing to arrive as quickly as possible. Like it or not, Bessie would have to accept Jesse's involvement. Between my being assaulted outside my own house, and a fire at Arleigh that might have been deliberately set, the dangers we faced were too great not to call upon the skills of a seasoned professional.

In the open automobile, I sniffed at the air to detect smoke. Bessie hadn't described the size of the fire or in which part of the house it occurred. The air along Bellevue Avenue, however, offered nothing more sinister than the ocean breezes, perfumed by the sweetness of roses and the light fragrance of the hydrangeas growing in so many of the gardens we passed.

"It can't have been a terrible fire, or our eyes would be stinging by now," I said to Derrick.

He nodded and gestured at the sparse traffic of both carriages and motorcars traveling up and down Bellevue. "Had the house gone up, the road would be clogged with spectators, fire engines, and police wagons."

The butler answered our knock and ushered us into the small parlor, where we discovered Bessie lying on one of the sofas, Hippodale on her lap, a rug wrapped around her legs. Her housekeeper occupied a chair close by. She came to her feet.

"I'll be in my sitting room, madam. Ring if you need me."

"Yes, thank you, Fisk." Bessie stretched out her hand to me. I saw it was bandaged. As I hurried to her, she moved her feet to the floor and made room for me beside her. Hippodale sniffed at me, but otherwise seemed uninterested. Before the housekeeper's footsteps had faded in the hallway, Bessie called out to her, "Fisk, do make sure Clara is all right. She had quite a shock, too."

Singe marks dotted Bessie's russet silk skirt. Otherwise, she didn't appear seriously injured, but certainly unsettled. Her fingers worked distractedly through Hippodale's ebony fur.

"Bessie, are you all right?" I asked her. "Were you hurt badly?"

Before she could reply, Derrick pointed to her hands. "Has a doctor been called?"

"Yes, he should be here soon, although I believe Fisk tended them well enough. The burns are superficial, hardly anything at all. She applied a carbolated salve to them. The bandages are really to prevent it from rubbing off on my dress."

I patted her forearm sympathetically. "What happened?"

Once again, her answer was forestalled, this time by Harry, who ambled into the room and stopped short upon seeing us. "What are you two doing here?" he asked with a tinge of annoyance.

Derrick was on his feet in an instant. Seizing Harry by the arm, he propelled him back through the doorway and into the hall. His voice, sharp and angry, reverberated back to Bessie and me.

"Goodness," she said, her eyes widening.

We could hear only disembodied words as Derrick demanded answers. I heard him utter, through gritted teeth, *Gull Manor, threats, assault.* I assumed Derrick was accusing Harry of sending whoever had attacked me, but I couldn't hear Harry's replies. Bessie sat immobile, her gaze riveted on the empty doorway, until our respective husbands reappeared.

Harry looked sheepish and visibly shaken, Derrick still brooding but temporarily mollified. At least I hoped so. It wouldn't do to become violent in front of Bessie, no matter what her husband might have done.

Bessie turned rigid as Harry approached her. As he leaned, I thought he meant to kiss her and found myself bracing for her reaction. But he only reached out a hand to stroke Hippodale's downy head. The papillon gave his fingers an affectionate lick. Then the two men distanced themselves, Derrick resuming his seat in the chair closest to Bessie, which forced Harry to move to the armchair placed beyond the far end of the sofa. I only hoped the distance proved adequate. Derrick continued to seethe.

Harry, pretending to ignore my husband's rancor, leaned forward as if to take his wife's hand, though he could not have reached it from where he sat. "How are you now, my dear?"

From beside her, I saw her jaw stiffen, her chin protrude. "I'm as well as I can be, Harry. You needn't trouble yourself."

"But, my dear . . ."

Derrick coughed. "Bessie, how did this fire start?"

She pushed out a sigh. "All I know is when I lit the match and tossed it onto the paper and kindling, the flames leaped out at me. It's a wonder they didn't set my frock on fire. I cannot imagine how I jumped out of the way quickly enough. Thank goodness I had already put Hippodale on the bed, or he might have been in my arms, directly in harm's way. And we're fortunate that Clara came in with my tea when she did. The clever girl snatched the comforter off the foot of my bed and used it to smother the flames that caught on the rug. Otherwise, who knows?" She waved a hand in the air. "The whole house might have gone up."

Harry appeared genuinely perturbed. "Why were you lighting your own fire? I thought Thorton did that for you every night."

"*Miss* Thorton," Bessie corrected him. "And I'd sent her off to bed."

"Why on earth?" Harry ran a hand over his pomaded hair.

Bessie opened her mouth to reply—probably to retort, if her expression was any indication, but footsteps, followed by the butler appearing in the doorway, silenced her.

"Detective Whyte, madam."

Bessie's gaze snapped to mine. A flush of guilt heated my face. "I'm sorry, Bessie," I whispered for her ears alone. Harry strained to hear what I was saying; I lowered my voice even further. "This has grown too dangerous. The police must be involved. But as I've told you, you can trust Detective Whyte."

The butler retreated, replaced by Jesse as he crossed the threshold, hat in his hands. Behind him stood two uniformed officers. "Good evening, Mr. and Mrs. Lehr. Mr. and Mrs. Andrews. I understand there's been trouble here tonight."

Harry came to his feet. "I don't know that I'd say it's the sort of trouble you're needed for."

Derrick stood as well. "There's been a fire upstairs, and it occurred under questionable circumstances." He aimed a glare at Harry. "Perhaps Mr. Lehr and I should allow you to speak with Mrs. Lehr privately. The fire was in her room."

Bessie clutched my hand. "I wish for Emma to remain."

"Don't worry, I will," I assured her.

"I'll stay as well." Though Harry didn't resume his seat, he appeared to dig in his heels. "I shouldn't like to leave my wife alone when she's clearly overwrought."

"I am no such thing." Bessie's chin jutted again. "Go, Harry. You're not needed here."

She spoke without rancor, merely stated a fact. Harry's skin became mottled; his eyes narrowed. "As you wish, my dear. But I won't be far. Call me if you need me."

She gave no reply, merely stared at him until he set his feet in motion. Derrick followed close behind him, and I perceived his effort not to give Harry a shove to hasten his retreat. They didn't make it far before coming to a sudden halt.

A third man had appeared in the hall, one I recognized immediately by his stoutness, his paunch, and the slope of his chin. It was all I could do not to call out his name: Ralph Noble.

"What's this?" Mr. Noble peered into the parlor, his eyes heavy-lidded and glazed. A lock of blond hair fell carelessly over his brow, giving him a disheveled look. "A party? When were you going to tell me, old chap?"

Bessie craned forward to see into the hall. "Who's here, Harry?"

"Just a friend, my dear. No one for you to worry about."

"No," Ralph Noble parroted, "it's no one for you to worry about, Mrs. Lehr. In fact, if anything, I'll keep your husband out of trouble."

Bessie scowled. Derrick did as well, apparently also having recognized Mr. Noble. Without attempting to disguise his next question as anything other than suspicion, he bluntly asked both men, "How long have the two of you been here? Where were each of you about an hour ago?"

"What?" Ralph Noble grinned widely, as if eager to engage in an amusing game.

Harry ignored him. "As I've already told you, we've been here."

"All night?" Derrick pressed, speaking directly to Ralph Noble now.

"We had a light supper in town and came straight here," Harry replied for his friend, looking and sounding none too pleased.

"Where did you sup?" Derrick demanded.

"The Casino Grill Room." The reply came quickly from Ralph Noble, lending credence to Harry's claim.

Quietly I gestured toward Mr. Noble and asked Bessie, "Did you know this man was here?"

She shook her head. "I've never seen him before."

Jesse crossed the parlor to them. "What's this about, Mr. Andrews? Why are you questioning them? Does it have anything to do with why I was called to Gull Manor earlier?"

Derrick regarded him, his lips pressed tight. Then he said, "It does. We had an intruder at Gull Manor just before receiving the telephone call from Mrs. Lehr."

Bessie turned to me in surprise. "Did you? What happened? Had I known, I'd never have insisted you come."

"It's all right." While I had no desire just then to go into what had happened to me earlier, I flicked my attention back to Ralph Noble. "In fact, it might be quite fortunate that we're here now."

He stared back at me, a subtle frown creasing his brow. Had it been him outside the barn?

My sights moved to Harry. And something occurred to me. Despite his shortcomings with humans, Harry appeared to be genuinely affectionate with dogs. At least he was with Hippodale, and the dog eagerly returned those affections. The day I'd searched his office, Harry had come home, gone to his room, and called for Hippodale. The dog had wasted not a moment in joining him, a sure sign of his devotion to his master. When Harry had entered the parlor moments ago, his first act had been to pet the dog, who rewarded him with a lick.

And earlier tonight, whoever had attacked me hadn't hurt Patch, although he very well might have. *Could* it have been a dog-loving Harry Lehr?

I shook off my conjecture. Jesse had been speaking, and now he said to Harry and his friend, "I'd like you both to remain in the house for now. I might have questions for you once I'm finished taking Mrs. Lehr's statement."

Yes, and so might I.

They shrugged and attempted to laugh off Jesse's authority. As they shuffled off to another part of the house, Derrick trailed them. A parting glance over his shoulder assured me he'd keep a close eye on them.

To his officers, Jesse said, "I want you to go up and examine the bedroom. Ma'am," he said to Bessie, "which room is it?"

"Third door from the landing, in the corner," she replied. "It faces the front of the house."

The two officers headed for the stairs. Jesse came and sat near Bessie and me. "Now, then . . ."

Bessie repeated what she had told Derrick and me when we arrived. But a question remained, one that troubled me. "You said you sent Miss Thorton off to bed. Why was that?"

"She had a headache. They plague her occasionally, so I told her to take a headache powder and get some sleep."

I found it terribly convenient that Miss Thorton had declared herself infirm on this night, of all nights. "How often does she have a headache?"

"I don't know." Bessie tilted her head at me in puzzlement. "Upon occasion. I don't keep track."

I met Jesse's gaze, and he gave a nod. "I'll need to speak with Miss Thorton."

"You can't." Bessie folded her hands primly in her lap. "Not tonight. She'll be asleep by now."

"You'll have to send someone to wake her, I'm afraid." Jesse's tone brooked no argument. "Do you always have a fire on a summer night, Mrs. Lehr?"

"I know it's unusual," she replied, looking almost apologetic. "But I enjoy it. Just a small one, you see, not one that would put out much heat at all. But the glow . . . comforts me." She tried to dismiss this last observation with a flick of her hand, but I caught Jesse studying her intently, no doubt making a mental note that this wealthy woman, reputed to be wildly happy in her marriage, and who enjoyed celebrated status among society, should need comforting.

He came to his feet. "I'll go up now and have a look at the room myself."

I excused myself to Bessie and followed Jesse into the hall. "Aren't you going to ask her why she thinks this happened?"

"No, I'm not. Not yet, at any rate. I'd like to speak with this maid and the other servants in the house. I'm assuming a footman laid the fire, to begin with. I'll need to see what he has to say for himself." He searched my features. "You know more than you've told me. And it has to do with Harry Lehr, doesn't it?"

"I've been sworn to secrecy about most of this."

"I'm not surprised. That's why I don't think it would do me a lot of good to question Mrs. Lehr about possible motives. I know how these swells operate. Avoid a scandal at all costs—even if the cost is a life. In this case, possibly her own." He shook his head again and started up the stairs.

Jesse didn't remain in Bessie's bedroom long. When he returned downstairs, he had one question for the Lehrs. "Do you keep gasoline on the property?"

"Of course we do." Harry treated the question as a stupid one. "What automobile owner doesn't?"

Jesse showed no response to the condescending tone. "Where is it kept?"

"In the carriage house, of course. Where we also keep the automobiles. Where else?"

"Can anyone gain access to it?" Jesse asked next.

Harry hesitated. Even Bessie appeared confused by the question.

"We never thought we needed to hide it," Harry impatiently explained.

We also kept gasoline on hand at Gull Manor, but Derrick kept it tightly sealed and locked in a cupboard in the barn. He did this as a precaution and sometimes I had wondered if his diligence was necessary, but I no longer would.

"It's a highly flammable substance." Jesse paused a moment, regarding the husband and wife. "Did it never occur to you that it could be dangerous and deliberately used to set a fire?"

Bessie, paling, hugged Hippodale tighter. "Are you saying gasoline was used to start the fire upstairs?"

"We believe on the kindling or the paper, or both. It had probably dried and was not as odorous as fresh gasoline. You didn't smell anything, ma'am?"

"Why, no." Her eyes went narrow, and then opened wide. Her nose wrinkled. "I suppose I did smell something unusual. But the windows were open and I assumed it was coming from outside. The front of the house is rather close to the avenue."

"I see." Jesse made a notation in his notebook. "I've had your housekeeper assemble the staff, including Miss Thorton, in the servants' hall. I'm going down now to question them."

Bessie raised her eyebrows. "Miss Thorton won't have anything to add."

"We'll see." Jesse turned to me. "Emma, I might need your help with the female servants."

"Yes, I'll come."

The servants stood at attention as we entered the room where they took their meals and relaxed between their duties. While he asked questions, I was at leisure to study each of the individuals present. Neddie Thorton stood amid the others, wearing her nightgown and robe, buttoned all the way up and cinched at the waist by a sash. This was my first view of her, and I took in every detail. I found her appearance unassuming. She was petite, and her hair, gathered in a braid behind her, an ordinary light brown. Her delicate features lacked beauty and might have been forgettable if not for her eyes, which were large and a luminous, silvery blue that seemed almost unnatural, as though lit from a source all their own.

While I pondered these details, Jesse didn't waste time on pleasantries or explanations. "Who laid the fire in Mrs. Lehr's bedroom tonight?"

A hand went up. It belonged to the dark-haired youth I'd encountered here before on several occasions.

Jesse regarded him. "Your name and occupation?"

"Asa Fullerman, sir. Second footman."

"How long have you worked for the Lehrs, Mr. Fullerman?"

"Just over three years, sir. I started as a hall boy. I was promoted to footman about a year ago," he added proudly.

"Do you always lay Mrs. Lehr's fire?"

"I do, sir. And Miss Thorton lights it later."

"Where do you obtain the wood?"

"The wood, sir? Why, from the log carrier brought in and left in the servants' vestibule each night."

"Who brings that in?"

"The groom's assistant, sir." Asa Fullerman raised a hand to point at the man. "John Dorey."

Jesse wrote down the name, eyed Mr. Dorey, and returned his attention to young Mr. Fullerman. "Do you remember smelling anything unusual on the logs?"

The footman tilted his head and considered. Then he shrugged. "Not that I remember, sir. I carried the logs upstairs in the carrier, laid the fire, and left."

Jesse shifted his focus to the groom's assistant, slightly older than the footman, with muscular arms revealed by his rolled-up shirtsleeves. He wore a tweed vest and trousers tucked into his boots. "And you, Mr. Dorey? Did you remember smelling gasoline on the wood?"

"*Gasoline?*" The young man looked startled.

"You heard me."

He looked down at his feet and wiped his palms on his trousers. "Thing is, sir, I'm the groom's assistant, but I also work with the motorcars. I'm usually the one who refills the gas tanks, so I'm so used to the smell of gasoline, I hardly notice it anymore." He breathed in audibly through his nose and scrunched his features. "But no, I surely don't remember the smell of gasoline when I gathered the wood from the shed and brought it into the house."

"Is it always your job to bring in the firewood?" Jesse asked.

The man's chin dropped a fraction, then in a low tone he replied, "Used to be our man-of-all-work did it, but he's gone now, sir, killed when the motorcar crashed."

"I see." Jesse continued to stare at him for so long, taking his measure, that Mr. Dorey began to fidget. "This shed. Can anyone get inside?"

"I suppose so, sir. There being only wood inside, we don't usually keep it locked, especially during the day."

Jesse nodded and darted his gaze back to Asa Fullerman, who stared blankly back, his expression revealing nothing. "I may need to speak to both of you again."

Jesse went up and down the line of servants, asking each what their duties were and where they were at various times throughout the afternoon and evening. He seemed satisfied with the answers they offered, especially when both the housekeeper and butler were able to corroborate each claim. There was only one exception: Neither could account for Neddie Thorton following lunch that day.

Chapter 11

The housekeeper cleared the rest of the servants away, leaving Neddie Thorton to face Jesse's questions alone, but for my presence. However, one servant—the groom—lingered outside the doorway as the rest dispersed. When he caught Jesse's eye, Jesse went out to speak with him. When Jesse returned, he took a seat across the table from Miss Thorton. I sat beside her.

After having the lady's maid state her full name yet again, Jesse got straight to the point. "I understand Mrs. Lehr released you from your duties this afternoon. Because of a headache?"

"Yes, that's right." Her vowels stretched in that languid way particular to Southern speakers.

"Where did you go after that?"

"Up to my room."

I noticed she didn't address Jesse as *sir* after each reply, as the other servants had.

"And nowhere else?" Jesse raised an eyebrow in a clear invitation for Miss Thorton to elaborate on her answer. "Are you certain of that?"

She hesitated, a corner of her lip catching between her teeth. Though I could only see her in profile, I detected the moment she realized she had probably been caught in a falsehood, no doubt revealed by the groom during his brief word with Jesse. "Oh yes . . . I'd forgotten. I went for a walk first. Sometimes fresh air helps relieve the pain."

"Of your headache," Jesse clarified, and she nodded. "How could you forget having taken a walk, Miss Thorton?"

After another hesitation, briefer than the first, she said, "Because when I finally went up to my room, I immediately fell deeply asleep. My headaches always exhaust me."

"Did your walk take you near the carriage house?"

"It did. Is that a crime, Detective?"

Jesse's mouth lifted at her question; a visit to the carriage house might well have been a crime in this case. "Did you go anywhere else in the house after returning? For instance, did you stop in your mistress's room?"

"No, I did not go to Mrs. Lehr's room." She stated this with certainty. "As you said, I'd been relieved of my duties for the rest of today."

"Were you in the servants' vestibule?"

Her intake of breath could almost have been a gasp. "Of course I was. It is the only way to reenter the house without using the front or terrace doors. But I merely walked through, and I certainly didn't tamper with the fireplace logs, if that is what you're implying, Detective."

Her defiance didn't surprise me, as it might have, coming from another servant. But based on what I had learned about Miss Thorton, about how she had manipulated her way into Bessie's employ, I knew she was no wallflower. That she had the ability to fight for her own survival.

Had I not entertained doubts about her loyalty to Bessie, I might have respected her for it.

Jesse and I conferred silently across the table. He nodded subtly.

"Miss Thorton," I said. She turned toward me, her surprise evident that I would speak during this interview. "You ordinarily spend quite a lot of time with Mrs. Lehr, don't you?"

"Mrs. Lehr has frequent need of my services." Again defensiveness.

"You've made yourself indispensable to her."

Her eyes narrowed as she apparently weighed the significance of my statement. "I don't know that I would say that. I try to be as helpful to Mrs. Lehr as possible."

"Beyond the usual scope of a lady's maid."

"Perhaps." Cool assurance replaced her defiance. "Unlike many personal maids, I know how to drive a motorcar, and that has come in handy."

I very nearly smiled at those last words. "Yes, about that. I understand you and she were to drive into town the day the Lehrs' man-of-all-work was killed in the crash, but that you noticed the automobile wasn't behaving normally."

A measure of her aplomb slipped. "That's true."

"And that when Mrs. Lehr nearly fell from her balcony at their Long Island home, it was you who prevented her from falling."

"It was fortunate I was there."

"Then there was the matter of the stair runner here," I went on. "It was loose at the topmost step, and Mrs. Lehr nearly fell. She might have broken her neck."

"I'd like to think not."

"I'm sure you would," I agreed. "Such a coincidence that you were there each time."

"Yes?" The word ended with a slight question in her voice.

I looked across at Jesse to signal that I had finished my part in the interrogation. The rest I would leave up to him.

"Miss Thorton." The sound of her name hovered awkwardly in the air before Jesse continued, prompting her to clutch her hands in her lap. "Have you created these incidents to ingratiate yourself to your employer?"

"What? How ridiculous! No, Detective, I have not."

His placid stare became relentless. "Are you sure?"

"Why would I endanger Mrs. Lehr's life when it would mean I'd be out of a job?"

"But you were there each time to rescue her, weren't you?" I reminded her.

Her head swiveled back toward me. "Not tonight, I wasn't. How could I have saved her from the fire if I was nowhere near her room?"

In lieu of a reply, Jesse came to his feet and opened the door to the hallway. He poked his head out, and a moment later, one of the maids entered as if she had been waiting for his summons. Which, of course, she had.

"You are Clara, and you're employed here as a housemaid," he said to the girl, who looked to be no more than eighteen or so. Jesse retook his seat, but he didn't invite Clara to sit; nor had he reclosed the door, which signified his interview with the girl would be a quick one.

"That's right, sir."

"It was you who doused the flames in Mrs. Lehr's bedroom tonight, yes?"

"Yes, sir. It was frightful."

"Were you hurt?"

"Not at all, sir."

"I'm glad. Now, Clara, is it usual for you to bring Mrs. Lehr her evening tea?"

"No, sir. That's Miss Thorton's job, but she took ill. Mrs. Fisk asked me to bring it up."

"And did you do that at the usual time—the time Miss Thorton usually brings it?"

"Yes, sir. Exactly the same time."

Jesse gave a nod. "Thank you, Clara, that will be all."

Once the girl had left, Jesse said to Miss Thorton, "You would have known one of the maids would bring Mrs. Lehr her tea, wouldn't you?"

"Of course," she replied with a shrug.

"Then you would have known that help would be arriving to save Mrs. Lehr from the flames."

"No, Detective. I didn't know that because I did not know there would be flames."

"You typically light Mrs. Lehr's fire in the evening. On the one night you didn't, there was a fire that might have consumed the entire house. Except that Clara conveniently arrived to douse the flames. Are you sure you didn't plan this all out as another example of why Mrs. Lehr cannot do without you? The case this time being that without you there to light her fire, Mrs. Lehr could have seriously injured herself."

For the first time, Miss Thorton's façade shattered. A flush consumed her cheeks. "You're determined to hold me responsible, aren't you? No matter what I say. No matter the truth."

"The truth is what I'm trying to get at, Miss Thorton." Jesse made a final notation in his notebook. "You may go, for now."

For a long moment, she didn't move. I believe Jesse astonished her with his sudden dismissal and she didn't quite know what to make of it. Then a realization set in, apparent in the shrewd look that came over her. She pushed to her feet and, without another look at either of us, strode from the room.

She had reached an obvious conclusion. Jesse had no tangible evidence against her.

Jesse and I lingered in the servants' hall after Miss Thorton left, reviewing her replies, as well as those of the others.

I still believed it possible that Neddie Thorton engineered these incidents for her own benefit, but if so, she played an exceedingly dangerous game, for herself, as well as Bessie.

"One mistake and Bessie might have been killed in any one of these occurrences," I said to Jesse. "The least consequence for Miss Thorton would be losing a good position; the worst, of course, being convicted of murder and going to the gallows."

"Could jealousy be her motive?" Derrick entered the room and slid onto the chair beside my own. "Is it possible she and Harry . . ."

Jesse's face, rather glum these last few moments, brightened with interest. "That's a very real possibility. Perhaps Miss Thorton wants Mrs. Lehr out of the way."

I tried to imagine Harry sneaking around with a maid, but the image refused to form. "I don't think so. Besides, Bessie says he's rarely home for long, whereas Miss Thorton is nearly always with her. When and where would they carry on?"

"What if Miss Thorton's headaches are a way for them to be together?" Derrick paused, considering. "With the rest of the servants going about their business, there would be no one on the third floor to catch them."

"I don't think this theory will lead to anything." I offered my husband an apologetic shake of my head.

"And according to Mr. Lehr and his friend," Jesse said, "they were at the Reading Room this afternoon and the Casino Grill Room this evening, which shouldn't be too difficult to verify. Did you get anything more out of them?"

While Jesse and I were dealing with the servants, Derrick had stayed upstairs with Harry and Mr. Noble. Despite his accusation toward Harry earlier, Derrick was still considered *one of them*, and they were far more likely to speak unguardedly with him than with the police.

"I didn't learn much more about their activities today," he

replied, "but I did get to know our Mr. Noble a bit better. Youngest son of a family that made a modest fortune in silver mining in the decade following the Civil War, but a combination of their main lode running dry and some bad financial decisions has left them pretty hard up. Sounds like business wasn't their forte. When I asked what business Mr. Noble was in now, he told me, 'The business of enjoying oneself.' I had the distinct impression Harry wanted to silence him, especially when he brought up a trip abroad planned for next spring."

"How is he going abroad if his family has no money and he doesn't have employment?" I asked, although the answer should have been obvious to me.

"He didn't say, but Harry looked very much like he wanted to change the subject."

"Bessie's money," I concluded with disgust. "Have either of you noticed how Harry is with the dog?"

My abrupt change of subject baffled them both. I explained my impressions of Harry's fondness for Hippodale and vice versa. Then I laid out my theory that it could have been Harry outside the barn tonight.

Jesse darted a perplexed look from one of us to the other. "I think it's time you told me what Mr. Lehr has to do with this matter. The *whole* truth, because you've already admitted to keeping things from me."

"I promised Bessie—Mrs. Lehr—that I wouldn't, but . . ." Plagued no small amount by guilt, I launched into an explanation of Bessie's and Harry's marital problems, her suspicions, and her appeal to me for help.

"She thinks her husband is trying to murder her—and no one thought to alert the police?" Jesse's eyes sparked with anger, something I'd rarely seen in him. "Instead, you've led me on wild-goose chases concerning her maid, her husband's friend, and one of your cousin's groomsmen."

"Those are *not* wild-goose chases," I said defensively. "Any one of them may be behind these incidents."

"And so might her husband," he persisted. "Especially if it's the wife accusing him. You could have told me in the strictest confidence, Emma. You could have trusted me."

"I wanted to. I practically begged Bessie to tell you the whole truth. But surely you can understand her position. Her family is Catholic and divorce is out of the question. She needs to be certain before she risks the scandal of accusing her husband. That's why she came to me for help."

Jesse scowled at Derrick. "I suppose you knew about this."

Derrick didn't blink. "I did."

Jesse turned away from us both, his lips tight. Then he shook his head. "All right, but I'm not sure I understand. What's this got to do with Patch and the Lehrs' dog?"

I explained again, and when I'd finished, Derrick said to me, "Not that I'm defending Harry, but you may be dwelling too much on a mere coincidence."

"I agree." Jesse shrugged. "I'm glad that loveable mutt of yours wasn't hurt, but I'd say it was pure luck."

"I realize it sounds as though I'm making something out of nothing, but you weren't there, either of you," I insisted. "The intruder easily could have delivered a bruising kick to Patch's side. I don't understand why he didn't, with Patch barking and jumping, as he was. Why did this villain spare him, if he wasn't someone with a deep fondness for dogs or animals in general? Some people much prefer animals over humans."

Jesse held up a hand. "Let's first verify whether Mr. Lehr and Mr. Noble were where they say they were today."

"There's also the matter of Ely Forrester," I reminded him.

"Despite Mrs. Lehr overhearing his conversation with your cousin, I don't see how he could possibly be responsible for the fire in Mrs. Lehr's room."

"I've discovered that he sometimes stays with the Berwinds right across the street, at The Elms," I informed him. "How easy would it be for him to slip across the street and tamper with the firewood that's kept in an unlocked shed? Especially if he did it under cover of darkness? I'm not saying he did. Merely that he's still a suspect."

Jesse snapped his notebook closed. "I'm going to assign an officer to stay here tonight, and the next several nights, until we learn more. Matters seem to have grown a lot more complicated."

Derrick and I lay awake that night, discussing possible scenarios, both of us too jumpy after the night's events to drift off to sleep. His arms were around me, my head on his shoulder.

He stroked my hair and sighed, long and deep. "Tonight proves these incidents concerning Bessie haven't been random occurrences. That she was right and not imagining things."

"About someone threatening her, yes, I believe so. But about Harry?" I sighed. "I still don't know."

Derrick's fingertips played up and down my arm, eliciting little shivers I had no desire to quell. "He seemed genuinely taken aback by the fire."

"He's an accomplished actor, remember? He has all of society fooled when it comes to his supposed affections for Bessie. But would he have used his own name to warn me off?" I pondered this, not for the first time.

"But even with the warning, I fear the haphazard nature of these attempts would create doubt in a prosecutor's mind, as well as in the minds of a jury. And that would make a conviction harder to achieve."

"I don't doubt that's the goal. Or maybe the perpetrator simply doesn't have the stomach to murder someone face-to-face. Wanting someone dead and causing that death are two very different matters. Perhaps this person feels a need to put distance between himself and the act." I thought back to another killer who had singled out society ladies two summers ago, who had used poison rather than face their victims directly.

"A squeamish killer," Derrick commented wryly. "That certainly leaves Harry squarely in the mix. I shouldn't think he'd have the fortitude to confront anyone face-to-face about anything."

"Except Bessie, when it comes to wanting her money. He has no qualms about confronting her then." The notion had me scowling into the room's shadows. "But no, in other matters, I'm sure he'd rather enlist someone else to do his dirty work." I thought about the possibilities. "Ralph Noble, for instance. But then again, Neddie Thorton could also have hired a man to threaten me tonight."

"Or Reggie's friend. When you arrived at the *Messenger* this afternoon, you were all but convinced he followed you from Sandy Point. Perhaps he did, and it was him waiting beside the barn." A brooding silence descended upon us, before I sighed and went on.

"Even so, I'd place him lower on the list, although I wouldn't strike him off it. Not yet."

He stroked the braid that fell over my shoulder. "We're going round and round, my darling, and ending up nowhere. At least for tonight. Perhaps things will look clearer in the morning. Or perhaps Jesse will dig up something new when he returns to Arleigh tomorrow."

"I hope so."

"Do you think you might be able to sleep?"

At the very thought, a chill raced across my shoulders. "I doubt it. I'm afraid as soon as I close my eyes, a faceless figure will reach out and grab me. Good heavens, Derrick, what if instead of going to the barn with Patch, I'd taken

Annamarie outside to look at the stars? Would that beast still have attacked? Would she have been hurt? I'd never have forgiven myself . . ." Sudden tears took me by surprise. They sprang from my eyes, hot and burning, to scald my cheeks before dripping onto Derrick's nightshirt. "I've been terribly selfish, haven't I?"

"Why would you ask such a thing?" He eased upright and gathered me to him, his arms tight and steady around me. "You've been attempting to help your friend—doing what you always do. That is, finding the truth and stopping people from being harmed. That's not selfish, my love."

"Isn't it? We have a child now. She should take precedence over all else—and everyone else."

"She does."

I shook my head like a stubborn child. "I've always needed to step in. It's a failing of mine, this obsession to take control of a situation. To take risks with my life. But it's not only my life anymore, and I must learn to back away, for her sake . . ."

"Emma, stop it. As much as I'd like to agree and urge you to step back, this is who you are. It's something I've had to learn to accept about you, when I would rather have kept you safe." His hands framed either side of my face, holding me still so that I had no choice but to look at him. "You're not one to sit back and wait for someone else to take charge. If you see something that needs doing, you do it. That's one of the things I love about you. That, and your courage and your refusal to be cowed."

"But Annamarie—"

"Is well protected, I promise you. Do you think Nanny or Katie would let anyone with ill intentions anywhere near that child?" I started to reply with more protestations, but he rushed on. "You're a journalist, and that means you have an insatiable curiosity and a thirst for the truth. To deny you that would be to deny your very nature and everything that makes you stand out among your peers. Not to mention everything I've always admired about you."

That did little to stanch my tears, but rather than tears of uncertainty and fear, they were of gratitude.

"I want you to be careful, but I want you to be you." Derrick drew me close and laughed softly against my ear. "Besides, my stouthearted darling, the only person who is going to grab you in the darkness of this bedroom is me."

With that, he scooped me up, rolled us both over, and proceeded to chase my fears away, or, at least, blanket them in a haze of pleasure until sleep eventually claimed us both.

Chapter 12

After the tumultuous events of the previous night, Derrick and Nanny tried to persuade me to stay home and spend time with Annamarie—a tempting prospect indeed. But while I resolved to return home early and to take extra precautions when it came to the well-being of my daughter, I also resolved not to be cowed. Not to hide.

Upon arriving at the *Messenger,* the larger world encroached upon our personal concerns, forcing us to set them aside for the time being. Word had reached the United States of a ghastly coup across the Atlantic in Serbia that resulted in its king and queen being assassinated in the most horrific manner, and a new king placed on the throne.

It reminded me of President McKinley, our nation's leader, shot two years ago by a deranged individual, a self-styled anarchist. But McKinley had been replaced in a civilized fashion by his vice president, Theodore Roosevelt, whose wife I had met only a couple of months prior. The United States Congress and cabinets had remained intact, continuing to carry out their functions according to the U.S.

Constitution. That assassination, unlike this latest, had been the act of a lone, unstable man, and not the result of a widespread conspiracy to alter the balance of power among rival families and political foes.

I spent the morning going through the Associated Press reports, as well as passing nearly two hours at the nearby Redwood Library, gaining as much background as I could about Serbian politics and their royal line. By the time I had a preliminary article drafted, I felt exceedingly lucky to live in this country, rather than in one of Europe's ancient kingdoms where the boundaries between power and justice were often dangerously blurred.

At midday, Ethan glanced up from his articles about the recent society functions he had attended. "Aren't you going?"

"Going where?" I murmured, still poring over my own article, scanning for accuracy and any mistakes I might have made.

"Aren't you supposed to attend a luncheon for the Ladies' Interchurch Meal Fund?"

I raised my chin and gasped. I'd received the invitation about three weeks ago, before Bessie had come to see me. How easily I had become sidetracked—especially when the Ladies' Interchurch Meal Fund, a cooperative, citywide project to aid Newport's poor year-round, had been my own idea. "I'd quite forgotten!"

In dismay, I glanced down at my attire. With little thought to fashion that morning, I had donned a plain gray skirt, adorned only by the thinnest of pinstripes, and a white shirtwaist, along with a jacket to match the skirt, which I had shed upon arriving at the *Messenger.*

My consternation grew as my gaze traveled to the cloak rack near the door, where my plain straw boater hung from a hook. "Oh dear."

The luncheon would be attended by ladies of the Four Hundred, as well as many of Newport's wealthy year-round residents, representing the various religious establishments across the city.

"I suppose it can't be helped." I came to my feet, retrieved my handbag from the bottom drawer of my desk, and went to the rack to claim my hat.

"Don't worry, Mrs. Andrews, you always look smashing."

"Ha. But thank you, Ethan."

Rather than telephone down to the livery, where Derrick and I housed Maestro and our carriage for the day, I walked up to Bath Road and caught the Easton's Beach trolley. Luckily for me, it was neither an overly hot nor rainy day. Before the trolley began its descent toward First Beach, I climbed out and walked up Cliff Avenue toward my destination, the New Cliffs Hotel on Seaview Avenue, overlooking Easton's Bay and the ocean.

Hotels such as this had become something of a novelty in Newport in recent years. Decades ago, they had been numerous, such as the Ocean House and Atlantic House hotels, both large, luxurious accommodations that attracted wealthy visitors. That had changed when people, like my Vanderbilt relatives, began building their cottages and no longer required the services of hotels. Nowadays wealthy summer visitors owned their own cottage, rented one, or were the guests of someone who did. The Four Hundred had happily watched Newport's grand hotels go out of business while creating their own exclusive resort area up and down Bellevue Avenue.

Yet, despite opposition from many of our summer residents, the New Cliffs Hotel had risen up on its rocky heights only four years ago, boasting every modern convenience and comfort this new century had to offer. The four-story, shingle-style building featured long verandas on each floor, which offered spectacular views of the water, as well as several cottages, which could be rented by private parties for the Season. And although they grumbled about it, the Four Hundred had decided not, after all, to ignore its existence, as evidenced by today's luncheon.

Not long after I stepped into the lobby, with its spotless marble floors and countertops, carved and gilded woodwork, and elegant yet comfortable furnishings, I found myself waylaid by an official-looking gentleman. He wore formal attire similar to a butler's, leading me to assume he must be a manager or perhaps the desk clerk. He planted himself directly in my path, forcing me to a sudden halt.

"Is there something I might assist you with, madam?" His gray eyes took my measure through a pair of tiny silver spectacles perched at the end of his nose. His tone belied his offer of assistance and suggested that I leave at once.

Yes, my workaday attire. Perhaps he shouldn't be blamed, for even I had to admit my appearance was not that of a typical hotel patron. One glance around at beribboned hats, silk day frocks, and pearl necklaces—*so many* strands of pearls looped around ladies' necks—confirmed that assessment. Then again, should anyone be judged solely on the merit of their clothing? I straightened my shoulders and tilted my chin in my most imperious imitation of Aunt Alice. "I am here by invitation to attend the Ladies' Interchurch Meal Fund Luncheon. Mrs. Derrick Andrews."

Recognition of the name flashed behind his spectacles and he looked immediately contrite. "Oh yes, I see. This way, if you please, madam."

He led me across the lobby toward the din of ladies' voices, which grew louder the closer we got. Through the doorway, I spotted Aunt Alice, with my cousins Gertrude and Gladys, and several other ladies of my acquaintance, including Minnie Berwind. Good—I would have a chance to ask her when Ely Forrester had stayed at The Elms. Before I crossed the threshold, however, I heard my name called out.

A glance to my left brought Bessie into view, hurrying toward me so quickly the tulle veil on her hat streamed out behind her. There was no sign of the bandages on her hands from last night, or anything else that suggested the fright she had suffered. Rather, she was a perfection of grooming and tailoring, as usual.

"Emma, you're late," she said more breathlessly than her brief effort to reach me warranted. "I was afraid you might not come."

"I'm rather surprised to see you, actually. After last night, I'd have thought you'd wish to relax at home today."

"And what, I beg to ask you, is relaxing about being at home?" She was only half joking and I had no answer for her. Not when it came to the life she shared with Harry Lehr.

I offered to link arms with her and said, "Shall we go in before my aunt Alice comes out to get me?"

"Not yet. Come with me." To my surprise, she seized my wrist and tugged me in the opposite direction.

Yet again, I crossed the lobby, diagonally this time, until I spied the gentlemen's lounge and heard the low hum of male conversation. Unlike the luncheon room, decorated in pastels and feminine textures, the tones here were dark and subdued, with a plethora of wood trim and leather. Men at tables wielded crystal tumblers of whiskey, snifters of brandy, or pints of ale, while others inhabited wingback chairs, newspapers held before their faces. Curls of smoke formed a languid cloud that drifted beneath the coffered ceiling.

It was a male sanctuary—no mistake. I dug in my heels. "Bessie, surely you don't mean to go in . . ."

"Shh!" She pulled me off to one side, turned me to face into the room, and pointed. "See there? At the small table near the chinoiserie screen? It's that man from last night. And Ely Forrester, from your cousin's wedding."

My gaze followed the rigid line of her arm. Several men milled past between the doorway and the object of her scrutiny, but then, suddenly, the way cleared and Bessie's quarry came into view. Surprise filled me. "What would Ralph Noble be doing here with Ely Forrester?"

"I cannot imagine. I had no idea they knew each other. And I'm surprised Mr. Noble is even awake, as when I left the house not long ago, Harry was still abed. According to my footman, he and Noble were up quite late last night and went through several bottles of wine. He should know, as they sent him down to the wine cellar on several occasions."

I didn't respond. I was too enthralled watching these unlikely companions. Ely Forrester hailed from a wealthy, well-connected family, while Ralph Noble seemed to have materialized out of thin air—or from wherever Harry Lehr managed to dredge him up.

It soon became evident theirs was not the most cordial of meetings. They sat across the table from each other, both in profile to Bessie and me. But I could still detect their frowns, their heavy-handed gestures, and Mr. Forrester's labored breathing as he fell back against his chair and uttered something to Mr. Noble I felt certain could never be repeated in polite company. I saw, too, Mr. Noble's shrewd curl of a smile in a pallid face that revealed the ravages of a late night. It would seem whatever had brought Ralph Noble to that table had superseded his need to sleep off a hangover.

"I wish we could hear what they're saying." I craned forward and eased as close to the doorway as I dared without being seen by them or any of the other men in the room. "Judging by their postures, I suspect Ralph Noble has the upper hand. Do you suppose he somehow knows about Saratoga?" I turned to regard Bessie. "Does Harry know?"

"Only what he's read in the newspaper, I would assume. And the articles have made no mention of Mr. Forrester."

No, so far they hadn't. I compressed my lips, watching for another few moments. With a leisurely air, Ralph Noble reached into his coat pocket and retrieved a cigarette case. A flick of his fingers sent the lid flipping open. He plucked one out, but didn't offer one to Ely Forrester. Mr. Noble lit his cigarette, took a long drag, and released a thick trail of smoke directly into Mr. Forrester's face. The other man snapped his eyes shut and whipped his face aside. When he turned back, the expression on his face made me recoil.

Standing at my shoulder, Bessie felt my grimace. "What is it? What happened?"

"I'm not quite sure, but it's safe to say these two men are not friends, and that Mr. Noble should tread carefully."

"Ladies, may I assist you?"

Bessie and I spun about to behold the same employee who had been keen to show me the door earlier. He looked no more amused now at finding two women staring so impertinently into the male dominion of the bar. He raised his eyebrows and peered at us through his tiny spectacles as if inspecting a couple of insects.

"Oh, we . . ." Bessie began, but faltered.

"We believed we saw an acquaintance go in, a relative of Mrs. Lehr's, actually." Pausing, I gave a haughty little sniff. "I do believe we were wrong, however. Were we not, Mrs. Lehr?" Without waiting for her reply, I added, "We'll be returning to the luncheon now, thank you."

"This way, ladies." He gestured for us to follow him; apparently, he wasn't content to leave us to our own devices. Before we'd taken many steps, I looked back over my shoulder into the lounge.

Mr. Noble was still sitting at the table, smoking his cigarette. Ely Forrester, however, stood in the doorway, holding me in a steely-eyed glare that raised the hair on my nape.

Our meeting proved fruitful, with the committees from the various churches around the city agreeing to a schedule whereupon our poor residents might find a free meal every day of the week come winter, regardless of where, or if, they attended services. I felt both gratified and proud that our summer Season and year-round ladies were able to work together so well. And I stole an opportunity to speak with Minnie Berwind.

She seemed genuinely pleased to see me. "It's been too long, Emma. Ned and I must have you and Derrick to the house for dinner soon. I'll plan an entertainment, although . . ." Here she looked sheepish. "Perhaps not a musicale."

The reminder of a series of heinous crimes that began at a musicale held at The Elms two summers ago brought a somber expression to my face. Here I was again, investigating crimes that originated just across the avenue. I didn't explain that to Minnie, however. Rather, I said, "I understand you may already have company staying with you. Ely Forrester?"

"Ely, yes. On and off. Such a nice young man. His family and ours go back nearly twenty years now."

"I met him at my cousin's wedding. Is he remaining in Newport for the rest of the summer?" Would Minnie find my curiosity about the young man strange?

"He hasn't said. You know how young people are. Although he did join us for dinner last night." Suddenly she cast me a shrewd look. "Are you matchmaking, Emma? Is there a young lady you'd like to introduce to Ely?"

I merely smiled in reply and let her think what she might. I had my information. From the sounds of it, Ely Forrester periodically stayed with the Berwinds, as Reggie had implied. More importantly, he had been at The Elms last night, close enough to Arleigh to have tampered with the firewood. Had he ridden the train from Portsmouth to return to Newport, the same train I had? And after dinner with the Berwinds, had he then made his way to Gull Manor to threaten me?

Another question, however, shed doubt on his being responsible for last night's near disaster. Would he have known that, despite this being June, Bessie preferred a small fire in her bedroom at night? Is that something he could have learned during the days leading up to the wedding? It seemed unlikely he would know about anything that went on behind Bessie's closed door. While Ely Forrester had proven himself to be no angel, had I been wrong to suspect him in relation to Bessie and Arleigh?

The luncheon began to disperse, and Bessie once more appeared at my side. "How did you arrive, Emma?"

"By trolley and on foot," I replied with a laugh.

"Then allow me to offer you a ride back to town. Or home, if you prefer."

I gratefully accepted the offer. She became caught up in some last-minute discussions, however; so, having had my fill of society matters for one day, I told her I'd meet her by her carriage and walked out with Aunt Alice and my cousins. Once they'd boarded their own vehicle, I scanned the premises for Bessie. She hadn't yet come out.

I began to wander aimlessly, taking in the shingle and Queen Anne–style architecture of the hotel's cottages, and the colorful flowerbeds that fronted them. This led me closer to the Cliff Walk, which stretched beyond the hotel in either direction, descending to Easton's Beach, to my left, and behind the mansions all the way to Bailey's Beach, to my right.

A multitude of rugosa roses tumbled along the ocean side of the pebbled path, their bright pink petals and cheerful yellow centers looking like butterflies flitting among the greenery. I stopped, breathing in the freshness of the sea air. My gaze drifted from where tiny figures dotted the sands of Easton's Beach and bobbed in the waves, to where the bay waters met the currents of the Atlantic. White sails flashed in the sun, vying with seagulls and terns for my attention. The brilliance of the sky and opalescent clouds, reflected with only slightly less vibrance by the water, made my eyes tear. I closed them and savored the firm caress of the breeze on my cheeks.

"You shouldn't stand so close to the edge, Mrs. Andrews."

With a gasp, I whirled to discover Ely Forrester standing not three feet away. "Goodness, you gave me a fright. What do you want?"

"My, is that any way to treat a good friend of your own cousin, Mrs. Andrews?" A corner of his mouth lifted. "Especially when I have only your well-being in mind."

I narrowed my eyes at him, taking in his slouching posture, the pencil-thin mustache that seemed more a failure to produce fuller results than an attempt to be fashionable. "I'm not standing near the edge, Mr. Forrester. I'm merely enjoying the view." I thought to confront him about his actions last night, but it seemed an ill-advised thing to do here, beside the rocky descent to the waves. "If you'll excuse me, I'll be rejoining my friend now."

"Not so fast." He blocked my attempt to step around him. "You and that nosy little Mrs. Lehr had better learn to mind your own business. First I catch the pair of you eavesdropping on Reg and me, and now here you are again, your curiosity leading you where women oughtn't go. Did you think I wouldn't see you? A gentlemen's lounge is no place for a lady. *Are* you a lady, Mrs. Andrews?"

"How dare you." My blood heated, fueling the beat of my pulse points. He had angered me, yes, but he also frightened me. What did he mean to do? There were others trekking along the walkway, though not in our immediate vicinity. Would he truly risk pushing me over and being seen? I doubted it, but I wished to end the encounter as quickly as possible. "Move aside, please, and allow me to pass."

"I shall, Mrs. Andrews, never fear. But know this. Whatever you and Mrs. Lehr believe you heard or observed that day, you do not understand the half of it. I'd advise you both to forget whatever it is you think you know. If I see a word of it in that rag of a newspaper you and your husband own—"

"Mr. Forrester, neither Mrs. Lehr nor I wished to overhear anything that day. If you recall, you were in *her* home. You and my cousin might have held your private discussion elsewhere."

"Do you care about your cousin? Do you wish to see him harmed?"

My heart clenched with fear. "Don't you dare."

"Not me, Mrs. Andrews. But there are others who won't deign to blink an eye before making sure their interests are protected, whether that involved Reggie Vanderbilt, his wife, or even you."

I should have accepted his words of warning and hurried back to the carriages, but the very reason we were there, having this conversation, held me to the spot. "What does Ralph Noble have to do with it?"

"Noble?" He tried to look unperturbed, but I saw the fear peeking out from the corners of his eyes. "Nothing. Nothing at all."

"I hardly believe that. The pair of you didn't appear to be enjoying a friendly drink together. Who is Mr. Noble and what does he want? Is he also connected to the Canfield gambling case? Is he blackmailing you, threatening to inform your family?"

He stepped closer, bending to bring his face in line with my own, his eyes beneath their thick brows flashing a stormy warning. "Keep out of what doesn't concern you. Do I make myself clear?"

Gooseflesh broke out on my arms and down my back; my stomach rolled into a tight ball. "It *was* you, wasn't it? Last night, outside the barn . . ."

"Barn?" He straightened, looking down at me once again from his greater height. "I don't make a habit of frequenting barns, Mrs. Andrews. Not even Reggie's top-notch one at Sandy Point."

"You were at Sandy Point yesterday when I was there," I persisted. "You followed me home to Gull Manor and threatened me on behalf of Harry Lehr."

"King Lehr? What's he got to do with anything?" He shook his head, clearly perplexed. "Perhaps you dreamed it. Do I inhabit your dreams, Mrs. Andrews?" His too-thin mustache twitched in something approaching amusement, but with malice, too.

I'd had enough of our conversation. I started forward, but he reached out as if to stop me. With a lurch, I shoved at him with every ounce of strength I could muster. As he stumbled, I hurried past until I'd cleared the walkway by several yards. Only then did I stop and turn. He'd regained his balance, as well as his temper, revealing itself in the blackest of scowls aimed in my direction. "Don't ever threaten me, my family, or my friends again, Mr. Forrester, or I shall see to it you are made very, very sorry."

He stepped toward me, but I lifted my hems and scurried away. I found Bessie standing beside her carriage, her hand adding its shade to her hat brim as she glanced around her. When she saw me, she called out, "There you are! I was beginning to think you'd left with Mrs. Vanderbilt and her daughters. Shall we be going?"

Her driver opened the door to the brougham and helped us in. I was glad for the carriage's enclosed interior rather than being an open buggy. I felt protected from harm and safe from prying eyes. As the vehicle turned down the drive onto Seaview Avenue, I peered over my shoulder to see out the back window. I saw no sign of Ely Forrester and let out a sigh.

"You seem agitated, Emma. Did something happen to upset you?"

As she searched my features, a brief debate played out in my mind. I could shield Bessie from the dangers posed by Ely Forrester and allow her to enjoy the remainder of her day, or I could be honest and issue a warning that could potentially keep her safe. Though I was loath to speak of it, the latter won out.

"I had an encounter while you were inside. With Ely Forrester."

"Goodness. What kind of encounter?"

"An unpleasant one."

"Don't tell me he confronted you right there on the Cliff Walk?" She pressed both hands to her bosom. "My dear Emma, how frightening. He might have killed you."

"I don't think he meant to harm me, at least not there. But he did mean to frighten me." I pressed her shoulder. "You must be careful, Bessie. He denied intending to hurt either one of us, but he said there are others who won't hesitate to protect their interests, as he put it. I'm not sure what I believe, except that this is dangerous business all around."

"This is my fault, Emma. If only I hadn't argued with Harry at Reggie and Cathleen's wedding, I wouldn't have gone off and overheard your cousin and Mr. Forrester's conversation. And you wouldn't have been there, either. You truly didn't hear anything, yet you're still being threatened."

"It isn't your fault, and you mustn't think so. It's the fault of the men who chose to do wrong. And it was Ely Forrester's fault in choosing to bring it up at the wedding."

Even the shadows hiding most of Bessie's face failed to conceal her fear. "What are we to do?"

"I'll speak to Jesse Whyte again and make sure he keeps a man at Arleigh to ensure your safety."

"There was an officer there all night, and someone new came to take over this morning. And Mr. Whyte himself came back to inspect the woodshed and speak with the entire staff all over again."

"Did he learn anything more?"

She stared blankly back and then shrugged. Of course Jesse hadn't told her anything. Silly of me to think he might. She frowned. "What about you? After what just happened, you should have protection, too."

I couldn't expect the police to spare yet another man to patrol Gull Manor or follow me about, so I said, "I'll be fine, I promise you."

With a jolt, I realized the homes lining Bath Road had given way to the business district of town. We turned onto Spring Street and soon arrived in front of the *Messenger.* Before I exited the carriage, I turned to Bessie.

"You'll go straight home?"

"I had planned to anyway, so yes."

"Good. I'll telephone over to the police immediately. Don't worry, you won't be alone at Arleigh tonight."

"Don't you be alone, either," she enjoined in an earnest voice. "You're very brave, Emma, braver than any other woman I know. And that makes me worry about you. Please don't do anything foolish, especially on my account."

"No, I promise I won't." But as I stepped down onto the sidewalk, I wondered if I would keep that promise. Because although Ely Forrester had frightened me there on the Cliff Walk, he had also raised my ire with threats designed to make me cower. And that made me indignant, which, in turn, made me more determined than ever to find the truth.

Once inside, I told Derrick what had happened, then nearly wished I hadn't.

"I will kill him. I will find him and strangle him with my bare hands."

I placed my own hands on either side of his face, ruddy with fury, and stared hard into eyes that flashed like a storm-tossed sea. "You'll do nothing of the sort. He didn't hurt me. He didn't even threaten to. It's almost as though he were cautioning me, telling me it's the people he and Reggie were mixed up with that we need to fear."

"What was I thinking last night, encouraging you to continue helping your friend?" He reached up, sliding my hands from his face and holding them against his heart. "I take it all back. Step away from this."

"My love, we both know I can't. But I promise to avoid cliffs from now on, as well as dark barnyards." I should have known better than to attempt to make a joke, for those angry, sharp edges returned to his features. Before he could speak, I hurriedly said, "I'm sorry. But as you yourself said, I can't sit by once someone has asked for my help. Especially when that someone is a woman. Bessie trusted me when she had no one else to turn to. She's very alone in the world, Derrick, and I'm determined to help her. But I *will* take better care and not put myself in dangerous situations, or ones that leave me exposed to the vagaries of others."

"I suppose I'll have to accept that." He didn't look as though he relished the notion. His hands held mine, were locked around them, but then they eased and he raised my hands to his lips. "You wouldn't be the woman I married if you did otherwise."

Chapter 13

I didn't expect to hear from Bessie so soon after the Interchurch Meal Fund Luncheon, yet the very next morning, she paid me an unexpected visit—all the more so because she arrived at an hour when most ladies of the Four Hundred were still abed. Coming into my office at the *Messenger* unannounced, she looked as though she had slept little the night before.

"Bessie, this is a surprise," I said, looking up from the articles strewn across my desk. I tried to temper any alarm I felt until I learned the reason for her visit. "What brings you here?"

"I hope it's all right that I came by unannounced. That nice man in the front room sent me back. Not your husband, the other one."

"That's Mr. Sheppard, our editor-in-chief, and of course it's all right." I came to my feet and dragged Ethan's chair over to my desk for her. "I hope nothing else has happened."

"I'm not quite sure." After sitting and adjusting her skirts around her, she pulled off her gloves. "Emma, I'm so unsettled I can neither sleep nor think straight. And I don't know whom to trust, except you, of course."

"Has Harry been haranguing you again?"

"Of course." She nodded without meeting my gaze. "It's what he does. He has utterly dismissed the notion that the fire was anyone's fault but my own. Can you imagine? He says I did it to myself so that I could lay the blame on him."

My eyebrows surged in surprise. "Did he not take into account that you might have been seriously injured?"

"According to him, I would have been if this had been the act of a malevolent individual. But my receiving only minor burns proves I'd staged it and was ready to leap out of the way."

"I'm sorry, Bessie. It must have been galling to hear this from your own husband."

"No more galling than what I hear from him every day."

"You said you don't know whom to trust." I frowned in puzzlement. "What about Miss Thorton? Is she well today? Did she come into town with you?"

"No, I had our driver bring me in the carriage." Ridges formed above the slender line of her aristocratic nose. "I'm not at all certain I can trust Neddie, not anymore."

"Oh dear. I'm sorry if I've planted seeds of doubt about her in your mind, but without evidence linking Harry to these incidents, you cannot blindly trust anyone. Not even Neddie Thorton. Until we know more, it's for your own safety that you proceed with the utmost caution."

"I have another reason to doubt Neddie and that's why I've come. That man, Ralph Noble, was at the house again last night."

"That can't have been pleasant for you."

She gave a small shrug and made an infinitesimal adjustment to the brim of her silk-covered hat. "For the most part, I didn't see him. Or Harry, for that matter. Although I heard them. They were drinking, heavily. No, it's what I found out this morning that has me in such a state. So much so that I refused Neddie's offer to walk with me in the garden. We do nearly every day, you see, but today . . . I simply couldn't."

When she paused, my curiosity prompted me to urge, "Please tell me what happened."

Her gaze flicked to mine, but only for the briefest instant. She pressed a hand to her breastbone, leaving me to surmise the topic she had come to discuss was exceedingly distasteful to her. Her next words proved me correct. "It appears Mr. Noble spent the night on the third floor . . . with Neddie."

"My goodness." My shock was unfeigned. Well enough did I understand that servants enjoyed little privacy, and few opportunities to pursue lives of their own, and that sometimes propriety suffered as a result. That Neddie Thorton might be engaging in a liaison didn't shock me, but that she had chosen such an object for her affections most certainly did.

Or *had* she chosen him? No sooner had my surprise begun to abate than a quite different, insidious suspicion took hold.

"Bessie, have you spoken with Miss Thorton?"

"No. I couldn't bring myself to raise such an unsavory subject. Her behavior has left me feeling betrayed, Emma. And very much alone, for who can I depend on in my own home?"

"But don't you see? Whatever happened last night might not have been her choice."

Her head tilted in puzzlement. "What do you mean?"

I had been told her life had been a sheltered one, but could Bessie Lehr truly be this naïve? I reached forward and placed my hand over hers. "She is in service, and this man, Ralph Noble, is a friend of her employer's. She may have feared dismissal if she protested."

Bessie's hand flew out from beneath my own and went to her lips. "I hadn't considered that. I was so hurt . . ."

"Miss Thorton deserves the benefit of the doubt, at least until she is given a chance to tell her side of the story," I said firmly.

"Then . . . I must . . . *speak of it* with her?" The hand slid back to her bosom. "I'm not sure I can. Actually, I'm quite certain it's a subject I don't dare raise, for fear of mortifying us both."

I sat back, considering. Neddie Thorton might well have been forced into a physical relationship with Ralph Noble. Women servants were rarely safe in the households in which they resided—a deplorable but inescapable fact. But another possibility existed, one that heightened my fears for my friend.

The balcony railing . . . the loose stair runner . . . the failed motorcar brakes . . . and the fire in Bessie's bedroom. My suspicions had led me to Neddie Thorton before; but without an adequate motive, those suspicions had been based merely on opportunity—her residing in the same house as Bessie. However, if she and Ralph Noble had been carrying on together, *his* possible motive, that of wanting Bessie out of the way to provide Harry better access to her money, might have become Neddie's motive as well.

And where had Neddie Thorton come from? By all accounts, out of nowhere. She had ingratiated herself with Mamie Fish's housekeeper—or perhaps blackmailed her. Had Mr. Noble put her up to securing employment with the Lehrs?

The two of them, working together, perhaps as far back as New York . . .

"Bessie, it's important to hear Miss Thorton's side of this. Today. If you like, I'll come with you."

Her face lit up with relief. "Oh, Emma, would you?"

I rose and collected my hat and handbag.

At Arleigh, when the butler admitted us, Bessie asked him to have Miss Thorton come to the parlor.

"Right away, ma'am. I believe she's walking in the rose garden. I shall go and get her."

"Thank you, Bagley. And please have someone bring up a tea tray." She led the way into the small parlor. "I suppose Neddie decided to take that walk without me," she mused aloud. Though she bade me make myself comfortable, she herself remained on her feet, nervously pacing the room. She went to the side-facing windows, open to the morning breezes, moved the lace curtain aside, then peered out. As she turned back around and began to say something, screams from outside cut her off.

Bessie went pale. "What on earth?"

"It's a woman." I came to my feet and we both hurried out of the room, Bessie leading as we followed the sounds of those screams toward the back of the house. When we reached the terrace off the dining room, several of the servants had already gathered on the lawn. They stood in a huddle as if immobilized by incredulity.

Having removed our hats while inside, we now shaded our eyes with our hands and attempted to see to the bottom south corner of the property, where the screams continued to emanate. The figure of a woman heaved as if possessed by a demon.

Bessie stood on her toes and craned forward. She suddenly gasped. "That's Neddie! What's happening to her?"

I ran down onto the lawn. A sense of horror rose as I watched Neddie Thorton zigzagging with short, spasmodic steps. She waved her arms, flapped her hands, and screamed as though her flesh were aflame.

Two of the servants, a maid and the head footman, were yanked from their stupor and ran down to her. The housekeeper hurried up beside me. "Dear God in heaven, it's bees. The neighbor's bees."

I spun to face her. "What?"

"The neighbors. They keep hives. They're just over those hedges." She pointed with a shaking finger. "What could have driven them to this?"

I started walking, then running, and as I did, I worked loose the buttons on my carriage jacket. My trembling fingers fumbled, but I kept tugging until the last button came loose. Then I yanked my arms from the sleeves.

Behind me, Bessie cried out, "Emma, no!"

"Stay there, Bessie," I shouted over my shoulder.

By the time I'd reached the rose garden, the head footman had filled a bucket with water and splashed it over Miss Thorton. Suddenly the Lehrs' second footman, the younger one named Asa Fullerman, appeared on the scene. He ran to the water pump near the greenhouse and frantically began filling another bucket. The maid had come to a halt, too frightened to know what to do.

I bypassed them all and, reaching Miss Thorton, began waving my jacket in the air around her. Bees scattered and flew off, then swarmed and descended again. Their angry buzzing filled my ears. Miss Thorton had fallen to the ground, and I tossed the jacket over her head to protect her face, already swollen from the stings. Her screams were muted to moans. Water flew, dousing me, as well as her. Pinpricks of pain erupted on my arms through my shirtwaist.

As the black swarm finally dissipated, I fell to my knees beside Miss Thorton and gently peeled my carriage jacket away from her face. I recoiled at what I saw and doubted whether she still lived.

* * *

"How is she, Doctor?" With Hippodale in her arms, Bessie came to her feet as Dr. Kennison entered the parlor. She and I had been sitting together on the sofa, Hippodale cuddled in her lap as she methodically stroked his fur.

I had made the telephone call to Newport Hospital, asking specifically for Hannah, and for Dr. Kennison, who had been my physician my entire life. They had spent the last thirty minutes upstairs in the guestroom, where Bessie had instructed the footmen to convey Miss Thorton. Surely, half an hour hadn't been sufficient time for her to recover. Her face had been swollen beyond recognition, her neck distended in the most dreadful way, and her hands ballooned to twice their size. Shock at what had occurred had left me barely aware of the pain of the stings I had received.

Dr. Kennison looked as mournful as I had ever seen him. "I'm very sorry, Mrs. Lehr."

She hugged Hippodale so tight against her, he let out a whine. "Surely, she cannot be . . . They were only bee stings."

"She'd received hundreds of stings," the doctor explained, his voice thick with apology. "The result was a condition only recently identified, called anaphylaxis. Her airways swelled and she suffocated."

"How horrifying." Bessie buried her cheek against Hippodale's head. "And there was nothing—nothing at all—you could do?"

"I'm sorry, ma'am. I administered a dose of adrenaline, but we were too late. Even if we had gotten here sooner, I don't know that it would have made a difference. Too much damage had been done."

I stood up beside her and placed an arm around her shoulders. "Bessie, I'm so sorry."

"I should have been there with her. She asked me to go."

Her features contorted with grief. "I turned my back on her and now she's dead."

"What could you have done if you had been there?" I let my arm fall to my side, then reached out again to grasp her shoulders. "You might be dead as well."

"Perhaps, but she was a faithful companion to me, and at the first misstep, I abandoned *her.*" That last word dissolved into sobs and she collapsed onto the sofa.

Poor Dr. Kennison had stood by in silence, no doubt feeling awkward and powerless. Now he said to me, "Mrs. Lehr has suffered a terrible shock on the heels of the earlier one, that of the fire in her bedroom. She must rest, Emma. She must have quiet and a chance to recover."

I caught myself scratching at the backs of my itchy, stinging hands and dropped them to my sides, only to clutch at my skirts. "I don't know that she'll find that chance in this house, Dr. Kennison."

He appeared puzzled by this statement, and I realized he could have no inkling of the state of Bessie's marriage. He only said, "Then perhaps she might go elsewhere. To the home of a friend, perhaps."

"Yes, I believe that might be best."

He came toward me and lifted one of my hands in his own. He glanced down at it. "You need to have these seen to."

"I'm fine."

"Don't argue. I'll send Hannah to you. She'll apply a salve." He glanced over at Bessie, who appeared to have shrunk in on herself, all her attention focused on the papillon on her lap. "I'll make the necessary arrangements to have the body removed."

"No, Doctor." Bessie regarded him with swollen eyes, her face streaked with tears. "I'll do that. She'll stay here until the undertaker can come for her. Then she'll have a proper funeral and burial." She looked down at the dog. "And . . .

I'll find a way to contact her family. It's the very least I can do for my dear, *dear* friend."

"Very well, ma'am."

While Bessie went upstairs to sit with the body, Hannah met me in the kitchen, where she cleansed the stings on my hands and arms and applied salve. Although I insisted I was fine, I had to admit her ministrations soothed the pain and helped me regain my equilibrium.

I confided in her what I had hesitated to say to Bessie. "I fear there is more to this than a tragic accident. Bees don't attack for no reason."

She twisted the metal lid back onto the can of healing balm. "I've certainly never known them to, and there are several families on the Point who keep bees. If they pose no danger in such close quarters, they shouldn't be a risk here, where there is so much property between homes."

"The hives will have to be examined."

"You suspect someone tampered with them. But why would they? Who would wish to harm a lady's maid?"

My first thought was to say nothing, but as I regarded Hannah, I remembered I had known and trusted her all my life. Moreover, she would soon be my sister. And then I realized Brady had probably already told her most of what I had confided to him about Bessie and the incidents that led her to fear for her life. I met her gaze. "Not Miss Thorton. Mrs. Lehr."

Her steady expression told me I had been right. Brady *had* kept her informed. "Do you think it was that friend of her husband's who lives on the Point? Or her husband himself?"

Obviously, she and Brady had had extensive discussions on the subject. "I don't know. There's someone else who might have even more reason to wish Mrs. Lehr out of the way. He's a friend of my cousin Reggie."

Hannah fiddled with the latch on the case that held her medicines and bandages. "You also suspected Miss Thorton of wrongdoing when it came to Mrs. Lehr." She shrugged. "Don't be mad at Brady. He swore me to secrecy."

I smiled. "I don't mind that he told you. But yes, I suspected Neddie Thorton, and I feel horrid about it now." My chin sank. "The worst of it is, I convinced Mrs. Lehr to suspect her, too. I don't know how I'll forgive myself for that."

"Don't do that, Emma." She put her arms around me in a fierce embrace. Her voice was equally vehement when she pulled away and said, "This is not your fault. You've been doing the best you can for Mrs. Lehr, and from what Brady has told me, Miss Thorton's circumstances *were* questionable. But what is this about one of your cousin's friends?"

"I don't wish to say too much about him, not because I don't trust you. I do. But because he may be dangerous, and not only toward Mrs. Lehr. The less people know about him, the better. Except for the police, of course."

"Goodness, Emma. Does your cousin know he's consorting with a dangerous individual?" She studied me. "Possibly a criminal?" she guessed.

"A criminal in the guise of a gentleman." I slanted my lips in distaste, remembering our confrontation on the Cliff Walk. "And yes, Reggie is well aware. He's no saint himself, as I'm sure you've read in the newspapers, but at least he hasn't a malicious bone in his body."

Hannah finished packing away her supplies. "Have you considered that, given Miss Thorton's mysterious past, perhaps it was she, and not Mrs. Lehr, who has been the target of these incidents?"

My chin dropped again, this time in astonishment. "No . . . I hadn't." Could I have been focused on the wrong victim all this time? The very notion startled me.

Which made the argument I walked in upon some minutes later all the more ironic. I'd taken a few moments while still below stairs to telephone Derrick at the *Messenger*, telling him briefly what had happened. He stated his intention of coming to Arleigh directly and we disconnected. Then, after thanking Hannah and Dr. Kennison again, and seeing them out to the ambulance wagon, I went upstairs to speak with Bessie and invite her to stay with us at Gull Manor until she recovered from her grief and from the upheaval of the last few days. But as I reached the room where Neddie Thorton's body lay, angry words rendered me mute.

"It was you, wasn't it, Harry? Who else would know Neddie and I walk nearly every morning in the rose garden? You thought *I* would be swarmed and stung to death. At least that was what you hoped. And you didn't spare a thought that Neddie might fall victim, too."

"I haven't the faintest idea what you're talking about, Bessie. This time, you've truly gone mad."

"What did you do to rile up the bees?" Bessie persisted. "How did you make them attack?"

"I did nothing to the bees. I didn't even know the Dyers *kept* bees." His denial ended in a shout. The Dyers lived in the Georgian-style mansion next door. The housekeeper had pointed to the hedges between the properties, from where the bees must have come.

"Really." Not a question from Bessie, but an expression of disbelief. "Elisha never told you they had bees?"

"Why would he? If he's got an apiary on the property, what's it to him? I'm sure he's hired a beekeeper to look after them. Good God, Bessie, are you accusing me of murder?"

I'd heard enough, or so I believed. But as I turned into the doorway, Bessie stood up from the chair she had pulled close to the bedside and regarded Harry with unconcealed loathing. "If not you directly, someone known to you. Someone with whom you have schemed and connived."

I stepped into the room, startling them both. They turned toward me, opening more space between them as they did so, as if they were co-conspirators who had just been caught. Except there existed nothing in their bearing that suggested they might cooperate on anything. *Ever.*

"This is hardly the place to be having this discussion." I looked down at poor Miss Thorton, laid out on the bed, the coverlet pulled to her chin, her closed eyes reduced to slits in her swollen face.

Bessie let out a sigh. "Heaven help me, you're right." After a moment, she added, "I'm sorry," though to whom—Miss Thorton, Harry, or me—I couldn't say.

Harry obviously believed her contrition was aimed at him. "You should be. The very idea."

Her lips flattened, then pursed, then opened. "Shut up, Harry." I thought she'd flee the room, but she only turned and swept to the window. Though she apparently stared idly out at first, something outside caught her attention. She pressed closer to the glass. "That's Elisha now."

No sooner had the words left her lips than the doorbell rang in the hall below.

Chapter 14

"Your butler ran over to tell us what happened." Elisha Dyer was a classically handsome man in his prime, with close-cropped, curly dark hair, a generous mustache that showed no sign of graying, and the kind of expressive eyes one often sees in actors onstage. Today those eyes held a mingling of disbelief and dismay. "Sidney—that's my wife," he added for my benefit, "is overwrought with remorse and lying down, or she would have come over with me."

"Please assure her we don't blame you." Bessie lowered herself into a corner of the parlor sofa. She held a crumpled handkerchief and occasionally dabbed her eyes with it. Harry slumped in the opposite corner, while Mr. Dyer and I took the upholstered chairs facing them.

Mr. Dyer needn't have explained to me who Sidney was. I'd met her before. I'd met them both previously, on several occasions, all social ones. His pretense of having only just made my acquaintance was his way of letting me know that—despite my marriage—I remained beneath his notice. Despite his somber demeanor today, his reputation was similar to Harry's, that of high spirits and the life of any party. It was he who had initially introduced Harry into society, making his acquaintance known to Aunt Alva, Mamie Fish, and others like them.

And eventually sealing Bessie's fate.

"My beekeeper is there now, inspecting the hives," he went on to say. "I've instructed him that after he is done, he's to come here to let us know what he discovers, if anything." He clasped his hands and leaned forward in his chair. He bowed his head, yet raised his eyes as he addressed Harry and Bessie. "For the life of me, I cannot understand what happened. They are well contained and have always gone about their business peacefully. The apiary is surrounded by hedges so that they're not disturbed by our gardeners or anyone walking on the lawn, or by traffic behind the house on Clay Street, such as it is."

"Merely a stroke of bad fortune, old man." Harry attempted to chuckle. "You mustn't worry about it overmuch. Tell Sidney—"

"*Not worry?*" Bessie slapped the hand holding the handkerchief to her thigh. "A woman lies dead, Harry, or have you forgotten?"

"Bessie, Sidney and I are so very—" Mr. Dyer left off and cleared his throat.

"I only meant the Dyers are not to blame, my dear." Harry reached toward her as if to lay a placating hand over hers. She flinched and pressed herself tighter against the curved arm of the sofa. To her credit, however, she made no accusations, not in front of Elisha Dyer.

Once again, the doorbell rang, and moments later, the butler ushered in a man dressed all in white, but for a pair of black boots that reached his knees. In his hand, he carried a white straw boater from which dangled netting attached around the brim. "Mr. Nivens to see you, sir and madam."

Mr. Dyer sprang to his feet. "Have you learned anything?"

"I have, sir." The man breathed in and out slowly, in such a way that I realized he was attempting to rein in his temper. "Black pepper, sir. There's evidence of it all over the hives. Someone doused them with black pepper. Probably right before the incident. It sent the bees into a frenzy."

Derrick arrived moments after Mr.Nivens, and he and I departed Arleigh shortly after hearing the beekeeper's report, but I hadn't left Bessie alone. Jesse and two officers had arrived and set about investigating the incident, and I stole a few moments to explain why I had accompanied Bessie back to Arleigh after she came to see me at the *Messenger.* Derrick took the information in stride, though his jaw tightened and his eyes flashed when I informed him of Ralph Noble having spent the night on the third floor.

"Blackguard," he'd murmured, and shook his head in disgust.

I'd also left Bessie to the ministrations of two companionable visitors. Mamie Fish and Tessie Oelrichs had rushed over from a garden club function at nearby Ochre Court. How they had heard the news so quickly, I'll never know, but they promised to stay and comfort Bessie, at least until her nerves had calmed. She had simply refused to leave Arleigh. She intended to watch over Neddie Thorton's body, insisting that to do otherwise would have been a betrayal of their friendship. Even so, I hadn't liked leaving her, and told her to come to Gull Manor should she change her mind.

Jesse turned up at Gull Manor about an hour later, just as I tucked Annamarie in for her afternoon nap. He hadn't much more to add to what we already knew, but I gathered from his mood that he needed to voice his frustration.

"This was a murder, to be sure." Jesse's pacing threatened to leave our parlor rug threadbare. Not that it would take much, as Derrick and I hadn't yet gotten around to replacing Aunt Sadie's old one.

"We shouldn't have left Bessie there alone," I fretted, wringing my hands. "Perhaps we should go back and get her."

"Don't worry, I've left an officer there—in the house this time," Jesse assured me. "She'll be safe enough for now." He shook his head. "Bees, of all things. Who would think of such a thing as turning bees into a weapon?"

"Someone horribly clever," Derrick murmured.

"And frighteningly unbalanced," I added. "You spoke to everyone at Arleigh again?"

"Everyone," Jesse confirmed. "The Lehrs, the servants, the gardeners, the Dyers, and *their* servants. According to the latter, no one from the house ever interferes with the bees. The beekeeper"—he flipped open his notebook, which he clutched in his hand, and consulted a page—"Mr. Nivens. He performs any maintenance on the boxes and collects the honey, which he then brings to the Dyers' kitchen."

"Were you able to grill Harry?" Derrick absently played with the embroidered antimacassar on the arm of the sofa. "I mean, really put his back to the wall?"

"Practically. Scotty and I went at it together. Took turns firing questions at him about where he was this morning and whether he knew Miss Thorton had gone out to the garden. Also, whether he knew his wife had left the house. He never so much as flinched over his answers. Said Miss Thorton and Mrs. Lehr usually walked in the garden in the mornings. As for this morning, he claimed to have slept late, had breakfast brought to his room, and spent the rest of the hours in his office, alone. He claims that's where he was when he heard Miss Thorton's screams. The servants corroborated his story."

"His claim of sleeping late agrees with what Bessie told me, that he and Ralph Noble had sat up drinking until the wee hours of last night. Did Mr. Noble's name come up?"

"It did. According to Mr. Lehr, he woke up and stumbled out of the house early, claiming he was going home."

"How was he going to get there? *Walk* all the way to the Point? He was probably still intoxicated." Derrick didn't seem to expect any reply, but swiftly asked another question. "Did you bring up Noble's jaunt to the third floor?"

Jesse let out a mirthless laugh. "Mr. Lehr said if such a thing happened, it had nothing to do with him. His last memory before dragging himself upstairs and passing out was of Noble slumped over the dining room table, mumbling some nonsense about a sweet Southern belle."

"Neddie Thorton was from the South," I reminded him. "And what about the servants? Were they aware of Harry's and Mr. Noble's activities last night? And where were they all when Miss Thorton was attacked by the bees?"

"They were supposedly given leave to go to bed last night while their employer and his friend drank their way through several bottles of assorted liquor." Jesse consulted his notebook again, although I suspected this to be more from habit than any true need to check his notes. "As for today, the butler and housekeeper were together in the servants' hall, going over the house inventories. The two housemaids were upstairs cleaning in the drawing and dining rooms. One footman was downstairs polishing the silver, and the other in the wine cellar dusting."

"Dusting the wine cellar?" I questioned with a dubious look. "Talk about fastidious."

Jesse shrugged. "Apparently, Harry Lehr doesn't like dust settling on his bottles."

"Sounds like Harry." Derrick made a face of derision. "By all means, drop everything else, but take care of the wine.

Don't forget, he *was* a wine salesman years ago, before the grand dames adopted him into society."

"Then everyone is accounted for," I concluded with a light clap of my hands. "At least everyone at both houses. Although Harry could have been lying about being in his office, despite what the servants believe. How difficult would it have been for him to leave the house and sabotage the hives?"

"Not very difficult, with the servants occupied," Jesse agreed. "Of anyone at Arleigh, Mr. Lehr is the most likely to have been guilty. But *only* if he didn't realize his wife had gone out, because what reason could he possibly have had to murder Miss Thorton? But if not him . . ."

"If not Harry, that leaves two of our suspects that don't reside at Arleigh. Ralph Noble and Ely Forrester." I came to my feet and began my own circuit of the room, prompting Jesse to step aside as I passed him. "Ralph Noble might certainly know Bessie's routine of walking in the rose garden in the mornings. Who knows how often he's been an overnight guest?"

"A good point," Jesse agreed.

"But then again . . ." I paused.

I felt Derrick's gaze on me, assessing. "What's going through your mind, Emma?"

"When Bessie told me about what occurred between Miss Thorton and Mr. Noble, I feared they might have been plotting together against Bessie. That Mr. Noble, who would certainly benefit if Harry controlled Bessie's money, seduced Miss Thorton in order to persuade her to help him. And that Miss Thorton has been responsible for each incident that threatened Bessie's life."

"But now Miss Thorton is dead," Derrick observed.

"Yes. She would hardly have roused the bees and then walked in the garden herself." I shook my head. "We no longer have any reason to believe Neddie Thorton was guilty of any act against Bessie. But Hannah made a suggestion earlier. She asked if perhaps Miss Thorton, and not Bessie, could have been the intended victim all along."

Jesse's expression revealed the extent to which I had surprised him. He made his way over to one of the easy chairs and sank into it. "Explain."

I rejoined Derrick on the sofa. "Miss Thorton has been more than a lady's maid to Bessie. She's been an almost constant companion, a badly needed one in a house where Bessie felt completely alone. She accompanied Bessie nearly everywhere." My brows converged as I realized I needed to speak with Bessie again to give credence to this new theory. I glanced from Derrick to Jesse and rose once again to my feet. "I must return to Arleigh at once."

"She's in her room, exhausted by grief," Harry informed me as he slowly came down the stairs. Derrick and I had driven back to Arleigh in his motorcar, not something I particularly cared for, but it saved time. He waited for me outside, as we had agreed it would be better for me to speak with Bessie alone, and he had no desire to spend a moment with Harry if he could help it. Jesse, meanwhile, had another matter to attend to, that of tracking down Ralph Noble and questioning him about his stay at Arleigh last night.

"She intends sitting next to the body all night, but her friends convinced her to lie down a while." Stopping a few steps short of the landing, Harry eyed me warily. "Mamie Fish and Tessie Oelrichs have only just left. I should think the least you could do for my wife is leave her alone until she's had a chance to recover."

It was all I could do not to purse my lips and narrow my eyes in cynicism. Since when did he give an owl's hoot about his wife's well-being? Was there something he didn't want me finding out about today's events? Perhaps that he hadn't been in his office as he'd claimed? But how could Bessie know that when she had been with me in town?

I stifled a sigh at his stubbornness. "I've come about an important matter that may have bearing on Miss Thorton's death."

"Are you going to convince my wife all over again that I did it?"

I met this question with my most direct gaze. "Did you?"

Our eyes locked for the briefest instant before he pulled his away. "Don't be ridiculous. Why would I want to murder the one person able to keep Bessie from falling completely apart?"

Part of me believed him, yet I still held him in suspicion. If not of murdering Neddie Thorton or making attempts on Bessie's life, at least of failing to safeguard her life, as was his duty as her husband. He didn't deserve her, had married her under false pretenses, and certainly had no business barring my way to her.

I put my foot on the bottom step. "Will you let me pass?"

"I hardly see why I should."

"Because finding the truth will go a long way in helping Bessie recover."

"And you believe you're the person to do that, do you?" Sounding bored, he reinforced the image by raising a hand and regarding his fingernails. Unlike me, he didn't bother restraining his urge to sigh. "All right. Come along if you must. If she agrees to see you, you may have ten minutes."

I followed him up the staircase, fully resolved to take all the time I needed. As we reached the upper landing, I saw the officer Jesse had left behind to ensure Bessie's safety. He presently occupied a hard-backed wooden chair right outside her bedroom door. At our approach, he stood, nodded to me, and moved aside.

Without a word to him, Harry tapped twice at her door.

"Yes?" came a weak reply from within.

"Bessie," Harry began, but I nearly pushed him aside as I pressed closer to the door.

"Bessie, it's Emma. I've returned because I have something I must discuss with you. May I come in?"

When no reply came, Harry turned a haughty look in my direction, which instantly vanished when the door opened and Bessie gestured for me to enter.

"My love, are you quite certain you're up for visitors?"

She ignored him, waited for me to cross the threshold, and shut the door perhaps a bit more firmly than was necessary. "I'm glad you've come back, Emma. But why did you?"

"Because I have more questions about what happened today. I hope you don't mind."

She drew me to the armchairs beside the unlit hearth. Hippodale, heretofore on the bed, jumped down and trotted over to us. He sniffed my hand and allowed me to pet him before jumping up onto his mistress's lap.

All traces of the fire had been cleared away. The rug had been changed, the scorched chair removed, and the fireplace and its tiled surround scrubbed clean. I discreetly sniffed the air. Beneath a distinctly floral scent, no doubt emitted by several sachets placed around the room, faint odor of smoke remained, soon to be swept away by the breezes entering through the open window.

"I don't know what else I can tell you." She absently stroked a hand down Hippodale's back. "Especially since I was with you when it happened."

"It's not what happened today that I have questions about. It's what occurred previously." She eyed me quizzically. I sensed she was about to remind me that we'd been over those details before, but before she could, I asked,

"The balcony railing that broke away. That was on Long Island, yes?"

She nodded, curiosity sparking in her eyes.

"Did Neddie often accompany you out onto the balcony?"

She cocked her head. Almost comically, the dog did the same. "Yes, especially at night. She'd help me into my nightclothes, and often the two of us would step outside to look at the stars." She smiled faintly. "Neddie was something of an amateur astronomer and she enjoyed pointing out the constellations to me. I'll bet you'd never have guessed that."

"No, I wouldn't have," I agreed in a gentle tone.

"Actually, she sometimes went out on the balcony alone." She paused with another sad smile and a glance down at her dog. "Those cigarettes of hers. Remember, she had that package in her room? She'd sneak out sometimes for a few puffs. I'd have preferred she gave the habit up, but I didn't mind. Not really."

I latched on to that bit of information. "I remember you telling me that Neddie sometimes accompanied you down the main staircase, especially in the mornings?"

"All the time, in fact. After getting me dressed, she and I would come down together and go into the parlor. She helped me sift through my correspondence every morning and even wrote out the replies to everything not of a personal nature."

My heart began to beat faster.

Bessie, unaware of my sudden animation, went on with her recollecting. "As I told you once before, if she hadn't been right beside me on the stairs that one morning, I'd have tripped over the loose stair runner and might have broken my neck."

Yes, or Neddie might have. "And the motorcar," I said. "It was Neddie who always drove?"

"Of course. She was . . ." A sob broke through her thready composure. "She was much braver than I. Oh, Emma, what shall I do without her?" She lifted Hippodale high enough to bury her face in his neck and let her tears flow.

I comforted her as best I could, then asked her for a favor. "May I take another look at Neddie's room?"

Bessie lifted her tear-streaked face to me. "Why?"

"In case there was something we missed. Something that might give us a clue to who did this."

"I don't understand." She shoved a damp lock of hair, come loose from her coif, away from her face. With a pang I realized the housekeeper or one of the housemaids must have dressed her hair that morning. "Neddie is gone because of me, Emma. Because someone wants me dead, and Neddie got in the way. If only I'd been here this morning . . ."

"Not this again, Bessie." I took hold of her hands and leaned closer to her, over Hippodale's small body. He raised his head, peering up at us with moist, quizzical eyes. "You're not to blame yourself. The person responsible shall pay, I promise you."

"But when, Emma? After someone else perishes? Let's not forget Jackson—our man-of-all-work. He was the first to die in my place."

"I haven't forgotten him."

She let out a gusty sigh. "If you feel it will help anything, you may go up and look around Neddie's room. But the police have already been. It's doubtful you'll find anything they didn't."

"Perhaps not, but thank you." I stayed another few moments, promising to return as soon as possible. Outside her bedroom, I stopped to speak to the officer on duty. "Please don't leave this spot for any reason, not without having the housekeeper or butler keep watch, and then only for as long as necessary."

"You can be sure I won't, ma'am. Detective Whyte was very clear on that."

I thanked him and continued up to the third floor. There I stopped and listened for signs that anyone else might be up there, but only the moan of the wind hitting the eaves of the overhanging roof met my ears. I made my way to Miss Thorton's room. The door was unlocked.

Little had changed since I had been there last. The discarded flowers were gone, of course, given to the young footman to be disposed of. Had Ralph Noble given them to Neddie? Were they part of a seduction, or an apology for an unwanted advance? Last night, had Neddie opened her door to him, or had he forced his way in?

Jesse and his men had been surprisingly gentle in their perusal of the room. The bed lay neatly made, the coverlet nearly wrinkle-free, but for a few rumples that suggested an officer had searched beneath the mattress. Two pillows had been left fluffed against the headboard. A colorful knitted afghan lay folded at the foot of the bed, again only slightly disheveled by the efforts of the police. I regarded the neat, zigzagging rows of yarn in alternating hues of light blue, yellow, and white. Had Neddie made the blanket herself? Or had she brought it with her from her old life—or one of her former lives, as she seemed to hail from an array of circumstances.

Remembering the makeshift jewelry I'd discovered last time, I opened the bottom drawer of her dresser. There it was, the small cardboard box. Yet, whereas previously the cover had been partly off, it now sat firmly in place. Had Miss Thorton not entirely forgotten them, as I had thought previously? I grasped the box and opened the cover.

The beaded bracelet and ring woven from hair were gone. Had the police taken them? I wondered why they would have thought them significant. I would have to ask Jesse the next time I saw him.

Had they been gifts from Ralph Noble? I shook my head. The man's predilection for life's finer things—entertaining friends, living in a house overlooking the harbor, and whatever else Harry Lehr provided him with—made it unlikely he'd bestow such tokens on a woman he wished to seduce. Even if he hadn't quite seduced her, if she had allowed him into her life willingly, I believed he would disdain such sentimental tokens and deem them unforgivably paltry.

I placed the box back in the drawer and regarded the room. Surely, if Mr. Noble had been here last night, there should exist some evidence of it. The rest of the dresser drawers yielded no new insights, except that a second package of Duke's Cameo Cigarettes accompanied the first, which was now half empty. It would seem Neddie had had no intention of quitting her habit, as Bessie had wished. Had it been her only vice, or one of many?

I went to the wardrobe, an oaken cabinet in a light stain, some six feet tall, with unembellished doors. Inside it, as last time, the same somber hues and simple styles of clothing met my scrutiny. I pushed them aside, hoping something might have been secreted away behind them, but there was nothing but the back wall of the wardrobe. Standing on tiptoe, I peered up at the shelf, then reached my hand along its surface as far as it would go. Nothing. Had the police discovered something and taken it with them when they left?

"Were you truly hiding nothing, Neddie Thorton?" I queried aloud. "Had you confessed all to Bessie? Except, perhaps, whatever had occurred between you and Mr. Noble?"

Once again, I contemplated the bed. Had Neddie and

Ralph Noble slept there together last night? Heat climbed into my face at the thought, but I moved past my chagrin to study the pillows, looking for . . .

Hair, perhaps. Short ones, which might identify that someone other than Neddie had lain here. But the pillows had obviously been shaken out. I turned them over, studied the backs of each one and the sheet beneath them. Again there was nothing. Neddie Thorton had been fastidious in keeping her room tidy. Once again, as I had when Bessie accompanied me here previously, I got down on all fours and peered under the bed. No reward met my efforts.

While down on the floor, I thought to run my fingertips over the rug, digging them into the nap, like the teeth of a comb. When I raised them, a few long, light brown hairs clung to them. Neddie's hair. Not a man's.

Using the bed as leverage, I pulled to my feet. I'd saved the dressing table for last. Three drawers were stacked, one above the other, to the right of the kneehole. To my surprise, I slid the first one open to behold an item that hadn't been there before. A box covered in shiny flowered paper, about the size of my hand, met my gaze—and my immediate curiosity. It was hinged on one side, and upon opening it, I gasped. Inside, nestled in a gold silk lining, lay a crystal bottle marked with a label: *Le Parfum Ideal, Houbigant.* A woman in profile, holding a sprig to her nose, was depicted in gold foil.

My gasp was not unfounded. I knew this to be some of the most expensive perfume in the world. Certainly beyond the reach of a mere lady's maid.

The remainder of the dressing table wrought no further surprises, but I contemplated the bottle of perfume, which Jesse and his men had apparently thought little of. The seal around the stopper remained unbroken, a sign Neddie hadn't possessed the bottle for very long. How could this be anything but a lover's gift?

But surely, not the same lover who had given her the makeshift jewelry—if indeed those had been gifts from an admirer and not mementos from her former life.

Though satisfied I'd looked everywhere something could have been hidden, I lingered, then made one more circuit of the room. The walls were solid, the floorboards firmly in place. Nothing lurked behind the dressing table mirror, or the room's single painting, a rather mundane rendering of a hilly meadow overlooking the ocean. It hung perfectly straight, as so few paintings did, unless adjusted nearly every day. Perhaps Miss Thorton had done so, keeping it, like her bedclothes and everything else in the room, in perfect order.

Everything but the forgotten, half-open box in the bottom of her dresser.

With a sigh of frustration I collected myself and made my way downstairs. Happily, I saw no sign of Harry along the way. After bidding goodbye to Bessie, I continued down to the first floor. The butler, obviously attuned to any movement in the downstairs rooms, entered the hall at the same time I did and saw me out.

Derrick met me halfway between the front door and the motorcar.

"Well?"

I shook my head.

"Nothing? You were in there so long, I thought surely you had found something."

"Yes, if you mean a complete lack of anything in the slightest bit telling."

"You speak in riddles, my dear Mrs. Andrews." He slipped an arm around me, halting my progress before I'd reached the motorcar. Derrick turned me to face him and regarded me with those dark, penetrating eyes of his. "Isn't a complete lack of anything in itself telling? What kind of woman was Miss Thorton? You must have reached some conclusion."

I gazed up at him, contemplating his question, as well as the chiseled features that continued, after nearly two years of marriage, to send me into a state of pleasant perplexity. Yes, my husband still held that power over me. I hoped he always would.

But as to his question . . . I quickly reviewed my impressions of Neddie Thorton based on the room I had explored. "An exceedingly neat one. One who liked everything in its proper place. One not given to excess. Or frippery," I added, remembering the serviceable clothing hanging in the wardrobe. "Although . . ."

He cocked his head at me. "Yes?"

"She did have a habit. A vice. She smoked cigarettes. And I found an expensive luxury item in her dressing table. One that hadn't been there the last time I looked. She might have purchased it herself in town but . . ." I frowned, considering. Derrick waited for me to continue, which I did presently. "I don't know how she could have afforded Houbigant perfume."

"Indeed. A gift, perhaps, from our Mr. Noble?"

"That's what I immediately thought."

"On the other hand, she might have been a woman who showed the world a sensible, rather plain exterior, but possessed another side. One given to the occasional flight of fancy. The occasional luxury. If she spent her money on little else, she might have enough for a treat of expensive perfume."

"And pre-rolled cigarettes," I added.

Derrick helped me into the Peugeot, then cranked the five-horsepower engine to life. As he stepped around to the driver's side and climbed onto the seat, he asked, "Shall we stop in at the office, or would you prefer to go home?"

"We've already lost the better part of the day. Let's go home and spend time with Annamarie."

"A sound plan." He sealed our bargain with a kiss to my cheek and shifted the vehicle into drive.

Chapter 15

When next I spoke with Jesse, it was to encounter his growing frustration with the case. Had Bessie been the intended victim of the bee attack or Neddie Thorton? Was Harry involved? His friend Mr. Noble? Reggie's friend Mr. Forrester? Did these events involve something even more sinister than two men wanting control of a considerable fortune, or the son of an influential family trying to shield his reputation? Were the members of a gambling ring in far-off Saratoga attempting to silence potential witnesses?

But how would they know Bessie had overheard anything—unless Ely Forrester had informed them of the fact? Yet, why would he do such a thing, when by doing so, he would plunge himself into an even more precarious position with these men? Criminals such as they didn't care for untidy circumstances, and Mr. Forrester certainly had created untidy circumstances when he'd allowed himself to be overheard at Reggie's wedding.

What did Ralph Noble know about these events? Although Mr. Forrester wouldn't admit to it, his meeting with Mr. Noble at the New Cliffs Hotel had all the makings of a confrontation in which Mr. Noble held something over Mr. Forrester's head. Here I fell to conjecture, but I had seen the apprehension in Mr. Forrester's eyes; albeit when I encountered him on the Cliff Walk, he had tried to appear confident and in control.

On our way to the *Messenger* the following morning, we stopped at Arleigh to check on Bessie, despite the continuing police protection. Physically, she might be safe, but I felt no such assurances about her emotional well-being. I went into the house alone, while Derrick, fearing he might be moved to fisticuffs should he encounter Harry, waited with our Peugeot. Yes, I had agreed to using the automobile on a more regular basis once I realized how much time it saved us traveling from one end of town to another. That didn't mean I had grown to enjoy it, however, and I felt not a little guilty at what I perceived as a betrayal of Maestro. Katie was now exercising both horses during the day.

Jesse happened to be at Arleigh when I arrived, and was on his way out as one of his officers let me in the front door. "I wished to question Mrs. Lehr again about her relationship with Miss Thorton," he explained with an exasperated tug at the lapel of his coat. We stood together in the hall; I could hear the quiet sounds of the servants preparing the downstairs rooms for the day. "It should be straightforward—a woman and her maid—but there is nothing simple about anything here at Arleigh. It's all sleight of hand, smoke and mirrors."

I couldn't have agreed more as he lowered his voice. "I tell you, Emma, I've never encountered such twisted goings-on as these among our summer population. He, such a wastrel and a rogue, and she, so lost and fragile."

"I dearly hope she's not as fragile as all that," I murmured, wondering how, without the possibility of divorce, she would withstand a lifetime of Harry Lehr.

"Anyway, I visited the housekeeper at Crossways to learn more about how Miss Thorton came to be where she was," he said. "She certainly had a devious streak and might have crossed more than a few people along the way."

"Do you think someone from her past murdered her?" I heard my own skepticism, and took no pains to conceal it from Jesse.

"I'm hardly convinced of it," he said, his weariness evident in the very lines of his face. "Perhaps she might have been the intended victim, and not Mrs. Lehr, but even that seems doubtful when you consider the other incidents."

I hadn't had a chance to confer with him after I'd visited Miss Thorton's bedroom yesterday, and indeed wondered now if it was worth mentioning, but that empty box in her dresser continued to niggle at me. "I went up to her room yesterday after you'd left—after your men had conducted their search—" I broke off at his admonishing look and shrugged. "As I said, *after* they'd conducted their search, so I could hardly have disturbed evidence before they'd had a chance to find it. But there were two items of jewelry I'd seen there previously that were missing. They were in a small cardboard box. Were they taken into evidence?"

I described the box and its contents to him.

"I remember seeing such a box in her dresser drawer." His brow creased. "And yes, it was empty. Tell me about the jewelry."

"A bracelet made from carved wooden beads, and a ring woven from hair. Dark hair. At the time, I believed it might be something from her former life, a token from a past sweetheart, or had come from a family member. But could the fact that it's missing now mean something?"

"You say it seemed discarded and forgotten in the bottom of her dresser." Jesse rubbed a hand across his chin. "Perhaps she merely disposed of it."

"But why now? And what if Mr. Noble had given it to her, and, upon engineering her death with the bees, reclaimed his gifts?"

A heavy footfall announced the butler's arrival in the dining room doorway. He stopped short, appearing surprised to find us there. "May I be of service to either of you, sir, madam?"

"I'm here to see Mrs. Lehr," I replied, well aware that I had incurred the man's disapproval by not ringing the bell when I arrived. Bagley's indignant expression did not prove me wrong.

"And I'm through here at the moment," Jesse told him with a nod. "I'll see myself out momentarily."

Bagley sniffed. "Madam, I'll let Mrs. Lehr know you're here." He retreated up the staircase, but not without another censorious glance encompassing the pair of us.

Jesse rolled his eyes. "Now, then, the jewelry. Did it look like something a paramour might have given her? A man like Ralph Noble?"

"No, it didn't," I admitted. "They were too simplistic. Too rough-hewn. But I found something else in her dressing table, and it hadn't been there previously. It certainly could have been a gift from a beau, provided he had a generous income." I described the bottle of perfume.

"I remember it, but I didn't think anything of it except that perfume is something a woman might have."

"A wealthy woman, not a lady's maid. It was French, very expensive."

Jesse shrugged. "I confess I don't know one perfume from another. If it did come from Ralph Noble, and if he *had* been her paramour, why would he have murdered her?"

"Perhaps she rejected him."

"A lover's revenge?" He looked skeptical. "Then what about the other incidents?"

My enthusiasm deflated. "I don't know, but I find it puzzling that the ring and bracelet should disappear now."

"We have yet another twist, throwing matters into deeper uncertainty." Jesse shook his head. "How can I find the culprit if I can't say for sure who the victim was?"

I conceded his point with a sigh. "At least we know now the culprit wasn't Neddie Thorton. I assume you've questioned Mr. Noble by now. What did he have to say for himself?"

"I haven't. There's been no response at his door and none of his neighbors have seen him since the day before last. I'd hoped to ask Mr. Lehr where his friend might be, but he's not at home, either. Mrs. Lehr doesn't know where he's gone."

"Not at home at this hour of the morning? How very odd for a man like Harry Lehr."

"Indeed."

"Maybe Brady can find out something."

"Do you think he'd mind poking around again? Would you ask him?"

"Of course I will, and no, I'm sure he won't. Brady loves a challenge. Now, if you'll excuse me, I'll go up and visit with Bessie for a few minutes, just to see how she is doing. Derrick is waiting by the motorcar"

"I haven't seen hide nor hair of Noble, either," Brady said about an hour later, after joining Derrick and me at the *Messenger.* "But I'll bet my favorite collar studs I know where to find Lehr today." He slid his watch from his vest pocket and flipped it open. "He should be there now, as a matter of fact."

Thus, I found myself back in the Peugeot, this time with Brady driving, retracing my earlier route down Bellevue Avenue, around to Ocean Avenue, and to Bailey's Beach. It was becoming dizzying, the speed at which one traversed one end of town to the other. Once again, I felt that twinge of betrayal, not only to dear Maestro, but to the island itself, dragged against its will into the hubbub of the modern age.

We were certainly not the only ones to descend upon Bailey's Beach that morning. Automobiles and carriages lined the road and filled the parking area, and a goodly crowd milled on the sand. The waves, however, appeared all but empty, but for a few figures wading or floating off to the sides, leaving the water directly in front of the pavilion empty.

Brady had told me precious little about what could have drawn Harry Lehr from his bed at such an ungodly hour, and as I glanced over at him, his amused smile drew my puzzlement. "Is there a swimming competition today?"

"Of sorts." He laughed outright. He brought the motor to a stop, cut the engine, and helped me out. "Your cousin Harold and Stuyvie Fish Junior are competing to see who can swim the farthest and longest as their friends attempt to reel them in on fishing lines."

"*What?*"

"Yes, and it's my understanding that Lehr is officiating. Come on."

Brady and I had never set foot on Bailey's Beach as children, as our family hadn't been able to afford membership. But now, as paying members, we were both able to pass through the pavilion doors without hesitation. From the patio, I spied Cousin Harold, the youngest child of Aunt Alva and Uncle William, and his friend, Mamie Fish's son, both still in their teens. They stood on the sand near the waterline, wearing sleeveless bathing costumes, and were being attended to by several laughing young men. I tried to make out what they were doing, but there were too many others in the way, some thirty or so other men of various ages, who appeared in high spirits and eager for this strange event to begin. There were only a few women about, and they remained on the fringe of the proceedings, curious onlookers who knew better than to stray too close to the boisterous gathering.

My gaze landed on Harry Lehr, dressed in white summer flannels and holding a megaphone. He was grinning, flushed from heat and enthusiasm as he shouted orders no one appeared to heed. I marveled at how quickly he had recovered from yesterday's tragedy. Bessie could hardly bare to stray from her room today, but here was her husband, looking the picture of exuberance as he presided over yet another of the Season's pointless antics.

"There he is." I started toward him, but Brady held me back.

"Not yet. Let them get started or you'll cause a fracas."

I hated to be forestalled, but Brady was right. Once intent upon one of their spectacles, young gentlemen of the Four Hundred did not suffer interruptions with grace.

Instead, I scanned the many faces, hoping to spot Ralph Noble. Wagers were laid and money exchanged hands as teams appeared to be formed, one group cheering on Harold and the other young Mr. Fish. Harry continued shouting directions through his megaphone. The cheering intensified, and the female onlookers backed farther away, toward the comparative safety of the pavilion. Once or twice, my hopes leaped as I thought I'd glimpsed Ralph Noble, but I was mistaken each time. I did, however, see Jimmy Van Alen of Wakehurst looking ridiculous in a bathing costume and top hat, a pipe clenched between his teeth, while a monocle in his right eye caught the sunlight in dots and dashes like a visual Morse code. Even at the beach, the man insisted on maintaining his English lord-of-the-manor persona.

A chronograph was procured from somewhere and handed to Harry. He held it high in the air, his thumb poised on the start button. Harold and Stuyvie, at the urging of their friends, shook hands, faced the water, and trudged into the surf. It was then I noticed the line attached to each of them by a belt, and how each line, in turn, connected to a fishing pole, the heavy sort used on commercial fishing boats, each held by three men—two to steady the rod, and one to man the reel.

"I thought you were joking," I said to Brady. "Surely, they can't mean to . . ." I stretched out an arm to gesture at the farcical scene taking shape before us. Harold and Stuyvie were waist deep now. They stopped and turned.

On the sand, Harry strode to the water's edge, holding the chronograph aloft. He raised the megaphone to his lips. "Gentlemen, are you ready?" At their exuberant replies to the affirmative, he shouted, "Begin!" and pressed the button on the timepiece.

The two competitors were allowed to swim out several yards before their designated "fishermen" began hauling on the rods and attempting to reel them back in. It might as well have been an official sporting event, given the volume of the cheers, jeers, and superfluous instructions shouted from all sides.

"This is ridiculous," I murmured to Brady.

"It's just the sort of thing Lehr loves," he replied.

I wished to turn and leave, rather than continue witnessing such a waste of time and effort, such a display of conceit as only the young men of the Four Hundred were capable of. Yet at the same time, I felt compelled to keep watching, lest some unforeseen accident occur—the tangling of their lines, or those lines holding them captive to an unexpected rip current, the giving out of their strength, or any number of other complications that might lead to one or the other of them succumbing to the waves. How little thought young men gave to the possible consequences of their follies. Was it my reporter's instincts, or concern for my younger cousin and his friend? An irrational conviction formed that should this not turn out well, I would hold Harry Lehr responsible.

And yet it did turn out well enough, and in short order. Before very many minutes had passed amid the continued encouragement of the spectators and the grunts of the "fishermen," it became apparent that the swimmers were tiring and could not hold out much longer. Stuyvie Fish Junior ceased his efforts first, prompting a burst of both laughter and groans on the sand. Harry Lehr pressed the chronograph to stop the time, declared Harold the winner in a voice made booming by the megaphone, which prompted Harold to immediately stop paddling and allow himself to be towed in.

"Thank goodness," I said with a disapproving shake of my head, a response that would have made Nanny proud. "Can we speak to Harry now?"

Brady, playing the protective brother, hadn't strayed more than a few inches from my side. "I think we should give it a few more minutes. Let them calm down."

As the swimmers came to shore, blankets were tossed around their shoulders and flasks thrust into their hands. I noticed several more similar containers reflecting the sunlight. "If I wait any longer, Harry might not be coherent. Besides, they'll think I'm here to cover their shenanigans for the *Messenger.*" I set out across the sand, Brady in quick pursuit.

"Em . . ."

As I had predicted, Harry assumed I had come in the capacity of a reporter. "Mrs. Andrews!" he exclaimed upon my reaching him, sending a brandy-laden burst of air beneath my nose. "So good of you to come. Quite sporting of you. Did Bessie come along as well? Where is the old girl?"

"Bessie is at home," I replied coolly.

"Yes, yes, I should say so. But what about that good husband of yours? A capital fellow. I like him exceedingly well." He pretended to search the crowd over my shoulder.

"No, Harry, he's not here, either," I said, allowing my impatience to enter my voice.

"A pity."

"Is your friend Mr. Noble here?"

Harry's frown was immediate. "I should say not. He's been ignoring me since yesterday morning, rude fellow."

"Have you had a falling-out?"

"Who knows? Ah, no matter. Would you like a quote for your paper?"

Though I made no reply to this, he supplied me with several quotes, none of which I bothered to jot down. Then I asked, "Would anyone else know where Mr. Noble might be found?"

"Is it so important?"

"It might be, yes."

He suddenly waved an arm high in the air. "Vanderbilt, Fish, come here and allow Mrs. Andrews to interview you. She's come all this way to cover our event for her little newspaper. Come here this instant! Mustn't keep a lady waiting. She is a lady, you know, despite her odd ambitions."

Brady, content to remain in my shadow until this moment, reached forward and clasped Harry about the upper arm. "You might settle down a bit, Lehr. Don't you think?" His words were calm yet firm, a warning for Harry to remember his manners.

Harry replied with an idiotic grin and shrugged. "Well, if it's Noble you're after, I'm afraid you'll have to look elsewhere."

"Hello, Emmaline." I turned to discover Harold beside me, looking sheepish. He still held a blanket wrapped around his shoulders and was dripping seawater onto the sand. Someone had jammed a straw boater on his head at a jaunty angle. "I don't suppose you're going to mention this to Mother, are you?"

I couldn't contain the laugh that burst from my lips. "Do you seriously suppose there's any possible way she won't hear about it?"

"I suppose not." Harold shuffled his bare feet. "She'll call it foolishness, and I'll never hear the end of it. Guess I'll just have to make a scarcity of myself for a few days."

"Stay with Willie," I suggested, referring to his elder brother, married now to Virginia Fair. But instantly I remembered they were soon to have their second child and had stayed in New York this summer. "Or with . . . someone."

"Capital idea," he agreed, but then, in a lower voice, said, "Despite what Harry wants, this doesn't really have to go in the papers, does it?"

"Not as far as I'm concerned, but surely there are other reporters here."

We spoke for another minute before he sauntered off to rejoin his young friends.

Brady and I left soon after, getting back into the Peugeot. We might have taken the more interior route of Coggeshall Avenue, which led onto Spring Street, but Brady once again opted for the broader, straighter Bellevue Avenue to take us back into town. We were negotiating the two sharp corners to get there—a hard right onto a short section of Coggeshall, then another ninety-degree turn left onto Bellevue—when the motorcar slid, spun, and slammed, front panel first, into the rock wall that separated the road from the southernmost entrance of the Cliff Walk.

Chapter 16

With a crumpling of metal and a startling jolt, the Peugeot came to a juddering stop. In the instant it did, I found myself pressed tight against the side of the seat, with Brady pressed against my other side. He still gripped the steering rudder in one hand, while his other arm had shot across me in an effort to hold me in the seat. He held it there like an iron bar, continuing to pin me to the leather squabs.

"Em, are you hurt? Are you all right?"

I felt no pain, at least none that I could discern at the moment. "I think I'm fine, Brady. You can let me go. You?"

His arm slowly snaked away and he sat up straighter, sliding back over to his side of the seat. "I believe so. What the devil happened? I wasn't speeding, Em, I swear it."

"I know you weren't. If I thought you had been, I'd have scolded you to slow down."

"That's the thing of it, Em. I did attempt to slow down even more around that second corner, but nothing happened when I pressed the brake."

By this time, a small crowd of people—men, women, and

a few children—had made their way up from the Cliff Walk path over to the Peugeot. A chorus of inquiries descended upon us from all sides as they surrounded the vehicle, voices I barely heard at first as Brady's revelation reverberated inside me. I began going through the motions of assuring our well-wishers that we were unharmed, but my thoughts latched on to a single thought: Could this have been deliberate?

"A shame, this," one man called out after walking around the vehicle twice. "It's brand-spanking-new, isn't it?"

"Sure is a beaut—or was," another said. "Although, I think all but the front panel is salvageable."

"Right front wheel's a bit bent. You'll need to replace it."

"This is why I'll not allow you to spend your hard-earned wages on one of these contraptions," a young woman admonished her male companion, who could only have been her husband.

"Derrick will have my head," Brady lamented. He climbed down and helped me down as well. I found my knees slightly wobbly, but I attributed that to shock rather than any injury I might have sustained.

"This was not your fault," I said firmly, and followed him around to where the front panel sat in intimate contact with the rock wall we had struck. One of the onlookers had been correct; the right front wheel had also taken the brunt of the collision. "So much like what happened to Mr. Jackson," I murmured as I surveyed the damage.

Brady stared at me. "You mean the Lehrs' man-of-all-work? The one who died?"

"The one who was likely murdered when the brakes on Bessie's motorcar failed."

Brady flicked a gaze at our audience and lowered his voice. "You think someone tampered with these brakes as well?"

I shook my head and shrugged. "I intend to find out."

Help came from nearby Beachmound, the neoclassical mansion owned by Benjamin Thaw, who happened to be enjoying the view of Bailey's Beach and the ocean from one of his upper verandas when our mishap occurred. He sent two servants running down to us, and after we'd finished our examination of the Peugeot, and declared it in no way fit to be driven, they escorted us back up to the house. From there, Mr. and Mrs. Thaw offered to have their servants push the car onto their property to await a mechanic. They also offered us the use of one of their carriages to take us to Gull Manor.

"It's a short walk," I began to demur, but Brady settled the matter.

"Thank you. We'd greatly appreciate it."

Some ten minutes later, Nanny had us ensconced in the parlor, a blanket around me, despite the distinct lack of chill in the room. She plied us with tea and a touch of brandy—does wonders for the nerves, she once again informed me—and then called back to the kitchen to ask Katie to bring us sandwiches and cake.

"Nanny, we're fine, I promise."

She waved off my protestations before slipping out of the room. Meanwhile, Katie shuffled in, bearing a tray laden with chicken salad sandwiches and other treats. She set it down on the sofa table. With nothing left to do but wait for Derrick, Brady and I tucked in and gratefully drank our tea. When Nanny returned some minutes later, it was with a chattering Annamarie, who, upon seeing us, held out her arms and squealed our names—"Mama, Unka Bee!" Nanny waited for me to set my now-empty plate aside before plunking Annamarie on my lap.

My arms went around the warm snugness of her and I

buried my nose in her hair. As my eyes fell closed, a sense of peace drifted over me as though Nanny had wrapped me in another blanket. When I looked up, she stood above me smiling with the knowledge that she had just administered the best medicine I could have asked for. The last of my jangled nerves settled.

Until the front door opened and Derrick shouted my name.

"Emma? Emma, where are you?"

I shushed him from where I sat on the sofa. "You'll frighten Annamarie."

"Papa!" my daughter called out, and laughed. It wasn't every afternoon, after all, that both her parents *and* her uncle Brady were available to play.

Derrick seemed blind to all else as his gaze locked on me and he crossed the room in very few strides. He threw himself down beside me and gathered both me and our daughter in his arms. "Are you certain you're all right? You're not hurt? Should we take you to the hospital, or have Dr. Kennison come here?"

"Yes, no, and *no.*" I spoke that last word adamantly, albeit it came out muffled against the side of his neck. I could barely breathe, he pressed me so tight against him, but I didn't pull away. "Brady and I are fine."

"That's right, fine, thanks for asking," Brady murmured from the chair opposite us.

Derrick's hold loosened marginally, just enough for him to turn his face toward my brother. I witnessed a storm gathering on his features and endeavored to forestall it before it broke in a torrent.

"Brady didn't cause the accident. You're not to blame him. The brakes failed just as they did for Ellis Jackson."

The tension in Derrick's arms eased; his jaw stopped

clenching . Nodding, he ran his hand over Annamarie's curls and kissed her forehead. "Sorry, Brady. I suspected as much, but I didn't wait for Oliver Prescott to examine the Peugeot."

"Is he at Beachmound now?" I asked him as I slipped the blanket from my shoulders.

"He is, with another mechanic. Drove me out in his own vehicle and brought tools to work on the vehicle enough to get it moving again. He'll take it back to his garage. Whatever he determines, he'll let Jesse know as well."

Brady reached for a leftover half sandwich from the tray. After consuming it in a few bites, he let out a sigh. "So then, what are we going to do about this?"

"*Do?*" Derrick laughed grimly. "We're going to find out who's responsible for this, hurt him badly, and turn him over to Jesse."

"If we find out who did this, we're turning him over to Jesse without the hurting," I said, well aware that I sounded like an admonishing schoolteacher.

Derrick said nothing, merely stared across the space at my brother, the two of them silently engaging in male understandings.

"The main question, besides who did this, is when," I said, as much to distract them from their intentions as to work out this latest puzzle. "When did someone have the opportunity to tamper with the Peugeot?"

Derrick shrugged while simultaneously reaching to take Annamarie's outstretched hand. "It sits on one side of the barn every night. It's sometimes in town, although I doubt anyone could have done it there on the open street. And it was at Arleigh only this morning. Good heavens, how long ago that seems now."

"But you waited with the car while I went inside," I reminded him.

His brow furrowed. "Not the entire time. I strolled over to the carriage house to have a look at their vehicles, and to speak with the groom."

"That wouldn't have given anyone enough time to fiddle with the brakes," Brady pointed out with a dubious expression. "Let's not forget the auto sat at Bailey's Beach for a good thirty minutes immediately before we crashed."

At that blunt mention of our mishap, Derrick flinched, then drew himself up. "Let's see what Oliver has to say. To me, it doesn't seem as though it would take much to walk by and give a good yank on the braking cables, especially if only one side is tampered with."

"The skidding seemed to indicate that only the right-side brake malfunctioned," Brady said with a nod. "Just as happened when Ellis Jackson drove Mrs. Lehr's motorcar."

I shifted Annamarie's weight from one side of my lap to the other, from where she could now play with Derrick's sleeve. He didn't seem to mind. "That someone would have to know what they were doing," I said. "And why would it take so long for an accident to finally happen? Assuming the damage wasn't done at Bailey's?"

"Remember what the other mechanic told us, the one at the Newport Engineering Works? Braking cables can come loose, little by little, over time." Derrick was silent a moment while Annamarie played with his cuff link. "If this had simply happened, without all of the other incidents before it, I'd be inclined to attribute it to the capriciousness of motorcars, have it fixed, and not think much more about it, other than to have it inspected on a regular basis." After another pause, he added, "Which I will, from now on, not to mention installing a lock on the barn door."

"I never thought I'd see the day when we'd need to lock up the barn." Despite Newport being no stranger to crime, horse theft wasn't typically one of them. On an island this small, where would a horse thief go that he wouldn't be caught? With a shake of my head, I smoothed the wrinkles from the side of my lap where my daughter had been previously sitting.

Derrick contemplated Annamarie with a pensive look, then ruffled her curls and tapped the dimple in her right cheek. She giggled and grabbed his finger in her fist.

Brady watched them with a gentle smile, which quickly faded. "Who do you believe did it?"

"If you're asking me," I said, "I'm still torn as to who has the greatest motive to want both me and Bessie, or perhaps Neddie Thorton, out of the way: Ralph Noble or Ely Forrester."

Derrick leaned forward to pluck a molasses cookie from the tray. He didn't immediately eat it, but used it to punctuate each point he made with little pokes at the air. "It only makes sense that Forrester's victim would be Bessie because of what she overheard at Reggie's wedding, and, by association, you. The Forrester family is as straightlaced as it gets. No scandals, no lawsuits, no divorces. They've used their impeccable record to increase their social standing, influence local politics, and even as leverage in some of their business dealings. Having a son involved with an illegal gambling ring would shatter their reputation, and I have little doubt they'd disown him rather than allow him to go on tarnishing their sterling credentials.

"Meanwhile," he went on, still waving the dark brown cookie, "Ralph Noble's intended victim would more likely have been Miss Thorton, especially if their last liaison didn't go well. They might have argued—with him, perhaps, breaking things off and she making demands. Or vice versa, causing him to want to be permanently rid of her."

"And because the two ladies were so frequently together," Brady reasoned, "it became near impossible to ascertain which of them was meant to die."

Derrick and I nodded, and Derrick said, "But I can't think of a reason why Noble would come after you, Emma, rather than simply lie low, now that Neddie Thorton is dead."

"And where does Harry stand in all of this?" I mused aloud. "If the Peugeot was damaged while we were at Bailey's Beach, he could not have done it. He was on the sand the entire time we were."

Brady laughed. "Surely, you don't consider Harry Lehr capable of murder? He's a buffoon, a jokester. The man hasn't a serious bone in his body."

"Except when it comes to Bessie's money," I murmured, more to myself than to them. "But even without that motive, could he have helped in her intended demise without quite realizing it?"

At that question, silence fell, if only for a moment. Derrick said, "I suppose he might at that. After all, he took Noble to Arleigh—who knows how many times? That meant Noble knew the house, and the routines of both the Lehrs and the servants."

"What about Forrester, though?" Brady asked. "As far as we know, he's no great friend of Lehr's, merely an acquaintance through Reggie."

"He was at Arleigh for Reggie's wedding," I replied, thinking back. "There was a week's worth of celebrations beforehand, many of which took place at Arleigh." Annamarie, having grown tired of sitting on Mama's lap, reached with both arms in an appeal for Derrick to slide her onto his. Once he had done so, she immediately went to work attempting to untie his necktie. "Before he ever had any reason to wish Bessie harm, he had an opportunity to learn the layout of the house. And despite what Reggie claimed, I believe Mr. Forrester took up residence at Sandy Point after the wedding. Possibly even while Reggie and Cathleen were in Europe. I don't think he ever left the island."

"Portsmouth is a long way to travel back and forth when one is plotting a murder," Brady pointed out.

"True," I conceded, "but he also has a close relationship with the Berwinds and sometimes stays at The Elms. I don't doubt he has other friends in town as well." I raised my eyebrows at Brady. "Perhaps someone can find out who those friends might be?"

"Someone might be able to do that," Brady replied with a chuckle. "But we still need to find Noble. It makes no sense that he's vanished into thin air."

"Jesse, of course, has checked with the outgoing ferries and trains," I said. "There's been no record of him leaving the island."

Derrick grinned at our daughter even as he said, in a somber tone, "That doesn't mean he didn't."

"No," I agreed. "Even Harry doesn't know where he is. Which means he could be anywhere by now."

I soon found myself once again targeted, this time by someone wholly unexpected. It was midmorning of the next day, and I had just left a city council meeting. I was still chuckling over the fact that one of the issues debated was a petition submitted by my aunt Alva and her husband, Oliver, to have Lakeview Avenue, which ran beside Belcourt, closed to local traffic. It would mean residents, as well as merchants and tradesmen, having to circle well out of their way to reach homes in the surrounding area. A small price to pay, apparently, to enable Oliver and Aunt Alva to enjoy exclusive use of the road.

I had reached the *Messenger* and was about to open the street door when a woman abruptly approached me. She could only have been lingering on the sidewalk, waiting for me.

"Mrs. Andrews?"

Her tone, less than cordial, made me stop in my tracks. She was a tall woman, made even taller by the silk flowers crowning her hat, with stern features and dark hair shot with silver. I immediately noticed the stateliness with which she held her trim frame, and she began to seem familiar, although I believed I had never set eyes on her before. Still . . .

"I am Mrs. Andrews," I confirmed, returning her bold scrutiny. "And you are?"

"Mrs. Drexel. Mrs. Joseph Drexel."

I'm sure my astonishment showed plainly on my face. She was Bessie's mother, who, from what I understood, rarely came to Newport. "A pleasure to meet you, ma'am." I waited for her to enlighten me as to the reason for our meeting.

"Have you a few moments to spare? There's something I'd like to discuss with you." No hint of amiability accompanied that invitation. In fact, her entire demeanor—rigid and unsmiling—assured me Mrs. Drexel was used to giving orders and having them obeyed.

She had my dander up and no mistake. But perhaps her antagonism wasn't directed at me. I could only assume that Bessie's troubles had come to her notice and she had traveled all the way to Newport for the sake of her daughter. But how much did she know?

"There's a tearoom just down the way." I gestured and we fell into step together. "You're not often in Newport, I understand," I said to break the silence. I wondered how she had gotten to the *Messenger,* for she seemed ill at ease walking along the sidewalk among the other pedestrians. Whenever anyone strayed too close, she leaned away as if afraid to make contact.

She didn't reply to my observation. A sideways glance revealed her to be gazing straight ahead, her features tense. When we reached the brick façade and gaily painted trim of Lily's Tea Emporium, she stopped short and surveyed the door and window overlooking the street. Though she said nothing, she gave me the distinct impression the place didn't meet her standards.

Then perhaps she shouldn't have waylaid me outside my place of business, but instead sent me notice and arranged a more acceptable place to meet. With an inner shrug, I reached for the knob and opened the door. Lily's had been there for years and I felt quite at home there.

We were shown to a table along the sidewall farthest from the door. About half the tables were occupied, mostly by local Newport women, perhaps a few visitors; but, judging from their well-made but relatively unadorned clothing, I surmised no one from the Four Hundred.

"The pound cake is very good here, as is the bread pudding," I said as we took our seats. "And I recommend the oolong tea."

"Hmph" was all she said. When the waitress came, she ordered a pot of oolong, accompanied with a plain scone. We shared the oolong, but I ordered the pound cake with blueberry compote.

After a bracing sip of tea, I saw no reason not to come to the point. "Mrs. Drexel, what is this about? Are you worried about . . . your daughter?" I had been about to say Bessie, but thought this woman might not approve of me referring to her daughter with such familiarity.

"Yes, I'm worried about Elizabeth," she nearly snapped as if I'd said something foolish. Then she gave herself a shake that restored her composure. "Forgive me, Mrs. Andrews.

I've been traveling since yesterday and only arrived in Newport within the hour. I'm tired and not at my best."

"You needn't apologize." Despite my assurance, I was rather relieved she had. Why should my friend's mother and I start off on the wrong foot? I could think of no possible reason. "Does Elizabeth know you're here?"

"No. Not yet. I came to see you directly from the ferry." She poured a thin stream of cream into her tea, but no sugar. Stirring it round, she met my gaze. "I read about Elizabeth's maid in the newspapers, including an article you wrote, and she sent a telegram explaining what happened. A horrible thing, bees behaving in that way. Practically unheard of."

"Yes, it was dreadful. B—uh—Elizabeth is very upset, as you can imagine. I'm sure your arrival will be a great comfort to her. And you needn't worry, the police *will* find who did it."

"Yes, of course." She gave a flick of her hand. "That's not why I wished to speak with you. It's about Elizabeth—and Harry."

My teacup stopped halfway to my lips. "You wish to speak to me about your daughter and her husband?"

"I do, Mrs. Andrews. I know about you." Studying her closely as she spoke, I recognized her daughter in her features. I saw the aristocratic lines, but none of the vulnerability or softness that in my mind defined Bessie. Without the easy acceptance that allowed Bessie and me to be friends. "I've heard all about your career as a journalist, not to mention your penchant for solving mysteries."

"I see my reputation is spreading," I replied, half in jest, but feeling utterly baffled as to where this conversation would lead.

"I might not come often to Newport, but I don't live an isolated life. I have friends and they tell me things. I hear all about the goings-on here and elsewhere. And I know you and my daughter have been spending an inordinate amount of time together."

"'Inordinate,'" I repeated, my guard now fully up. I wondered how much she knew beyond the basic facts of Neddie Thorton's death. I waited for her to continue, having no intention of supplying her with answers to questions she hadn't asked yet.

"I cannot help wondering *why* you and Elizabeth would have any reason to forge an alliance, much less a friendship. What could you possibly have in common? Elizabeth was raised with the utmost care, from her earliest days through her education and finishing. While you . . ." She sipped her tea and placed the cup carefully back in its saucer. "Please, I mean no offense, Mrs. Andrews, but even you must admit that despite your marriage, you hail from a very different sort of world than Elizabeth. And even now, with your newspaper business, your life is on a course vastly different from my daughter's."

"I wouldn't say *vastly.* We are both wives and mothers," I pointed out more calmly than I felt. Had she asked to speak with me for the express purpose of insulting me?

"Yes, wives. Which brings me to my point."

Finally. I waited for her to elucidate.

"With such differences between you, I could think of only one reason Elizabeth would associate with you." She folded her hands on her lap and leaned toward me. "Did she hire you to investigate her husband?"

My eyes widened. Had she somehow discovered why Bessie had initially come to see me? Surely, Bessie herself would not have told her. She had made it quite clear to me that her mother must never learn about her suspicions—unless they proved true. I waited in silence for her to continue, lest I give too much away.

"Well, Mrs. Andrews? Is my daughter hoping to catch her husband in an indiscretion?" She sat back with a haughty tilt of her chin. "Ever since Alva Vanderbilt, *your own* relative, dared divorce her husband, women everywhere think they can simply walk away from their marriages. From their obligations. But it isn't right. It's immoral. It's a *sin,* Mrs. Andrews."

Ah. I perceived now that Mrs. Drexel did not know the truth of why Bessie had come to me. No, her purpose here was entirely of her own making, the result of an overactive imagination entertaining notions that her daughter could be led astray. Not to mention suspicion of any woman brash enough to engage in a career outside her home.

"Mrs. Drexel, I can assure you Elizabeth contacted me for no such reason. She has no intentions of divorcing her husband."

She studied me for a long moment before saying, "I'm no fool, Mrs. Andrews. I know what Harry Lehr is. Oh, I didn't when he and my daughter were first married, or I'd have put a stop to it beforehand, but as I said, I know people and I hear things. And while Elizabeth puts on a brave face, I know my daughter. I know when she isn't happy. And she is not happy in her marriage with Harry Lehr."

"Then why hold her to it? As you said, my aunt Alva ushered in a new freedom for modern wives who wish to escape unhappy marriages. One word from you and Elizabeth would find relief." I stopped abruptly, having said too much. But from Mrs. Drexel's expression, I hadn't said anything she didn't already comprehend.

"I will never speak that word, Mrs. Andrews. *Never.* As I said, divorce is a sin. My daughter might be unhappy now, but that is nothing compared to the eternal damnation of her soul. No, I will do everything in my power to protect Elizabeth from that. She must simply learn to carve out a life for herself that brings her some measure of satisfaction and contentment, if not outright happiness."

I wanted to tell her how sad a prospect that was, how tragic, that Bessie, through no fault of her own, should be meant to live a life of constant adversity, bitterness, and ill use, with no end in sight.

It seemed very much a purgatory to me.

Chapter 17

Mrs. Drexel's sudden appearance wasn't my only surprise that day. A message arrived from Brady about an hour after I returned to the office, which sent Derrick and me hurrying to the Point. I went as both a reporter and Bessie's friend.

As we arrived on Washington Street, at the property Harry Lehr had rented for his friend Ralph Noble, we saw Brady waiting just inside the honeysuckle hedge bordering the road. A small crowd filled the sidewalk, their buzzing speculation blending with the clamor of horns, steam engines, bells, and the sharp cries of gulls from the harbor. Three police vehicles stretched in a line along the roadside, Jesse's included. In their midst, the ambulance wagon waited with its rear doors open.

Chills of foreboding ran down my arms, raising gooseflesh. I hardly needed to ask Brady what happened, but I hurried to him after we alighted from our carriage. "It's Ralph Noble, isn't it?"

Brady opened the gate for us. "He's dead." I slipped my hand from Derrick's and was about to move closer to the open front door when he added, "I found him."

The revelation stopped me cold. "You? How?"

"I'd been going through a parcel of papers sent up from the New York Central, was at it all morning, so I decided I needed to take a break." Even though Brady might spend time in Newport during the summer months, his work for the New York Central Railroad continued to fill a good part of his days. "As long as I was out and about, I thought I'd do a little poking. Since the police hadn't had any luck banging on Noble's front door, I went around back. Everything looked secure, but it wasn't. The kitchen door was unlocked."

"So you went in?" I prompted when he paused.

"Of course I did. At first, the house seemed empty. You know that utter stillness you only experience in an empty house? I almost left, but something prickled at the back of my neck. When I called out and no one answered, I went farther in, moving from the kitchen into the dining room . . ." Brady breathed in sharply, his shoulders shaking as though he'd felt a sudden draft. "And then I smelled it."

I felt the blood drain from my face. Derrick placed a steadying hand at the small of my back. I knew the answer, but felt compelled to ask, "What did you find?"

Haunting shadows darkened Brady's eyes. "I found Ralph Noble on his parlor floor, facedown, a kitchen knife protruding from his side."

"Good heavens."

"Any idea how long he'd been there?" Derrick's somber gaze traveled over the red clapboard façade.

"Only that it hadn't just happened, if you know what I mean."

"I do." I had seen death before—countless times. I knew all the signs and could no longer be confused as to whether someone was merely unconscious or the life had drained from their body.

"Well," Brady said, "now you know everything I know."

The three of us fell silent. Moments later, a commotion inside the open front door drew our attention, along with that of the neighbors gathered on the sidewalk. Jesse appeared, along with Scotty Binsford, another former neighbor of Brady's and mine when we were children. They stepped aside and two men carrying a stretcher came out and down the two steps that gave onto the short walkway. The coroner and his assistant followed. Brady, Derrick, and I moved out of their way as they approached. On the other side of the hedge, the onlookers' voices rose, with questions being called out about who lay beneath the white sheet stretched over the body.

Neither the grim-faced coroner nor his assistants offered replies. They continued out through the archway in the hedge toward the ambulance wagon, carefully slid the stretcher into the vehicle, and firmly shut the doors. They didn't leave, however. The men who had carried Ralph Noble's body folded their arms and stood guard as the coroner went back inside.

I followed him, despite Derrick calling me back in a whisper and Brady's louder, "Em, maybe now isn't the best time."

I kept going. Of the three of us, I had the most reason to be there; I was, after all, the *Messenger*'s news reporter.

I found Jesse and Scotty in the parlor. More voices came from the kitchen. Brady had said the murder weapon had been a kitchen knife. I didn't stray beyond the parlor doorway, but took in what I could from there. A chair had been knocked over, a small table as well. Against one wall, the glass panes on a curio cabinet had been smashed. Shards of glass littered the floor in front of it, while the items inside—figurines, teacups, small vases—lay askew, some of them shattered. There had been a struggle, a fierce one; Ralph Noble hadn't gone down quietly.

"Emma, that's far enough," Jesse called to me unnecessarily from across the room. He and Scotty had been examining the spot where the body had lain, each holding a cloth bag in which to drop any evidence they found. Jesse held a magnifying glass as well; Scotty, tweezers. My gaze fell to the patch of rug between them, to the uneven stains congealing to shades of rust and brown. My stomach momentarily roiled. Steeling myself, I dug my notebook and pencil out of my handbag and began making notes.

"Don't worry," I said, taking shallow breaths to avoid the odor of death, "I know better than to disturb the scene."

"Gosh, Mrs. Andrews—Emma." Scotty often stumbled between addressing me in the proper way and reverting to the familiarity of our childhood. About my age, his hulking size belied a gentle nature, but I had learned that Scotty, as a policeman, shouldn't be underestimated. "You shouldn't be here. You don't want to see this."

"I'll be all right, Scotty, thanks. You know it's nothing new for me."

"That's the shame of it," he murmured.

I watched and listened in the next minutes, my pencil scratching across several pages. Finally I went back outside to where Derrick and Brady waited and told them what I'd witnessed. Jesse joined us soon after giving the ambulance permission to take the body away. Scotty and the other policemen climbed into their carriages to leave.

"The coroner estimates he's been dead for more than a day." Jesse slapped his derby on his head. "Which means when we came knocking, he was here, lying on his parlor floor. Makes me feel pretty ineffectual."

"You only came to question him," Derrick said. "Without proof he'd committed a crime, you couldn't very well break down his front door."

"I should have," Jesse replied with a grim shake of his head.

Brady clapped his shoulder. "And done what? He was already dead."

I continued holding my writing implements and, like any good reporter, asked, "Could you determine anything by the angle of the wound?"

"Only that it was probably someone of similar height, and right-handed, as the wound is on the left side of his torso. Noble was probably facing his attacker when the knife went in. Then it looks as though the force of it spun him around, and he fell face-first." Jesse quirked his eyebrows. "None of that tells us much, at this point."

"What evidence did you find?" I asked, as much to facilitate my coverage of the murder as to help Jesse sift through the details he had gathered so far. This was a process he and I had fallen into in the past several years, and while many men might have found my questions impertinent, he welcomed them.

"There were signs of a tussle in the yard behind the house, so it looks like Noble was out there when the killer arrived."

"Enjoying the view," Brady mused. "His last."

"There's a crack in the window in the kitchen door," Jesse went on, "indicating Noble had perhaps tried to run inside and shut the door, but the perpetrator used force to open it. The kitchen is also a mess, with whatever had been on the main work counter scattered on the floor."

"What about in the parlor itself?" I glanced at my notes. "I saw the disarray in there. They fought hard, or, at least, Mr. Noble struggled hard to elude his killer. But did you find anything identifying?"

"Only dirt and scuff marks on the rug. The dirt could have come from the yard, or anywhere. The scuff marks don't indicate the size shoe."

"So, in short, nothing." Derrick let out a frustrated sigh. "Why did I know that would be the case."

"Because it so often is," I replied. I closed my notebook. "But I believe I know who did this. Ely Forrester. Mr. Noble threatened him at the New Cliffs Hotel. He obviously found out about Mr. Forrester's involvement in the Canfield gambling scandal, and we all know how much Ely Forrester wants to protect that secret."

Jesse tempered his nod of agreement with, "But you didn't hear outright what they were discussing. And Forrester didn't shed any light when he confronted you on the Cliff Walk. They could have been talking about anything."

"Doesn't the fact that he confronted me prove he's aggressive? He didn't push me off the cliff—how could he, with other people around? And he *claimed* he wouldn't hurt me, but is that to be believed?" I thought back to what I'd seen in the gentlemen's lounge at the hotel. "Ralph Noble obviously had the upper hand that day. His expressions and mannerisms were of someone who controlled the situation, who was backing his opponent into a corner. And Ely Forrester's reaction exuded fury."

"Not to mention what happened to the Peugeot ," Derrick added. "Noble couldn't have tampered with the brakes, having been dead more than a day. But if Forrester believes Emma heard his conversation at the wedding, or believes Bessie told her, he's just as likely to come after her as not."

Jesse nodded again, but this time with more certainty. "I'll mount a search for him. If he's on the island, we'll find him."

"I'd start with The Elms," I said, "and from there, Sandy Point. And don't take my cousin's word that Mr. Forrester isn't there."

"Believe me, I won't."

"Let me come with you," Brady offered. Jesse balked at that, but Brady pressed on. "I might not hold any sway with the Berwinds, but with Reggie, I do. Even if Forrester isn't staying at Sandy Point, I don't believe for a minute Reggie doesn't know where to find him. And I can make him tell us." He cast me a sheepish glance. "I know things about him not many others do. Not even you, Em."

"Men" was my only comment.

"I'm going, too." Derrick showed Jesse a determined expression. "If this is the man who threatened my wife's life, I want to help bring him to justice."

"I can't have any vigilantes on the scene," Jesse said firmly. "I have enough policemen to help bring him in."

"Your policemen are of better use scouring Newport and the points of exit," Derrick swiftly countered. "If Brady can help you with Reggie, I can help you with the Berwinds. And you know it."

Jesse's mouth flattened. Both Brady and Derrick had him on all counts, and he couldn't deny it.

I settled the matter. "Jesse, let them go with you. Derrick, I'll take the carriage back to the *Messenger,* write my articles, and then I'll drive over to Arleigh to see Bessie. And to let her know we believe Ely Forrester is responsible for everything. Perhaps, after all, it *was* she, and not Neddie Thorton, who was meant to fall victim to the bees. But with one of your men at Arleigh," I said to Jesse, "she's safe for now."

Chapter 18

Any certainty I felt about Ely Forrester being a murderer abandoned me by the time I reached the *Messenger.* I couldn't say why. I only knew the notion didn't sit completely right with me. Was it due to his manner when he confronted me on the Cliff Walk? His denial that he would hurt anyone?

It wasn't as though he would admit to being a killer.

I found Ethan in our office, busy at the typewriter as usual. The summer Season kept him supplied with a steady stream of articles to write. He glanced up when I entered and immediately stilled his fingers. He hadn't been in when Brady's message came, so he didn't know why Derrick and I had left the office.

"You look as if you've seen a ghost."

I threw myself into my desk chair. "Not a ghost, at least not yet."

"But someone is dead," he surmised, his eyes narrowing on me.

I told him about Ralph Noble. As my office mate and fellow reporter, Ethan already knew the basics about what had been happening. I explained the rest, along with the conclusions we had reached less than an hour ago.

He continued to stare at me across the small space. "This Mr. Forrester . . . you're not convinced, are you?"

"That obvious? No, I'm not. And I don't know why." Again, I went over the evidence that pointed toward Ely Forrester.

"It's all circumstantial," he said when I'd finished.

"Yes, well. One circumstance is, he detained me on the Cliff Walk making subtle, and not so subtle, threats that had me fearing for my life. He has a lot to lose, should anyone—Bessie, me, my cousin, and yes, Ralph Noble—give his secret away."

"But?"

We had worked together for several years now, and Ethan had come to know me well. I showed him a rueful smile. "I just don't know . . ."

"You think it's too easy?"

"Perhaps."

"Why?" His expression turned shrewder than one might expect of a society journalist. "And that's not a question I expect an immediate answer to. If you think it could be someone else, review your impressions again. After all, I'm a fresh set of ears. I haven't been in the thick of it as you have and perhaps I can see the forest for the trees."

"That's an excellent idea, Ethan."

"Then tell me, is there someone you haven't considered, at least not seriously, but who has been there since the beginning?"

"Someone we haven't considered . . ." I stood up and began pacing our tiny office as I often did when caught in a particularly perplexing matter. I thought about the day Bessie first came to see me, to enlist my help finding evidence that Harry meant to kill her. I'd followed up her suspicions by hiding in their dining room and listening in on their conversation. After that, I'd gone upstairs to search Harry's office, where I had found the invoice that led us to Oliver Prescott at the Ocean House Automobile Garage. Harry had taken Bessie's car in to be serviced and lingered to watch every test and adjustment Oliver had performed on the vehicle. Had he been learning how to sabotage the motorcar?

"Harry Lehr," I said, pausing my steps. "He's been there since the beginning, doing inexplicable things and making his wife's life miserable."

"But isn't that what Harry Lehr does?" Ethan picked up a pencil and began tapping one end against his desk. "According to what Mrs. Lehr told you, it's been the same since the day they were married. Except now, he seems to need more money. Wasn't some of that extra cash needed to pay his friend's expenses—the same friend who was murdered today? Would he have murdered a friend he was willing to support?"

"Perhaps . . . if they'd had a falling-out." My hands on my hips, I walked again as I reasoned it out. "Perhaps Ralph Noble discovered Harry meant to murder his wife and was going to expose him." All along, I had doubted Harry's involvement in anything besides being a drain on Bessie's emotions and her pocketbook. Had I been wrong? Was he more than a jokester, a spendthrift, and a carouser?

"All right, that's Harry Lehr. Who else have you suspected, besides Ralph Noble, of course?"

With a shrug, I said, "Another victim. Neddie Thorton. She was with Bessie when every incident occurred. Except the last one, with the bees."

"We can safely cross her off your list," he said with a mirthless chuckle. "But her involvement made you wonder who the intended victim was."

"Yes."

"What put Miss Thorton there at each incident?"

I spread my arms, as if the answer was obvious. "She works for Mrs. Lehr. She was both lady's maid and companion."

"But if she had been the intended victim . . . what was it about her that might have prompted the killer to try the means he did each time? Consider each attempt."

"I see what you're getting at." I circled my desk and lowered myself back into my chair. "It began with the balcony railing that came loose, nearly sending Bessie over if Neddie hadn't been there to catch her." I groped at the air. I'd been over the same details countless times. "But Neddie smoked, and she sometimes smoked on the balcony. Bessie didn't approve of the habit, but never admonished Neddie to quit. So yes, Neddie sometimes went out there by herself and someone might have known that."

Ethan nodded thoughtfully. "What next?"

"The loose stair runner, I believe. Mrs. Lehr and Neddie went down the main stairs each morning to the small parlor, where they would go over the morning's correspondence together."

"Miss Thorton was expected to be on the staircase at least once every day, first thing in the morning."

I nodded.

"And next?"

"The automobile accident that killed the Lehrs' man-of-all-work."

"Miss Thorton did the driving, didn't she?"

"Yes, but only when Mrs. Lehr was in the car with her."

"That doesn't mean Miss Thorton wasn't the target." Ethan leaned his elbows on the desk and tented his fingertips beneath his chin. "Tell me everything you've learned about Miss Thorton."

"Precious little, I'm afraid."

Ethan's eyebrows went up. "Probably more than you think."

I took that as a challenge. "All right. She hailed from a poor Southern family, but pretended they had been wealthy before the war, to lend herself an air of gentility. She came to New York to find work and used any means she felt she must to survive, including stealing and blackmail."

"Someone like that makes enemies."

"Most of her targets were men who didn't wish to risk the scandal of having her arrested."

"She must have had a way with men. Are you sure she wasn't resorting to the same tactics here?"

"I doubt it." I thought back to a conversation with Bessie. "Neddie told Mrs. Lehr what she had been up to in New York. If she'd planned to continue her scheming, I don't think she would have admitted to it."

"Still, though . . . you said she had some kind of relationship with Ralph Noble."

"According to Mrs. Lehr, they spent at least one night together. And I discovered a bottle of expensive perfume in her dressing table that could have been a gift from him. There were other—" I'd been about to say other possible gifts in her dresser when my mind latched on to a notion. The makeshift jewelry at the bottom of her dresser . . . the discarded and forgotten flowers . . .

I went very still, my extremities tingling. Why hadn't I made the connection before?

"She had more than one beau." I'd considered the possibility before, but now I had a sense of who it might be. With a jolt, I snapped out of my thoughts. I whisked open my desk drawer, retrieved my handbag, then hurried to the door, grabbing my hat from the rack as I went.

"Where are you going?"

I didn't stop to explain.

My carriage awaited me outside. Though typically I would have brought it to one of the liveries in town, knowing I'd be leaving the *Messenger* again had prompted me to park it on the street.

I drove up to Bellevue Avenue, praying the thoroughfare wouldn't be jammed with afternoon traffic, especially when I reached the Casino. Those prayers went unanswered, and I found myself drawing on every reserve of patience I possessed as I waited for other vehicles, horse drawn and motorized alike, to drop off or pick up passengers or simply maneuver their own way through the throng. I thought I heard my name being called from somewhere in front of the Casino's entrance, but seeing no familiar face as I glanced over, I kept my hands tight on the reins and my gaze hard on the road, waiting for a space to open up that would allow me to drive through.

It took an eternity, but I finally found myself leaving the Casino property behind. The trees gathered overhead, their branches arcing from either side of the road. I passed Kingscote, resisting the impulse to urge Maestro to a canter. Bessie was in no immediate danger, I reminded myself. A police officer guarded the house, shadowing her in whatever room she entered. Her mother would surely be there as well, offering, possibly, even fiercer protection than any policeman could.

I peered in through the wrought-iron fence as I drove past The Elms, searching for Jesse's carriage. He, along with Derrick and Brady, must have already left. Gone to Portsmouth to search for Ely Forrester. Even if they found him, it would do neither Bessie nor them any good. Not if I were correct in my hunch.

I turned onto Arleigh's driveway and stopped a few yards short of the portico. At the front door, I raised the knocker and let it fall, and when nothing happened, I tried again. The clang reverberated inside, bouncing off the walls and ceiling of the hall. Should I try the latch? My fingers were wrapping around the handle when suddenly the door opened and the butler looked out.

"Mrs. Andrews . . . uh . . ." His hesitation took me aback.

"Might I come in?" I asked when it seemed we were locked in a staring contest. I started to step across the threshold, but he failed to move aside.

"I . . . uh . . . must see if Mrs. Lehr is receiving."

"Mr. Bagley, you know Mrs. Lehr will always receive me. Hasn't that been made abundantly clear these past many days?" When he continued to balk, realization dawned. Mrs. Drexel must indeed be here and had issued orders of her own. I could just hear her: *Do not let that Andrews woman in.* Well, I would not be deterred. "Bagley, I have important information for your mistress. I suggest you allow me to come in and let her know I'm here. Where is she now?"

"I . . . er . . . believe in the garden with her mother."

Taking him by surprise, I placed the flat of my hand on the partially open door and pushed it wider. At the same time, I crossed the threshold with a determined stride, forcing him to step back whether he liked it or not. "I'll wait here while you inform her of my visit. Thank you, Bagley."

"Yes, ma'am . . . I'll . . . uh . . ." He closed the door and turned on his heel, disappearing into the corridor that led to the morning room and service pantry. Needless to say, I did not wait in the hall, but made my way to the dining room, from where I could look out the French doors over the rear of the property. Would Bessie walk in the rose garden so soon after what happened to Neddie?

At first, I saw no one, but movement near the fountain drew my gaze. Only one figure revealed itself, a woman in a beige skirt with black trim along its hem. Mrs. Drexel had worn just such an outfit earlier, except that she had removed the jacket to show the shirtwaist beneath, trimmed with the same black embellishment at the collar and cuffs.

Why was she alone, especially when Bagley had just told me Bessie was with her? I pondered that question for a scant few seconds before turning about, retracing my steps into the hall, and climbing the stairs. As I went, I listened for voices. Harry's, Bessie's . . . I heard neither. At the top of the stairs, I turned hard left and strode to Bessie's bedroom door.

The first thing I noticed was that a chair no longer occupied a space beside the door, where each policeman assigned to guarding Bessie took up position at night, or whenever she spent time in her bedroom.

Why had that changed?

I flung the door open and bounded inside. The room was empty.

Back downstairs, with no Bessie awaiting me in the hall, I went through each room: the small parlor, drawing room, morning room, wherever she was likely to be. Neither she nor Harry appeared to be anywhere in the house. Not the public rooms, at least. As I doubled back into the hall, Bagley was just entering, followed by an annoyed-looking Mrs. Drexel.

"Mrs. Andrews, I thought we understood one another. I must insist—"

"Where is Bessie?" I went to stand directly before her. That she found this disconcerting was plain in how she stepped abruptly back.

"My daughter has gone upstairs for a parasol, not that it's any business of yours."

"No, she hasn't. She's not there, I just checked. Where else might she be?"

"I . . ." She trailed off as her features realigned into a look of perplexity.

"Mrs. Drexel, think. Where might she be? And where is the policeman assigned to guard her? His chair is no longer outside her room. Why is that?"

Her irritation with me returned, flickering in her eyes. "You should have been frank with me earlier, Mrs. Andrews. You should have told me everything. But I'm here now and I'll protect my daughter, if indeed protection is needed. I sent the policeman away."

"You did *what*?" Of their own accord, my hands went to the sides of my head, and I only just refrained from tugging at my hair. But Mrs. Drexel's ill-advised actions were beside the point. We had to find Bessie. To Bagley, I said, "Search the house. And telephone for the police." Then I gave him further, quite explicit instructions.

He looked aghast. "Are you certain? *Quite* certain?"

"I am, yes," I said, sounding perhaps more convinced than I felt. I was acting on a hunch. But a strong one.

Clearly astounded, he appealed to Mrs. Drexel. "Ma'am?"

The woman scrutinized me for an instant before nodding. "Do as she says."

As Bagley turned to go, I demanded of Mrs. Drexel, "Where is Harry?"

"He's gone out. I don't know where."

The significance of the silence upstairs and all through the first-floor rooms suddenly struck me. "Where is Hippodale? Did Harry take him, or was he outside with you?"

"He was with us. Bessie took him with her when she went inside. She carries that dog everywhere. Oh, I know." She let go a relieved chuckle. "Perhaps she's taken him for a walk.

They could be strolling along the avenue as we speak. And all this ado for nothing."

I was shaking my head before she'd completed her suggestion. "Leave the property without telling anyone? Bessie wouldn't do that." No, Bessie wouldn't, but she very well might go anywhere, do anything, if someone threatened to harm Hippodale.

The truth of my assertion wiped the relief from Mrs. Drexel's face. She pressed her fingertips to her lips. "Good heavens, where could she be?"

At the sound of footsteps, we both turned toward the entrance to the small corridor.

"Bessie, dear, is that you?" Mrs. Drexel called out.

It was the housekeeper, Mrs. Fisk. She approached us calmly, her hands folded at her waist, but I detected the tension in the clenching of her fingers. "Mr. Bagley has reported that Mrs. Lehr is nowhere to be found. May I suggest a search of the attic—"

"*The attic?*" Mrs. Drexel interrupted. "Don't be daft, woman. Why would my daughter go up there?"

Mrs. Fisk's composure didn't slip. "If you'll excuse me, madam, Mrs. Lehr expressed to me her intention of searching for more of Miss Thorton's personal effects. She said Miss Thorton stored some things in the attic when they first arrived for the Season, and that she now wished to retrieve them and see what might be sent to her family and what given away to charity. She decided last night that she'll pay the expense of having the body transported home for burial."

"She mentioned nothing about this to me," her mother said, a hand on her hip.

Mrs. Fisk ignored the woman's admonishing tone. "The attic is rather extensive, a warren of rooms. I'll go up with

Clara. Our other housemaid is off for the rest of the day and has left the property."

"Search *everywhere.* Even places you think a person couldn't be," I instructed the woman. "And remember, she might not be able to respond to your calls." I saw the questions in her eyes, but Mrs. Fisk merely nodded. As she left us, her steps taking on a new urgency, I turned to Mrs. Drexel. "Stay here in case Bessie turns up." Then I hurried away, back up the stairs, leaving the questions she called after me unanswered.

I returned to Bessie's room. Had there been a struggle? Had she been forced at knifepoint, as Ralph Noble had? Nothing in the room pointed to a scuffle. Had she even made it this far before being sent on a detour? I went into her dressing room and began opening doors. In one, several parasols stood on end, off to one side. I counted five in all. They didn't look as if they had been disturbed.

In the main room, I again looked for any sign that Bessie had been taken against her will. Had she left any clue as to what happened to her? Only an utter stillness answered my questions.

I decided I'd wasted enough time and went back into the hallway, where I stopped to listen. No footsteps, no voices. The attic rooms were two floors above me. If they were being searched, I couldn't expect to hear the activity from here. Another door filled my vision. At the end of the hallway, just feet beyond Harry's office, stood the entrance into the second-floor service corridor. I hurried to it.

I had passed through this door the day I'd searched Harry's office—and been intercepted before I'd gotten very far. I hurried through now, went to the end, and turned the same corner as then. There was no one in sight, only the doorways into the sewing room, linen room, and the back staircase.

Up or down? I stood poised on the landing and heard the faint echoes of voices coming from the attic. But the third floor lay in between. Which way should I go?

Bessie and I had been intercepted another time, outside Neddie Thorton's bedroom on the third floor. I remembered the rustic jewelry. The flowers.

Those forgotten flowers, left to wilt on a chair. Bessie had retrieved them, then handed them off. *Please see that these are properly disposed of.*

The memory thrust my wildly beating heart into my throat. Which of them had been the intended victim? I suddenly believed I knew. Not one or the other.

Both.

Gripping the banister, I hauled myself onto the second step and took the rest two at a time.

Chapter 19

Even as I reached Neddie's room, I knew I wouldn't find Bessie inside. Still, I threw the door open.

An overwhelming flowery scent enveloped me, so strong and sharp my eyes teared and my nose began to run. I pressed my sleeve to my nose and mouth and took a step inside. There, on the floor in front of the dressing table, lay the shards of a crystal bottle in a pool of liquid. The stopper had rolled across the uneven floorboards, leaving a trail of Houbigant perfume in its wake. I stared down at it for several seconds as I comprehended the magnitude of the anger that could prompt an individual to behave in such a manner.

Had Bessie been here when it happened? I didn't think so. No, I believed this person had come here to . . . to mourn Neddie, perhaps? To regret her death? To imagine life as it might have been if Neddie had been a different sort of woman? Or to fantasize that she was still alive and happy to welcome her visitor?

But reality had come crashing down and Neddie's would-be suitor snapped; had become as enveloped in his fury as I had been just now in the wreckage of Neddie's expensive perfume.

Once again, I hurried along the corridor and back to the staircase. Down I went, meeting no one along the way. Where were they all? But as I passed a window, I saw the butler and head footman out on the rear lawn. They had decided to search for her outside. I heard them shouting, "Mrs. Lehr! Mrs. Lehr!" I stopped long enough to watch their progress to the base of the lawn, where the tall hedges separated the property from Clay Street.

Could she have been forced from the house in broad daylight? If so, to where? Clay Street ran north and south, with no clear path to the Cliff Walk without first walking up to Narragansett Avenue. Too long a walk, surely, to force an unwilling victim. Where then? Perhaps to the empty patch of land between Clay Street and Annandale Road, where she might be disposed of behind some trees, or in a dip in the land?

I continued down to the kitchen area. Here, the cook and her assistant were also calling out Mrs. Lehr's name, and I heard one of them say, "That's everywhere, and she isn't here."

"Are you sure?" I reached the bottom of the stairs and found the two women conferring in the kitchen. "Are you certain you've checked everywhere, even in the most unlikely of places?"

"We even checked the small storage cupboards," the cook said, "where a person would have to crawl to get inside. She isn't here."

I thought a moment. "Is there a subbasement beneath this floor?"

"We checked down there, too," the assistant said. "Called out at the top of our lungs." Both women nodded as if that settled the matter.

What if Bessie isn't able to answer? "From where is it accessed? And what's down there?"

The cook tucked her thumbs into the waistband of her apron. "The laundry facilities, although they're not used anymore. The Lehrs send most of their laundry out. There's also the ice storage room. And the wine cellar. But that's kept locked, so she couldn't be in there."

I barely heard that last assertion. The wine cellar. I remembered something significant about it, something that had me asking, more urgently, "How do I get down there?"

The cook and her assistant let out sighs of resignation, as if I were a pesky houseguest they were forced to humor. The cook said, "Come, I'll show you."

She led me past the kitchen and servants' hall and down a couple of steps. Here the corridor became far more rustic than previously, with stone flooring and cement walls, rather than tiles and paneling. We passed several doors.

I pointed to them. "What are these?"

"The larders, for cold storage. We checked them, I promise. Even though we knew Mrs. Lehr wouldn't be inside. And she was not."

At the end of the corridor, the woman opened yet another door. Cement steps descended into darkness, until she reached in and turned a switch. The dull wattage of a bulb hanging overhead cast an orange glow.

"The laundry, the ice storage room, and wine cellar are down there," she said. The corners of her mouth turned down. "Do you want me to go with you?"

"No, I want you to go upstairs and see if the police have arrived. If so, tell them where I am. If not, let Mrs. Drexel know I've gone down."

"I doubt you'll be gone long. Probably back up before I reach the first floor. There's nothing down there." When I showed no sign of relenting, she shrugged. "There's another light switch at the bottom of the stairs, though the bulbs barely give off any light. Go right for the laundry, left for the ice room and wine cellar." She reached beneath her apron to a pocket in her dress. She drew out a key and handed it to me. "This is for the wine cellar. Mrs. Fisk gave it to me when she asked me to search for Mrs. Lehr."

"Is this the only key?"

"No, there are two others. But Mr. Bagley has those."

Did he? I wondered how securely the keys were kept and if someone might have stolen one. I thanked her and started down, feeling the temperature drop the deeper I went. At the bottom, a damp chill permeated the air and raised chills on my arms and down my back. As I had done previously, I listened, ears pricked. As then, I heard nothing.

I turned left, to the wine cellar. The key slid into the lock with the well-oiled precision of frequent use, reminding me that Harry often sent his footmen down here multiple times during the course of a night.

Had anyone inside heard me? I listened with my ear to the door; with my fingertips, I felt for vibrations. Would signs of life penetrate the heavy pine planking? It seemed doubtful, but even so, upon hearing nothing, I carefully pressed the latch and pushed inward, just enough to peer in with one eye.

The silence continued. Detecting no movement, no breathing, I pushed the door wider and took a step inside. The chill in this room deepened. Shelving, much like bookcases, lined the walls, extending well above my head. But instead of books, innumerable bottles reclined on their sides, corks facing out, each resting in its own half circle carved into a lip that lined the front of the shelves. I didn't bother searching for a light switch, and the bottles glinted in the pallid light from the hallway. Of Bessie, I saw no sign. My hopes plummeted. Where could she be?

With a rising sense of panic that I had been wrong, and

Bessie would not be found in time, I hurried back past the staircase and reached the double doors that led into the laundry. They opened readily into a vast darkness. I walked in a step or two, felt beside the doors, first on one side, then the other, and found the switch. Several overhead bulbs groaned their way to an anemic glow, illuminating a row of sinks on one wall, abandoned drying racks, and a large vat, lined in copper, in the middle of the space.

"Bessie, are you here?" I didn't expect an answer. Rather, I made my way to the vat, braced myself, and leaned over, afraid of what I might see. Had the cook and her assistant done more than call their mistress's name? Would they have known if she lay at the bottom, unconscious . . . or dead?

The paltry light revealed only the floor of the tub. I breathed out a sigh of relief. Even so, I checked the corners of the room, opened cabinets, and peered beneath worktables until I was satisfied my friend wasn't here.

In the hallway, I checked for other doors, ones the cook might not have thought to inform me of. But there were none, so I traversed its length once more, to the other side of the stairs, to the ice room.

As the cook had said, the door was unlocked. Inside the room, the walls consisted of smooth stone. Blocks of ice, harvested during the winter, rested on wooden shelves and were tightly packed with straw and sawdust. The room sat against an outer wall of the house. An air shaft near the ceiling, which prevented the accumulation of moisture, must have led outside. A dry and relentless cold wrapped itself around me, and I shivered at the thought that a human being wouldn't last long trapped in such a place.

I left and closed the door behind me, then merely stood with my arms wrapped around myself, with a sense of defeat. "Bessie, where are you?" I whispered urgently. One notion, a memory, continued to tug. Surely, its significance could not mean nothing. My gaze crossed the corridor and landed once again on the door to the wine cellar. But how could she be inside? I'd detected no hiding places, just an open space lined with shelves. Still, I stepped toward it again, but halted at the sight of tools hanging from nails on the wall beside the ice room: a straight pick, a curved hook—both with lethally sharp tips—and a pair of tongs with equally sharpened points.

Without quite forming a purpose, I grabbed the latter down from its nail, tested the weight in my hands, opened and closed them, and decided to carry them with me. I had no clear idea how I might use them to defend myself, other than as a heavy implement with which to thrash my opponent if necessary.

That is, if I found him.

Shifting the tongs to one hand, I opened the wine cellar door. This time, I walked all the way inside until I stood in the center of the room. I slowly turned to view its entirety. Was there a cabinet? Another doorway? Gazing up, I saw no light fixture and realized I should have brought a lantern. With only the light from the corridor to guide me, I went closer to the far wall.

A faint, flowery scent tickled my nose. It was nothing compared to the overwhelming, cloying aroma of the shattered bottle of Houbigant in Neddie Thorton's room. And yet . . .

I drew in a long breath, attempting to separate the aroma from the room's other smells: the wood of the wine racks and the slightly musty odor particular to all cellars. Yes. When the bottle splintered, the perfume must have splashed, sending droplets onto whatever—whoever—stood nearby.

They had been in this room—I was sure of it now. And not very long ago. But where had they gone? Logic told me to search elsewhere, but I lingered, held by some elusive, prescient instinct. I hesitated . . . and then I heard a sound that propelled my heart into my throat.

A distant, muffled bark—or had I only imagined it, conjured by my desperate hopes? It came again, the high-pitched bark of a small dog. My breath suspended, I waited, hoping for another, praying for the little papillon to call out to me again. When he didn't, I began to examine the room more closely. After setting down the tongs, I went wall by wall, running my hands over the shelving. I'd gone halfway around when a sharp pain pierced my left palm. I snatched my hand away to discover a bleeding gash.

I ignored the pain and wiped the blood on my skirt. Had I swept my hand across a broken bottle? I examined the shelf, found the smeared evidence left by my wound, but no shattered glass. Rather, to my astonishment, I discovered a hinge. A large one, half hidden by the darkness and the fact that the metal had been painted over to match the wood of the shelves. Upon further examination, I discovered two more, one above me and one close to the floor. Someone had intentionally concealed them from casual view.

A door? I stood back to study the contraption, then moved to the other side of the case. Here I found, hidden in a recess in the wood, a vertical bolt that, when secured, would prevent the case from moving. The bolt had been left unsecured, and the recess also provided a handgrip. I placed my fingers in it and pulled. Like a door, the case of shelves eased away from the wall. Except there was no wall behind it. There was an opening.

I retrieved the ice tongs. With only inches to spare on either side of me, I squeezed through and found myself in a narrow corridor. Or perhaps *tunnel* was the more precise word, with walls and a floor of uneven stone. In the wine cellar, I had relied on the scant light from the corridor. Now I no longer had even that. As the fear of becoming trapped, buried alive, closed around me, my heart pounded like the beats of a bass drum in my ears. I reached out my hands to either side and pressed them to the walls. I had negotiated a tunnel years before, at Fort Adams, where I'd thought I had become lost—impossibly, irretrievably lost.

But in the end, I had found my way. And I would today, with the walls to guide me. I had only to follow the walls, to put my trust in them.

I hadn't proceeded many yards before I began to surmise where this tunnel might lead—to Clay Street behind Arleigh's property. A suspicion took hold. When the bees attacked Neddie Thorton and the servants came running outside, one of them had been missing. Had the culprit used this tunnel to gain access to the neighbors' property without being seen? Had he—

Voices, somewhere up ahead, sent my thoughts scattering. Rising on my toes to make as little sound as possible, I hurried along as best I could in the utter darkness and the roughness of the stones beneath my feet. Soon a weak shaft of light guided my way. Up ahead, I could see that the walls curved slightly to the right. I slowed my steps, realizing whoever was up there wasn't far away now.

The voices became louder. Bessie's and her young footman's.

"Keep going, missus, or I'll hurt him. I promise I will."

"All right. But let him go. He's just an innocent dog."

A cruel laugh bounced along the walls. "You love this dog more than you love anyone else on this earth. Your husband is right. You're a cold and heartless woman."

"You may say anything you like about me. Only don't hurt Hippodale. Hand him back to me. He's never done you any harm."

"No, but I'd enjoy seeing you lose something you love, the way I lost what I loved—because of you."

"I never told Neddie not to love you."

"You didn't have to. You turned her head with notions that she was as good as her betters, that she deserved the finer things in life. Things a footman couldn't give her. You pushed her into that other man's arms. That Noble character. So unworthy of a woman like Neddie. It sickens me to think of his hands on her."

"I certainly didn't want Neddie with him. She made up her own mind. Surely, you must realize that."

"All I realize is that she rejected every honest overture I ever made. I'd have married her, taken care of her. But she threw my regard back in my face. Because she wanted to be like you. And because you treated her like an equal, she believed she *could* be like you."

"Please, Asa . . . couldn't we go back upstairs and talk this over? I could help you. I could make sure you lived comfortably for the rest of your life. You could have any woman you—"

"Shut up. We're almost there."

Bessie's voice dropped to a shaky whisper. "Where?"

"You'll see."

Had I not been there, I knew that wherever Asa Fullerman took Bessie, she—her body—would not be found for a very long time. *If ever.* I doubted anyone else in the household knew of the door in the wine cellar. Only Asa, whom Harry had sent down so often he'd discovered the room's secrets. The house's original owner died before the completion of the construction, leaving it to her daughter, Florence Pratt. Mrs. Pratt and her husband had never lived here, and might not have known the tunnel existed. I wondered if perhaps the passage had even preexisted the house, part of a homestead established early in Newport's history, the house long gone from memory.

All I knew was that being left down here was akin to

being buried in an unmarked grave. I wasn't about to let that happen.

Once again, I tested the weight of the tongs in my hands. Could I manage to swing them in the air and bring them down on Asa Fullerman's head? The thought sickened me, but the man had already murdered three people, two of them in the most hideous, painful manner. And now he held Bessie's beloved Hippodale in his arms.

I would need an element of surprise. None of them—not Asa, Bessie, or even Hippodale—must know of my presence until I was ready to strike. Especially Hippodale, who might discern my presence well before the others and give me away.

That meant I had to maintain a safe distance and be utterly silent.

"Keep moving," Asa ordered. "Do you think I don't notice how you're trying to stall? Do you think someone is coming to save you?"

"It's dark. It's hard to move any faster."

The light coming from around the tunnel's curve brightened slightly. "There, I'm holding the lantern higher. But now I have to hold your beloved mutt in one arm, tighter than is comfortable for him. Can't you hear him whining?"

I heard him. Faintly. Breathy little squeals that indicated Hippodale's discomfort and his confusion that someone who had always been kind to him should be so unaccommodating now. My anger surged. Ire scorched my cheeks and fingertips and turned each breath I drew into a dagger point.

I heard, too, Bessie's pleas. "He trusts you. Besides my husband and me, you're the only person in this house he'll let handle him. Please don't betray that trust now. Let me hold the lantern so you'll have both arms free."

"And let you hit me with it?"

"I wouldn't . . ."

"Of course you would. Now walk!"

Was he taking her to the end of the tunnel? She would never make it out to the other side—that, I knew for certain. No, he would dispatch her possibly within feet of the entrance and then make his own way out, with or without Hippodale. My instincts told me he would not harm the dog unless he felt it absolutely necessary. I suddenly understood something Bessie had told me days ago, that no one but one of their footmen could bathe Hippodale. I now realized the identity of that footman: Asa Fullerman.

The night I was accosted outside our barn, my attacker hadn't hurt Patch. Asa Fullerman apparently had a fondness for dogs, perhaps for all animals, and I guessed he would take Hippodale to safety and concoct a story of finding him somewhere near the cliffs. Of Bessie, he would claim, there had been no sign . . .

I stole a glance over my shoulder in the hopes that help had followed me. That the police had arrived at Arleigh, had been directed to find me down in the subbasement, and had discovered the door in the wine cellar that I had left ajar. Surely, they had arrived by now. Surely, Jesse and Derrick . . .

No, they were in Portsmouth on a useless errand to apprehend Ely Forrester. Help might not be coming anytime soon. It was up to me to act, and soon.

What kind of weapon would he have brought? A knife made the most sense. But if he was holding a lantern and Hippodale, that knife must be in a pocket. I crept farther forward until I reached the curve. Now I could see them some yards ahead of me. Bessie walked first, with Asa close behind her. She looked back at them frequently, as if afraid of taking her eyes off her beloved pet. With both of his hands engaged, Asa would be hard-pressed to fend off an attack from behind. What would happen to Hippodale? I had no choice but to find out.

Drawing a breath deep into my lungs, I bolted toward them. Bessie turned at the sound of my footsteps, her face filled with alarm. To take Asa off guard, I screamed as I ran, the sound filling the tunnel, reverberating tenfold in volume. Asa turned, but I was already upon him. Before he fully faced me, I raised the tongs and brought them down, hard.

In the instant before contact, I involuntarily shut my eyes. When I opened them an instant later, I saw that I had struck his shoulder. His expression registered pain, coupled by a murderous fury, but the blow had rendered him so off-balance his arms had fallen to his sides. The lantern clanged to the ground and fell over, the flame fluttering and struggling to stay lit. Hippodale scrambled away from his captor, his little feet slipping over the stones of the floor. Bessie cried out his name as she bent and scooped him up.

Asa Fullerman blocked Bessie's escape. He raised his good arm, the one I hadn't struck, and his hand went to his coat pocket. Guessing what would happen next, I swung the tongs again, this time blindly as the lantern flame sputtered and we were plunged into inky darkness.

Chapter 20

Asa's outcry died as a gurgle in his throat, followed by the thump of his body hitting the floor.

"Emma? What just happened? Where are you?"

Having no desire to trip over Asa, I stretched out my arms above where I judged him to be. In the narrow tunnel, he likely lay from one wall to the other. "Take my hand. Do you have Hippodale?"

Bessie's sob echoed around us. "I do. I think he's all right."

His panting reached my ears. "Good. Reach toward me." I felt the graze of her fingertips against my own. Then she clutched my hand. "Hang on tight," I told her. "You'll have to step over Asa."

"I can't see anything."

"I know. Shuffle forward until you feel him. Then take a big step over him. I'll steady you."

"All right . . . yes . . . Oh! Here he is." Her hand tightened around mine. Letting the tongs drop, I braced myself as she used my arm for leverage by pressing my other hand against the wall beside me. Our skirts brushed as first one foot, and then the other, made its way over the fallen footman, until Bessie stood at my side. She released my hand. Hippodale whimpered.

"We'd better go quickly," I urged in a whisper. "We have no idea how long he'll be unconscious." I wondered, but didn't muse aloud, whether he would wake up at all. How hard had I struck him?

A moan brought an answer, both welcome and alarming.

"Come!" I turned and started walking as quickly as the darkness would allow, once again running a hand along the wall to guide me. I'd taken several steps when I realized Bessie wasn't behind me. I stopped and hissed out her name.

"But I can't see. I'm afraid I'll fall and hurt Hippodale."

Hippodale, with his canine vision, could probably find his own way out easily enough on his own. But telling her so would be of no help. I retraced my steps until I could clasp her hand.

"What happened . . . ?"

Bessie gasped at the sound of Asa's groggy question. Without a word, I reached out, grasped her hand, and tugged her along. We hurried back toward the wine cellar as fast as I dared. The going was precarious, with both of us stumbling, and Bessie often bumping up against my back and threatening to knock us both off our feet. Hippodale, unused to such frenzied treatment, began to bark, and none of Bessie's shushes would quiet him.

"Please, Hippodale, you'll give us away," she pleaded. But the papillon could bark all he wanted. Asa knew exactly where we were, and that we could not escape his pursuit until we reached the cellar. Our success hinged solely on whether or not he was able to follow us.

And follow us, he did. I could hear him blundering along behind us, his feet dragging laboriously. The blows I'd struck him had apparently left him dazed and clumsy, but for how much longer?

We eased around the curve in the tunnel and maintained the straight course toward the entrance to the wine cellar. The faintest hint of light promised refuge up ahead. Would Bessie and I make it to safety and be able to close the secret door before Asa reached it?

I had left him a second weapon, the tongs, in addition to whatever he had with him. Had he realized? Did he have them?

His voice came at us as a roar. Bessie cried out and Hippodale's barks surrounded us as they echoed off the walls and ceiling and floor. I kept Bessie moving, almost running. Though I knew better, I kept glancing over my shoulder to see if I could catch a glimpse of Asa against the blackness of the tunnel. He moved faster now, footsteps a sharp staccato in counterpoint to Hippodale's barking.

We were close to the entrance now, so close to safety. "Bessie, we're almost through."

In that moment, I again looked back over my shoulder—and ran smack into something.

Someone.

Had he somehow gotten ahead of us? Knew of another passage? I released Bessie's hand and beat my fists against anything they could find. I heard a voice—a deep, rumbling voice. It called my name, told me to stop, but I didn't. I kept striking, punching, as hard as I possibly could.

And then Bessie's voice blended with the other, telling me to stop, that it was all right. Hippodale yipped loudly, as if to drive the point home. Gradually I did stop as realization sank in. I let strong arms close round me, briefly, before one released me to reach for Bessie as well and drag us through the doorway into the wine cellar.

"Help me push it closed," Derrick urged, and I darted to

his side. Together, with Asa's footsteps loud in our ears, we shoved the door back in place. Derrick slid the bolt home.

Turning, he leaned his back against the shelving, causing bottles to clink against one another, and reached for me. I collapsed, breathless, against him and allowed myself to melt into the safety of his arms; meanwhile, behind us in the tunnel, Asa shouted thunderous curses and vowed to make us sorry. Hippodale woofed in haughty defiance.

A message had been sent to Portsmouth, to Reggie's Sandy Point, advising Jesse to return to Newport as soon as possible. Meanwhile, Derrick requested that Asa Fullerman be brought to us in the servants' hall, rather than directly to the police wagon awaiting him in the driveway.

While we waited for him to be brought in, I asked Derrick how he came to be in the wine cellar at just the right moment, even though he had been determined to go to Portsmouth with Jesse.

"It didn't feel right," he said, holding tight to my hand, "going so far from you after what happened earlier. I telephoned over to the *Messenger* from The Elms and discovered you'd already departed. I assumed you went home, and Ned Berwind offered me the use of their carriage to follow you there. But when I went outside, I saw our carriage here in the driveway. And so here I came."

With Bessie safely back upstairs, being tended to by her mother, I felt able to speak with candor. "It's a good thing you did. I don't know that I could have secured the door before Asa reached it, and I'm quite sure I couldn't have held it closed with him pushing against it from the other side."

"A good thing, too, that you left that door open, or I might have looked in, seen no one, and gone to search elsewhere."

"When I think of what might have happened . . ." I shuddered at Bessie's and my narrow escape.

"You did slow him down considerably," Derrick reminded me with a grin. "A lesson to me not to leave the ice tongs lying around where you might find them." We laughed at that, but then I sobered.

"It was all him. All Asa. The sabotage of the motorcars—ours and Bessie's—the tampering with the balcony railing and the stair runner, and then the fire, the bees, my being attacked outside the barn—all of it. It was as if he could be several places at once, but now that I know of the existence of the tunnel, I believe he's been using it all along to leave the house without being seen. What do you suppose it was for?"

"Seeing as Bessie knew nothing about it, that passage hasn't been used in a very long time. Not like the Berwinds' coal tunnel at The Elms."

"I think perhaps another house once sat on this property, long ago."

"Very possible, especially considering how many houses were burned by the British. There may be records of it, although much of those were burned, too." Derrick lifted my hand, turned it to study my palm, then brought it to his lips. "It could even have been part of a series of tunnels, leading to the cliffs."

"Yes, for smuggling, perhaps." I had read about such activities in Newport's history. There were many such tunnels leading from town and private homes to the water's edge, but their purposes could only be surmised now. "It might have been used during the Revolution as a way to elude the British."

"Perhaps."

At that moment, we heard footsteps, two pairs that stepped briskly, another that shuffled to keep up. The two police officers turned into the room, propelling a scowling Asa

Fullerman between them, his hands shackled behind his back.

Had I ever considered him an amiable-looking young man? Now I only saw the sinister intentions, the complete disregard for the lives of others. Unable to possess Neddie Thorton, he determined no one else would, and he hadn't cared whom he harmed in the process.

Derrick came to his feet. "Do you have anything to say for yourself?"

Asa's scowl darkened, and he snarled out a threat. "You better hope they lock me up tight, or you and yours will never be safe."

The words send a chill through me, my thoughts turning immediately to Annamarie. Derrick's hands curled to fists, but he didn't lift them. His jaw tightened, beaded with tension, but he held his temper in check. "Know that I will use every shred of influence I and my family possess to ensure you never see the light of day again. Not that you have many days left to you, my boy. It's all but certain what your sentence will be."

"I'm no *boy,*" the footman growled in response.

That almost drew a laugh from me—that out of everything Derrick had just said, it was the insult of being called a boy that most riled him. I came to my feet. I might already have known the answers, but I wanted to hear them from him. "You attacked me outside our barn that night. Why? I didn't suspect you. In fact, I'd just returned from Portsmouth in search of another suspect, someone who had far more reason than you to wish Mrs. Lehr harm."

"Mrs. Lehr." Asa seethed. "This is her fault—all of it. She turned Neddie's head, gave her grand ideas. She's persuasive and relentless, and I knew she'd urge you, on and on, until you finally found your way to me."

I couldn't help a small smile. "I did, didn't I? It came together for me only today, the clues and loose threads. The jewelry, the flowers . . . and you turning up in places in this house you shouldn't have been. I came here today convinced it was you, and if anything persuaded me of the fact, it was the broken bottle of perfume in Neddie's room. It made you so angry, you smashed it."

"Neddie didn't need gifts from that reprobate. What she needed, I would have given her."

I remembered about the makeshift jewelry and cast a glance at one of the policemen. "Did you search his pockets?" At his nod, I asked, "And what did you find?"

He reached into his own coat pocket and drew out exactly what I expected to see: a ring woven from hair and a bracelet made of hand-carved beads. Studying the familiar pieces that lay in his palm, I could only shake my head. A small silence fell, until Derrick spoke again.

"You couldn't give her what she needed, could you, Asa?" Derrick caught the young man's gaze and held it. "Because now she's dead. You killed her."

"Did I?" His tone mocked. "Or was it the bees?"

"Bees you enraged by tossing pepper on their hives," I challenged him. When he opened his mouth to counter me, I shook my head. "I wonder . . . perhaps you didn't mean for her to die. Perhaps you only meant to teach her a lesson, make her feel pain—as you were feeling. But you didn't realize so many stings could kill. Is that it, Asa? Was Neddie's death a mistake?"

His mouth opened upon ahowl of fury, and before the officers could react, Asa broke out of their grips and charged forward. He came like an animal blinded by bloodlust. I instinctively lurched backward, and Derrick stepped between us, his arms out to either side to shield me. But with his hands restrained behind him, Asa had little control over his footing. He stumbled, his right foot tangling in the legs of a chair. It toppled and so did he, falling hard to the floor, face-first.

Derrick stood over him. "That's the last time you'll ever threaten anyone." To the officers, he simply said, "Get him out of here."

They seemed only too happy to oblige, dragging him back onto his feet and propelling him out the way they had come. I assumed they took him out through the service entrance and away to Marlborough Street.

Derrick and I stood for some moments, our arms around each other.

"Are you all right?" he murmured into my hair.

I tipped my face to look up at him and, from somewhere, found a smile. "No, but I will be soon enough. Let's go up and see how Bessie is doing."

Reluctance filled his eyes, but he didn't protest. I'm certain he wished nothing more than to get me home, but he took my hand and together we climbed the stairs to the main part of the house.

We found Bessie, not in the small parlor, which had been her favorite room, but in the morning room. She and her mother sat together at the table. Mrs. Fisk had supplied them with tea. They both looked up as we entered the room.

"It seems I owe you an apology, Mrs. Andrews," her mother said, but I waved the notion away.

"No one owes me anything. I'm just glad Asa Fullerman will never hurt anyone again."

Bessie beckoned us to sit at the table, and once we'd settled, she said, "I don't know that I can ever sit in the small parlor again . . . not with the memory of Neddie still so pervasive in there."

"Give it time," I told her.

She shrugged noncommittally. "Did you learn anything more from him?"

As we had left the wine cellar earlier, leaving the arriving officers to deal with the footman, Bessie had unequivocally stated her desire to never set eyes on Asa Fullerman again. I completely understood her sentiments, just as I understood her wish now to know if we had gained any insight into the horrors he had committed.

I shook my head sadly. "Nothing we didn't already know or guess. Except that he truly didn't mean to kill Neddie. He wanted to punish her, yes, but he didn't understand the effect hundreds of bees could have on the human body."

Staring down into her teacup, Bessie didn't say anything for a moment. When she lifted her face to us, her expression was grave. "But he did mean to kill me."

"Bessie, don't say such things." Her mother placed a hand over her daughter's. "He is a deranged individual. Even he probably doesn't know what he wants."

"No, Mother," Bessie replied firmly. "He meant to take me to the end of the tunnel, kill me, and leave me there. There's no use pretending otherwise. He hated me and he wanted me dead—"

Before her mother could protest again, I broke in. "Whatever Asa's intentions, everyone within his reach faced danger, whether they knew it or not. But he's gone now and will never return."

Bessie drew a deep breath and released it as a sigh. Her aristocratic features were careworn. Suddenly I realized she wasn't necessarily continuing to fret over Asa, but over Harry and *his* intentions. No, I didn't believe Harry Lehr would ever attempt to take Bessie's life, but he very much had the power to prevent her life from ever being happy. Why he would want such a thing, I still didn't quite understand. I wondered if Bessie understood it fully, or if she had merely come to accept what was.

With promises that Bessie and I would see each other

soon, Derrick and I left for home. Once there, we settled on the parlor rug with Annamarie and spent the next hour or so cuddling and playing with our child. It's said parents chase away their children's fears, but that day, it was quite the opposite, with Annamarie's dear face and chubby hands smoothing away our cares and helping us feel renewed.

Not many days later, just as we had reestablished the normal rhythm of our lives, a letter arrived. Katie placed the small stack of morning post between Derrick's and my places on the morning room table, along with the variety of newspapers we perused each day. It was just the two of us, as Nanny had Annamarie in her feeding chair in the kitchen and Katie had already eaten.

I picked up the letters and thumbed through, separating out those addressed to him from those addressed to me. Halfway through, I came upon one that made me pause. It was addressed to Derrick from our attorney in Providence. While it could have been a matter that pertained to my husband only, that had been rarely the case since our marriage. We conducted the greater share of our affairs jointly, yet the office insisted on addressing all correspondence to Derrick alone. As if I didn't exist. Or couldn't read. Or was too dimwitted to understand.

I thrust it at him as he sipped his coffee. "Here," I said peevishly, "it's for you."

He peeked over at it. "From Robert Harwood, I see."

"Yes, addressed exclusively to you. As usual." I slapped the letter on the table in front of him. As if the omission were his fault.

He gazed up at me, compressing his lips to hide the smile struggling to break free.

I relented with a sigh. "Sorry. I know, it's the way of the world. It's just so vexing."

His reply was to pick up the envelope and letter opener Katie had also left on the table. He took his time reading, his eyes widening and his brows quirking dramatically, until I reached over to snatch the letter from his hands. This had him laughing, and I soon joined in. But as I laughed, I perused the lines. And went silent as my mouth dropped open.

"Well?" my husband prompted.

I let out a cry of happiness. "I can't believe it. Finally!" With that, we both jumped up from our seats and tossed our arms around each other. Our laughter continued, loud enough to bring Nanny hurrying in, one arm around Annamarie, who straddled her hip.

"Land sakes, what's gotten into you two?"

Derrick held out the letter as if that explained all. Which it did. "It's happening, Nanny. The sale of the property next door is finally underway."

"There are no more obstacles," I added, doing a little pirouette in my happiness and relief. "Our dream of a school will finally become a reality."

"That's wonderful!" She looked down at Annamarie. "Do you hear that, baby girl? Your mama and papa are going to build you a school."

"No, not quite," I corrected her. "We're going to build a new home for all of us and use Gull Manor for the school."

Suddenly we all three went still. Katie, with Patch trotting in behind her, strolled in to see what the fuss was about. By the time she reached us, a dead quiet had descended on the morning room.

Her gaze darted from one to the other of us. "Is somethin' wrong?"

Derrick and I regarded each other, before our gazes converged on Annamarie. Nanny stood with her lips pursed, her head tilted as if she had only just solved a tricky puzzle and waited to see if we would do the same.

"But . . . we have no ballroom here," I murmured.

"And no drawing room," Derrick added, raising a hand to his chin. "Only the parlor."

"Which is far too small for any significant company." I looked about the room where, years ago, my great-aunt Sadie and I used to plan our mornings together over breakfast, where she had encouraged me to start writing articles and submitting them to the local papers. Here, now, Derrick and I mapped out our days over coffee and eggs; and at night when we arrived home, it was in our inadequate parlor that we relaxed and played with our little girl. Why, she had taken her very first step in that room . . .

"Derrick," I whispered, feeling bemused, "I think . . ."

"We need to build a school next door, because Gull Manor is home," he finished for me, looking equally befuddled.

"Thank goodness that's settled," Nanny said with a dramatic sigh. "A grander house—is that really what either of you want?"

Derrick and I shook our heads simultaneously. "If we wanted that," I admitted, "we could have had it long before now."

My husband nodded as he reached an arm around me. "Would we even want the ability to entertain some two hundred people at a time?"

"I certainly do not," I replied, slipping an arm around him as well.

"Me neither. I much prefer socializing on a quieter scale." He planted a kiss in my hair. "Nanny's right. It's settled. A new school next door, and this old home for us."

We sealed it with a kiss—a proper one—effectively sending Katie scurrying back to the kitchen. Nanny sat with Annamarie at the table, while Derrick and I resumed our breakfast. The three of us spoke of a few changes we'd like to make to Gull Manor. A new rug and sofa for the parlor, a new sink in the kitchen, an upgrade to the coal furnace in the cellar. Electricity? We all shrugged at the suggestion and continued our breakfast.

Halfway through my plate of fluffy scrambled eggs and fruit, I realized some of the mail still lay unopened. I retrieved the next on the pile.

I frowned in puzzlement. "This must be a joke. It's addressed to Patch."

"Patch? Let me see that." Derrick reached for the missive. Patch ambled over from where he had been lying in a patch of sun near the window, the sound of his name having woken him from his half slumber. Derrick read the address and then glanced down at our mutt, who stood waiting to find out why he'd been summoned. "Seems you've got friends, boy."

Our spaniel mix opened his mouth, his tongue lolling out. I took back the envelope and used the opener to tear the seal. I frowned again. "It's an invitation. For Patch. To Arleigh."

Nanny stared as if I'd lost my wits. "Patch has been invited to Arleigh?"

"That's what it says." I shrugged, baffled. "Next Tuesday afternoon at four. White-tie optional . . ." I trailed off, positive we were the recipients of a practical joke. But I soon discovered that a handwritten note from Bessie had been included. " 'You're all invited, especially your little girl, who is sure to be delighted,' she writes." I looked up. "How very odd. What do you think this could be about?"

"A birthday party for Hippodale?" Derrick gave a roll of his eyes. "With Harry Lehr, the sky's the limit. We'll just have to wait until Tuesday to find out."

When Tuesday came around, we left the *Messenger* early to go home to prepare for the Lehrs' party—or whatever it was going to be. Since it was an afternoon and not an evening affair, I wore a simple pale blue muslin dress with lace sleeves and tiny seed pearls embroidered onto the bodice, from House of Paquin. I dressed Annamarie in a darling sailor dress and matching dark blue cap, which had been a gift from Cousin Gertrude.

Then it was Patch's turn. The invitation had said white-tie optional. I was no less mystified now than I was when I'd first read the invitation. Was I truly going to subject my happy mutt to being dressed up like a doll? Surely, Bessie had meant no such thing. But I thought back to the night of the Fishes' first Harvest Festival at Crossways four years ago. They had promised an Austrian prince, but a monkey had come in his place—dressed in silk and satin. Well . . .

I removed Patch's leather collar and replaced it with one of Derrick's white silk cravats, one that had seen enough use that he needn't wear it again. For the next part, I consulted with Nanny.

She held up a hand to silence my ideas and said, "I've got just the thing."

She disappeared upstairs, where I could hear her rummaging in her sewing room. When she came downstairs, she held a piece of black velvet about two feet square, along with a length of ribbon. Poor Patch sat still while Nanny draped the velvet like a cape over his back, then attached it with some quick basting of the ribbon that scooped beneath him behind his front legs and in front of his rear legs.

Would he tolerate his costume for long? I doubted it. But for now, I praised him for his patience, gave him a thorough tummy rub, careful not to dislodge his cape, and handed him one of the jerky treats Nanny made especially for him.

With Patch thus arrayed in white tie and black evening wear, and Derrick in a sack suit and bowler, the four of us set out in the carriage for Bellevue Avenue. Annamarie, snug on my lap, pointed with her dimpled hand at dozens of fascinating sights along the way, babbling in her baby way as if holding a coherent conversation. And perhaps she was. Luckily, all she required of her clueless parents were replies of *Oh, how lovely,* and *Yes, darling, we see,* and *Isn't that wonderful?*

Mr. Bagley greeted us, along with several other newly arrived couples—and their canines—at the front door and escorted us through the house to the dining room and out through the French doors. Stretching nearly the length of the terrace was a dining table—about a foot and a half tall, laid with fine linen and china. While no utensils graced the table, each place setting included a silver bowl of water beside the plate. There were no chairs. None were needed, as each guest of honor sat comfortably on cushions spread over the terrace stones. On the table, bowls and platters were piled high with stewed livers, rice, fricassee of bones, and shredded dog biscuits. Two footmen presided—the head footman, who had been here previously, and a new one, who had taken Asa Fullerman's place.

Holding Annamarie on my hip, I glanced over at Derrick, who held Patch's leash. "What on earth?"

"I see now why they said white-tie optional," he murmured back. Indeed, each poodle, terrier, pointer, and a host of other pedigrees had been decked out similarly to Patch, although many with finer fabrics that had been tailor fitted, and a few with gems attached to their finery.

"Goggie, goggie!" Annamarie began shouting, pointing this way and that with a look of glee. Patch, meanwhile, pressed tight against my leg, clearly unsure what to make of the scene. Would all these dogs get along?

Beyond the terrace, tables and chairs of ordinary heights were set up on the lawn for the human guests. I spotted several acquaintances and waved.

"Emma, Derrick!" Bessie, elegant in red silk with a high neckline of gold-threaded lace, came hurrying over to us. "I'm so glad you could come. And hello, you." She kissed Annamarie's cheek, then bent low to pet Patch's head. "And you, sir. Welcome to the Dog's Dinner."

To look at her, beautiful in her crimson silk, with her dark hair piled high on her head and topped with a little hat and veil that matched the gown, one would never think she had feared for her life such a short time ago. Tonight her dark eyes sparkled with merriment, quite rivaling Harry's. I could see him out on the lawn, showing the group of people around him some trick he had taught Hippodale. He caught Bessie's eye, waved, and blew her a kiss. Did he mourn his friend? I hoped so, because if not, he was even more of a scoundrel than I had come to believe. Bessie responded to his gesture in kind, as though it was the most natural thing in the world. Then she turned back to us, the façade of a happy society wife fixed firmly in place.

"Did you know a group of us are forming the Newport Dog Show Association? We plan to hold Newport's first-ever dog show later in the summer. Are you interested in joining us?"

Derrick and I exchanged a glance before looking down at our mutt of dubious origins. We laughed, and so did Bessie.

"Perhaps not, then," she said, still chuckling. "Make yourselves at home and enjoy. There's a lovely dinner about to be served to the humans, and I encourage Patch to find a place at the canine table and dig in."

With that, she turned away to greet other guests, and while Patch did indeed nose his way up to the dogs' table, Derrick and I, with Annamarie, went down onto the lawn to mingle.

Aunt Alva found us before too long, holding a stout pug in her arms, its leash trailing. "Quite a hoot, isn't it?" She shook her head fondly and stroked the dog's head. "Leave it to Harry and Bessie to come up with the most original affair Newport has seen in years. They're quite a team, aren't they? I still congratulate myself, every time I look at them, on a match well made."

A match well made. The world might never know the truth about Harry and Elizabeth Lehr. Ellis Jackson, Neddie Thorton, and Ralph Noble had lost their lives, but in a sense, so had Bessie. She had lost her true self and the life she would have led, had she not been saddled with a man who cared for her not one whit. But she would put up a brave front and suffer through, smile and be gracious, and pretend to love her husband through all their years together, until one or the other died.

It was a living death, a tragedy.

That evening at home, I held my daughter longer than usual before putting her to bed, and afterward, I held my husband long into the night. And I was both joyfully and humbly grateful.

Author's Note

Arleigh is one of Newport's lost houses, having burned down under "suspicious circumstances" in 1932, shortly after being sold to a new owner. In its place now stands a modern brick structure that houses the Heatherwood Nursing Home. Originally the house was commissioned by Mary McGonigal Matthews, the mistress of Isaac Singer, founder of the Singer Sewing Machine Company. By the time the house was completed in 1894, however, she had passed away in 1893 and her daughter inherited the property. She and her husband used it only during the first year they owned it, choosing instead to lease the house to members of the Four Hundred from then on. Erected on the site of an older house, Arleigh was built in the Queen Anne style, but I've been able to learn little about the interior other than finding a sketch of the main stair hall inside. Even an inquiry with the Newport Historical Society about its architect, John Dixon Johnston, failed to turn up anything enlightening. I therefore used my imagination in describing the interior of the house, based on the layouts of other houses of similar Queen Anne design from the period.

The most famous, or perhaps infamous, couple to rent Arleigh were Harry and Elizabeth Lehr, who lived there during the summer Season, from 1901 through 1904. Married in 1901, they were considered one of society's "it" couples. Harry was wildly popular, especially among society's grand dames, most notably the Four Hundred's Triumvirate: Alva Belmont, Tessie Oelrichs, and Mamie Fish. They apparently adored Harry, and Mamie, in particular, recognized in him a fellow practical joker who made any party an affair to remember—including that of the Dog's Dinner in 1904, upon which the Dog's Dinner in the story is based. His impersonation of the czar of Russia at another party earned him the moniker King Lehr. He was also known as America's Court Jester. Harry possessed a keen imagination, a flair for fashion, a sharp sense of humor, and an ability to charm others when he wanted to.

What he lacked was a fortune of his own. As the son of a tobacco and snuff importer, and himself having been a wine salesman, Harry's origins were certainly modest compared to most members of the Four Hundred. That didn't stop him from referring to full-time Newport residents as society's footstools.

He and the newly widowed, wealthy Elizabeth Wharton Drexel Dahlgren met through a mutual friend, Edith Gould, wife of John Jay Gould, but it was the approval of society's Triumvirate that convinced Harry to marry her. During their courtship, he treated Bessie with affection and respect, leading her to believe theirs would be a successful marriage. Upon their wedding night, however, he entered the eager bride's bedroom and explained he had only married her for her money. She repulsed him, and while he would continue to treat her with respect in public, they would have no relationship at all in private. Because divorce was out of the question for Bessie, they would remain married until Harry died of a brain tumor in 1929.

Later, in her book, *King Lehr,* she would reveal in so many words that her husband was gay, abhorring the idea of physical intimacy of any sort with women. After his death, Bessie would marry again and become Lady Decies, wife of an Anglo-Irish peer, but this marriage, too, would be an unhappy one.

In 1903, Reginald Vanderbilt, aged twenty-three, married his first wife, eighteen-year-old Cathleen Neilson. At the time, Reggie was under subpoena in the state of New York to testify in the Canfield case—not, as I depict in the story, as someone actively connected with the scam designed to fleece gamblers, but as one of its victims. Whatever the case, Reggie opted to ignore the summons and flee New York rather than become involved. He and his bride accepted the Lehrs' offer to hold their wedding at Arleigh. As in the story, Reggie ran into trouble with local police days before the wedding for racing his car through Middletown, which lies between Newport and Portsmouth. He was a notoriously reckless driver, and it was said neither pedestrians nor sheep were safe when he got behind the wheel.

He and Cathleen had one child, a daughter also named Cathleen, and less than ten years into the marriage Reggie, heavily in debt, abandoned his family. Cathleen sued him for divorce in 1920. Three years later, Reggie would marry the beautiful young socialite, Gloria Morgan. They would also have a daughter, Gloria Vanderbilt, who would become a successful fashion designer and the mother of Anderson Cooper. Only two years after the birth of his daughter, Reggie died of cirrhosis of the liver at Sandy Point Farm.

At the time of the story, the keeping of pets was taking on much greater importance than previously in this country. With urbanization and fewer people living on rural farms, the longstanding working relationship between people and animals, such as dogs and cats, slowly diminished, as did the connection of people to nature in general. However, the bonds of affection and trust between humans and animals persisted, resulting in pets becoming, essentially, part of the family, much as they are today.

The existence of the tunnel connected to the wine cellar near the end of the story may seem a little too convenient, and did, in fact, spring from my imagination, but not without some basis in fact. Tunnels have been uncovered in various places in Newport leading down to the water, probably used in smuggling before the Revolutionary War as a way to elude British tax laws, and during the war to bring in supplies under the noses of the British occupiers.